A Sinful Calling

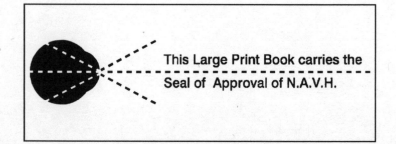

This Large Print Book carries the
Seal of Approval of N.A.V.H.

A SINFUL CALLING

KIMBERLA LAWSON ROBY

THORNDIKE PRESS
A part of Gale, Cengage Learning

GALE
CENGAGE Learning·

Farmington Hills, Mich • San Francisco • New York • Waterville, Maine
Meriden, Conn • Mason, Ohio • Chicago

LIBRARY OF CONGRESS CATALOGING-IN-PUBLICATION DATA

Names: Roby, Kimberla Lawson, author.
Title: A sinful calling / by Kimberla Lawson Roby.
Description: Waterville, Maine : Thorndike Press, 2016. | Series: A Reverend Curtis
  Black novel | Series: Thorndike Press large print African-American
Identifiers: LCCN 2016023723| ISBN 9781410493187 (hardcover) | ISBN 1410493180
  (hardcover)
Subjects: LCSH: Triangles (Interpersonal relations)—Fiction. | African American
  women—Fiction. | Large type books. | Urban fiction.
Classification: LCC PS3568.O3189 S57 2016b | DDC 813/.54—dc23
LC record available at https://lccn.loc.gov/2016023723

Published in 2016 by arrangement with Grand Central Publishing, a
division of Hachette Book Group, Inc.

Printed in the United States of America
1 2 3 4 5 6 7 20 19 18 17 16

For my mother-in-law and two uncles

Lillie C. Roby
July 4, 1935 – April 1, 2015

James Henry Tennin, Sr.
September 9, 1925 – October 29, 2015

Deacon Earl Lee Rome
November 4, 1933 – November 2, 2015

I love and miss you all.

CHAPTER 1

As the choir sang, Dillon gazed across his 1,000-plus-member congregation and could barely contain himself. His heart raced with excitement, and it was all he could do not to break into laughter. The reason: He felt more like a rock star than he did a pastor, and his plan was working brilliantly. Even from the pulpit, he could tell that the members of New Faith Christian Center loved and worshiped everything about him, and he couldn't have been more pleased.

And who would have guessed that a man of his character, someone tainted with such a sinful past, could achieve this kind of glorious success? Especially with the way Dillon had tried blackmailing his own father, the infamous Reverend Curtis Black, and had slept with his own brother's wife. Those two indiscretions alone had occurred just over three years ago, however, thank-fully — for whatever reason — Curtis and

Matthew had forgiven him. Dillon and Matthew certainly weren't the best of friends, and Dillon could tell that his dad still didn't trust him either, but again, they no longer held his past crimes against him. Although, it wasn't like they ever called or spent time with Dillon the way he would have liked.

But the best news of all was that his sister Alicia had turned out to be his favorite person, and she was now closer to Dillon than she was to any other family member. The two of them could easily serve as poster children for popular clichés, as they were definitely thick as thieves, two peas in a pod, bosom buddies, and the list went on. They were as close as any brother and sister could be, and they stood up for each other — probably because they were now both the black sheep of the family. Still, they'd made a pact, and because Dillon didn't have much of a relationship with anyone on his mom's side, God rest her soul, he cherished the one he had with his sister. This was part of the reason that he'd decided very quickly that she would be New Faith's chief operating officer. He was also grateful to his brother-in-law, Levi, who'd invested all the initial funding to get the church up and running.

Because of drug-related charges, Levi had

done time in prison, but he was a changed man and anyone could see that he loved Alicia with his entire being. Levi had also proven beyond question that he would do anything to protect Dillon and the ministry, and he was the perfect chairman of the church's elder board.

Although, it wasn't only Alicia and Levi who genuinely cared about Dillon, because he now had a gorgeous wife who loved him, too. Raven, who sat smiling at him in the front row, was his everything, and he couldn't be more grateful to have married her. He was thankful to finally have found a woman he trusted and appreciated, because before Raven, it had been no secret that he'd never had much respect for any woman, not even his own mother. Of course, there was no denying that, like his own, Raven's past wasn't pretty, but she loved, honored, and respected Dillon, and that was all that mattered to him. Yes, Raven had once served as chief financial officer at his dad's church, and she'd served a few years in prison for embezzling a hundred thousand dollars from the ministry — out of desperation to repay her gambling debts — but today, she was a different woman. She'd been completely delivered from her casino addiction, and she was the ideal first lady. The women of New Faith Christian Center certainly thought so, and they viewed her as a stellar example. To them, she represented the fact that anyone could change for the better if he or she wanted to, and they admired that. Dillon was also happy to say that part of his success as a pastor, as well as the growing of the congregation, was a result of Raven's notable business acumen. She was exceptionally good with numbers, and while she wasn't New Faith's CFO, she'd given Dillon daily advice in terms of how to handle church finances in an entrepreneurial fashion. Dillon had listened to every word and had carefully followed her suggestions, and as a result, the church leadership as a whole had very few complaints when it came to his operational decisions. It was the reason the membership was solid and increasing weekly.

But on a more personal note, Raven was the kind of woman most men would be proud to have. Not only was she head-to-toe beautiful, she was also highly intelligent, confident, and sophisticated. She didn't seem at all like the woman he'd heard about before meeting her — nothing like the felon who'd finished a stint in prison. It was as if she'd taken lots of time to learn everything she could about culture, class, and elegance, because along with her dressing the part, she decorated their home in the same manner. She carried herself with total refinement, and Dillon was glad she'd contacted him right after he'd become estranged from his dad and siblings and had been forced to move back to Atlanta. Raven had told him that she didn't want anything from him, but that a friend of hers had filled her in on his situation. She'd certainly understood what he was going through, particularly since she'd made her own mistakes and had been ousted from her CFO position by his dad. She'd then shared that because she'd had the opportunity to work so closely with his father and his church, she knew the ins and outs of Deliverance Outreach's daily operations. This conversation alone had gotten the wheels spinning in Dillon's head, and it was then that he'd decided he was going to become a minister. It was true that he'd learned a long time ago that it was much more customary for a minister to be called by God to preach, but truth was, Dillon hadn't been called by anyone. He'd called himself, and he wasn't ashamed of it. He'd founded his own church in the living room of his tiny apartment, and he was prospering nicely because of it.

This, of course, made Dillon think about

his former fiancée, Melissa. What a dimwit she'd been, and while he hadn't seen or heard from her since that night she'd confronted him three years ago, he hadn't forgotten what she'd done to him — and he wasn't planning to leave this earth before paying her back. Just thinking about the way she'd taken all his money and run off with their idiot lawn boy, Country Roger, made him cringe. Yes, Roger was a grown man, but to Dillon, he'd been nothing more than a raggedy-mouth child who'd needed tons of dental work. Dillon had known from the time he'd hired him that he was a knucklehead, but Country Roger had come cheap and he was good at what he did. Still, not once had Dillon imagined that Melissa would be foolish enough to start sleeping with Roger behind his back and then run off with him, taking just about every dime Dillon had.

Not long after Dillon had met his dad for the first time, Curtis had given him five hundred thousand dollars, trying to help make up for all the years he hadn't been a father to Dillon, and his aunt had left him a hundred fifty thousand when she'd passed. But after spending two hundred thousand buying a condo and furnishing it, that had left him around four-fifty, and Melissa had gotten into all his bank accounts and taken the money for herself. She'd then betrayed him even further by giving proof to his dad that Dillon had been trying to blackmail him. Worse, the night she and Country Roger had left, Country Roger had held Dillon at gunpoint so that Melissa could say everything she wanted to him. Melissa had somehow, out of nowhere, discovered that she had a backbone, and she'd spoken to Dillon as if he were some moron. She'd acted as though she'd never loved him and was no longer afraid of him. The latter had shocked Dillon the most, because for years he'd controlled her every thought and move and had kept her in line. He'd made sure she'd known who ran things in their relationship, and sometimes when she'd acted stupidly, he'd had no choice but to physically remind her. But on that final evening, she'd turned into a woman he hadn't recognized and had seemingly lost her mind.

That was okay, though, because again, Dillon would eventually seek retribution. It was true that three years had passed, but he hadn't forgotten, and there were times when he lay awake at night thinking about it. He wished he could simply move on the way he knew some good Christians would, but no one stole from him or humiliated him and got away with it. He just couldn't live with something like that, and when the time was right he would handle things the way he saw fit. He'd made a promise to himself that he would never put his hands on a woman again the way he had with Melissa, but he would still find a way to get his revenge.

After the choir finished singing its last song, a few church announcements aired on the TV monitors, and Dillon got up. He buttoned his Italian-made black pinstripe suit and stepped in front of the glass podium.

"This is the day the Lord hath made, so let us rejoice and be glad in it." He began with the same scripture he quoted every single Sunday. He didn't speak these words because the scripture meant any more to him than any other scripture he'd read; he did it because this was the scripture he'd always heard his father open with. He'd even once heard his dad say that he also quoted it each morning when he woke up, so Dillon decided that if this particular scripture was working for his dad, it would certainly work for him, too. But Dillon had taken his approach a step further, as he had taught *his* members to quote it back to him.

"This is the day the Lord hath made, so let us rejoice and be glad in it," his parishioners spoke in unison.

"It is truly a blessing to be alive," Dillon said. "It's a blessing just to be able to say we woke up this morning in our right minds and in good health. Amen?"

"Amen," everyone said.

"You know, for some reason I feel like sharing my testimony this morning. Many of you have heard it before, but today I feel led to share it for our new members and any visitors who are present."

Dillon looked toward the ceiling of the sanctuary and closed his eyes. He did this to gain sympathy, and he didn't open them until he'd mustered up real tears. He wasn't in the mood for doing any crying today, but he'd learned early on that his church members pitied him a lot more when he did. It was one thing for a woman to shed tears, but it was something totally different when a grown man did it, and he gave them a great performance.

Dillon opened his eyes and sniffled.

"Take your time, Pastor," more than one person said.

Dillon took a deep breath, and tears streamed down his face. "I'm so sorry, but I just feel full today. God has been so very good to me, and He's brought me a mighty long way. My aunt used to say those very words all the time, and now I know what she meant. Life hasn't always been this great, though, because no matter how much I've forgiven my father and moved past what he did, it's still very hard sometimes. It's hard to imagine that any man would sleep with a woman, get her pregnant, and then cut her off like a piece of trash. But that's exactly what happened. Then when my mom gave birth to me and asked my dad to take care of me, he refused. And not only did he refuse, but when he was forced to take a paternity test, he somehow worked it out so that his play brother took the test instead. But even that wasn't enough, because then my dad paid off a couple of strippers my mom worked with. He got them to say my mom had been stealing money from the strip club she worked at, and she was fired."

When Dillon saw a couple of women already wiping tears, he swallowed hard and sniffled again for deeper effect.

"Please excuse me, but telling this story never gets easier."

Many people nodded with approval and gave their full attention to Dillon.

"After my mom got fired, though, and then learned that the paternity test showed my dad wasn't my father, she begged him to tell the truth. She begged him to help take care of me. She also threatened to tell his fiancée everything. And that's when I suddenly ended up missing one day. Then, about an hour after I was taken, my dad called my mom and told her that if she ever wanted to see me again, she would sign a document stating that he wasn't the baby's father. She then had to agree to never contact him again. Of course, my mom signed it, but she couldn't live with losing her job and having my dad deny me the way he did. So she borrowed a friend's car and crashed it into a tree. She killed herself when I was only a newborn. My mom was a stripper, and knowing what she did for a living caused me a lot of pain — it was the reason I grew up having no respect for any woman except my aunt — but she didn't deserve to die."

Dillon shed more tears, and although his initial tears had been forced and phony, the ones he shed now were very real. His heart ached terribly, and it was all because he'd never gotten to know his mother. His mom's sister had been the best mother figure she could be, but Dillon still longed for his birth mother. He also wasn't sure he'd ever stop blaming his father. He'd tried to love his father and forget about what Curtis had done, but he couldn't. Maybe if Curtis had welcomed him with open arms and immediately loved him the way he loved his other three children, Dillon could have felt better about things. But that hadn't happened. Instead, his dad had made it very clear that his precious Matthew was the son he truly loved and that his two daughters, Alicia and that brat Curtina, were the loves of his life also.

"I'm sharing this story because I want people to understand that when parents make selfish decisions, they affect a child for the rest of his or her life. Being forced to basically grow up as an orphan is the reason I made so many bad choices. I committed a lot of sins and hurt a lot of people, but today I'm a completely different man. God has delivered me from sin. He called me to minister, and I thank Him for giving me another chance. He'll give everyone in here another chance as well. He's a good God, and none of us would be *anything* without Him," he proclaimed, speaking louder than he had been. "We don't deserve his grace, mercy, and favor, but I'm here to tell you that He gives it to us anyway. He forgives us because He loves us, and if you agree, you ought to give Him a huge amount of praise today! Praise His sweet, holy name!"

The entire congregation applauded and most stood up. Many shouted their words out loud, all while in tears.

Dillon smiled and was glad to know his testimony still worked. It made people take notice and feel sorry for him. He watched the reaction of his parishioners and day-dreamed about the ten-thousand-member congregation he wanted. His goal and dream was to have the largest church in Mitchell, Illinois. More than anything, he wanted to have a church larger than his dad's, and he wanted this sooner rather than later. His dad's existing sanctuary seated two thousand people, so to accommodate five thousand members — four thousand of whom attended regularly — he had to hold two services. Every week, Deliverance Outreach operated at 100 percent capacity, and for this reason, Curtis was finally building a five-thousand-seat building adjacent to the current one. That way, all his members could worship together at one service, and there would also be room for new parishioners. New Faith could hold two thousand people as well, but since Dillon only had one thousand members, the church never filled more than half its space. This wasn't good enough for Dillon, and his plan was to have twenty-five hundred members by the end of this year, a total of five thousand twelve months from now, and another five thousand within two years.

He wasn't sure what he'd have to do to make this happen, but he'd decided a while ago that he was willing to do whatever it took. Nothing was off-limits . . . not even sleeping with the woman he now glanced at in the audience. Her name was Porsha Harrington. He'd tried his best to ignore her, and until three months ago, he'd been successful. But now he couldn't get her out of his mind or his system, and he saw her as much as possible . . . regardless of how much he loved his wife. He didn't fully understand why his genuine love for Raven wasn't enough or why he had this burning desire to sleep with someone else, but he couldn't help it. For now, though, he had to refocus on the matter at hand. He had his congregation right where he wanted them, and as soon as everyone settled down and took their seats, he smiled and said, "I know you've already given your tithes and offering this morning, but when God speaks to me I've learned not to disobey him. So let us turn our Bibles to Second Corinthians nine, verses six through seven."

Dillon waited for everyone to open their printed editions or pull up their electronic versions.

"Are we all there?"

"Yes," everyone replied.

"And it says, 'The point is this: Whoever sows sparingly will also reap sparingly, and whoever sows bountifully will also reap bountifully. Each one must give as he has decided in his heart, not reluctantly or under compulsion, for God loves a cheerful giver.' "

Dillon gazed at his members and never said another word. He didn't have to. Not when they were already pulling out additional cash and writing new checks.

He'd heard lots of stories from Alicia about how when she was a small girl, their dad had been loved by all. She'd told him that members of his church seemed to have no problem doing anything he asked, including giving whatever amount of money he requested. She'd insisted that it was simply a gift that their father had been blessed with. He was handsome, charismatic, and very smart, and people gravitated to him. Dillon hadn't been sure he'd believed her, but when many of his congregants had begun saying how much he looked and sounded like his dad, he'd known he could use his father's good genes to his advantage.

He'd decided that not only could he be

his dad, he could be better. When it was all said and done, the good Reverend Curtis Black would be history and Pastor Dillon Whitfield Black would be all the city of Mitchell cared about.

CHAPTER 2

Alicia sat at the elegant twelve-seat mahogany dining room table, something that was much too large for four people, wishing time would pass by quickly. Dillon and Raven had invited Alicia and Levi over for dinner after church, but Alicia didn't want to be there. Not because she didn't want to spend time with her brother, but because she didn't care to exchange small talk with his uppity wife. As a matter of fact, Alicia was getting to the point where she could hardly stand the sight of Raven, and secretly, she wished her brother would divorce her. In a perfect world, he would fall out of love with her for good, and that would be the end of it. Alicia knew it wasn't right to want someone's marriage to break up, but she couldn't help the way she felt about Raven. Of course, Dillon had made it very clear how much he loved his wife, but this woman was proving to be a real piece of work. Actually, as far as Alicia was concerned, she'd always been that way, and Alicia just couldn't see why her brother was so taken with her. It was true that Raven was a gorgeous woman who was very smart, but she also couldn't be trusted; not when she'd stolen a hundred thousand dollars from the church where Alicia's dad was pastor. The woman had stolen from God's house, of all places, and she'd done it as though it were nothing.

Raven did claim to be a different person, but Alicia didn't believe her, partly because Raven spent a lot of time focusing on status and material possessions and partly because she seemed more concerned about gaining total control in the church than she was about building it as a whole. Actually, it was her history of stealing money and her deceitful character that had caused both Alicia and Levi to speak against her becoming New Faith's CFO. Raven had insisted she was the best person for the job, but when neither Alicia nor Levi would agree to it — which had made all the difference, since Levi was steadily covering all the church's operational expenses — she'd finally backed down. Raven hadn't been happy about it, but Dillon had seemed relieved. He'd never gone as far as saying it out loud, but Alicia could tell that, to some degree, Dillon was glad she and Levi had spoken up, because he didn't fully trust his dear wife to handle all the church's finances, either.

As far as Dillon and Raven's personal relationship, however, Raven did seem to support Dillon on every level, and she also seemed to genuinely love him. But Alicia still didn't like her. To be fair, Raven didn't care much for Alicia, either, even though she pretended to because she knew how much Dillon loved Alicia. Alicia faked with her, too, for a similar reason: She didn't want her brother to have to choose sides.

Dillon and Raven's sixtysomething weekend cook, Martha, set the final dish of food on the table and smiled. "Can I get you all anything else?" she asked.

Dillon glanced at everyone. "No, I think we're good, and thank you for everything, Miss Martha."

"You're quite welcome, Pastor. I'm glad to do it."

"Yes, thank you," Raven said in a demeaning tone while straightening the pearl necklace that lay against her St. John suit. "And I hope the rolls are warm this time. Remember, last Sunday you forgot to warm them up."

"I'm really sorry about that," Martha said. "And yes, I warmed them up today for sure."

Raven picked up the metal tongs and lifted one of the rolls from the bowl. She purposely checked to see if Martha was lying, and Alicia wanted to shake her head. So pathetic.

"Yes, you definitely remembered today, and I appreciate that. Especially since we have guests. Wouldn't want to be embarrassed when there's no reason to be."

"Yes, Lady Black, I understand."

Dillon seemed uncomfortable with the way Raven spoke to Martha and finally said, "Why don't you call it a day and head on home. Enjoy the rest of your Sunday, and we'll put the dishes in the dishwasher."

"Excuse me?" Raven said.

Dillon looked at Raven and then at Martha. "Like I said, Miss Martha, we can handle the dishes."

"Are you sure?"

"Absolutely."

"Okay, if you really don't mind."

"Not at all. We'll see you next weekend."

Alicia watched Raven's every move, but Raven didn't say anything else. She always acted as though certain people were beneath her, specifically the "help," so to speak, and

Alicia didn't like it.

When Martha left, Alicia scanned the dishes of turkey and cornbread dressing, macaroni and cheese, fried chicken, and turnip greens, and Dillon reached for his wife's hand. Levi grabbed Alicia's. Normally, when Dillon and Raven had more guests, Dillon sat at the head of the table and Raven sat at the other end, facing him. But with there only being four of them, it didn't make much sense, and Alicia wondered why they couldn't just eat in the kitchen at their smaller table. Of course, Raven would never allow that, not with her always feeling the need to do everything in a big, formal way.

Dillon bowed his head, and so did everyone else. "Dear Heavenly Father, we come now thanking You for the food we are about to receive. Thank You, Lord, for giving us this great day of rest and for allowing us to honor and praise You during service this morning. Thank You for my dear wife, sister, and brother-in-law and for bringing us together for this wonderful fellowship. Also, dear Lord, thank You for Martha as well as for the food she has prepared for us. Let it serve as nourishment for our bodies in Jesus's name. Amen."

"Amen," the others said.

"Down-home cooking just the way I like it," Dillon affirmed. "Miss Martha is the only person I know who can cook as well as my aunt, Susan, used to. I just love her."

Raven didn't seem too impressed. "Yeah, I'll give her that. She can definitely cook, but I'm glad she doesn't cook like this all the time. If she did, we'd be as big as elephants. And eating this kind of food is way too unhealthy."

"Whatever, woman," Dillon said, laughing and lifting a large spoonful of dressing onto his plate and doing the same for Raven. "But on a different note," he continued, "I really think it's time we figure out a way to roll out our next marketing campaign. We need to bring in a lot more visitors than we have been. The kind who won't just visit but will ultimately become members."

"I agree," Raven added. "We need to market Dillon and the church like never before, and if we put the right kind of dollars behind it, we can do that."

Levi scooped some greens from the large bowl. "I think it's time we do a lot more marketing and advertising as well, and I also think we need to bring in a new marketing firm. We have a couple of good ones we've worked with in the past, but I think we need the best of the best this time around."

"Exactly," Raven said. "Bringing in the best is the only way to get things done in a top-notch manner."

"I'm going to put together a few more ideas so we can begin discussing them on Tuesday at our elder board meeting," Dillon said. "Especially since all the ministries will need to be included in the ads."

Alicia pulled her thick, shoulder-length hair behind her ear and ate a forkful of macaroni and cheese. She was COO, but she didn't say anything.

Until Dillon looked at her. "So, what do you think, Sis?"

"I think doing a new campaign will be great, and I look forward to hearing some of your ideas."

"I look forward to hearing them as well," Raven said, sounding as though she was worried that Dillon might share his ideas with Alicia first. This was the reason Alicia hadn't commented initially.

"Baby, of course. Since when do I work on anything relating to the church without asking your opinion?"

Raven playfully bumped her arm against his, and Alicia wanted to roll her eyes. She could barely stomach Raven, and her feelings toward her were getting worse as time went on. It also didn't help that while Dillon, Raven, and Levi had been talking, Alicia had glanced over at one of the curio cabinets and spied new vases that looked antique and pricey. It was true that Dillon earned a six-figure salary from the church and Raven was on payroll as well — since she was the head of the women's ministry — but they didn't bring home the kind of money where she could keep spending hundreds and sometimes thousands of dollars on things they didn't need. Not to mention, they had to be paying a pretty hefty mortgage for this richly constructed five-bedroom home that had six bathrooms. It wasn't Alicia's business, of course, and yes, her and Levi's house wasn't shabby, either, but she didn't see how things would end well if Raven kept buying everything in sight. Alicia also wondered why Dillon wasn't paying attention to the amount of money his wife spent, but it was likely because he was so taken with her. He was blinded by his feelings for her, but Alicia knew all too well what could happen when a person became obsessed with clothing, jewelry, and household goods — what it was like when someone spent beyond their means. She'd done the same thing in the past, and sadly, Raven's shopping addiction was much worse.

But to be honest, Raven and her excessive spending habits should have been the last thing on Alicia's mind, because Alicia had her own problems and worries to contend with. She loved, loved, loved her husband, Levi, mind, body and soul, but for the life of her, she still couldn't shake the guilt she'd been struggling with since Phillip's death. She'd had an affair, Phillip had snapped because of how hurt and betrayed he'd felt, and the gun the two of them had tussled over had accidentally gone off and killed him. Two years had passed, yet she still blamed herself. This had also been the reason it had taken her a full year to actually marry Levi. And while she'd accepted the fact that her parents and stepparents blamed her as well, knowing she was no longer close to them still hurt her to the core. From the time she'd been born, she'd been a daddy's girl, but even he didn't talk to her as much as he once had. He didn't treat her badly and had stated more than once that it wasn't his job to judge her regarding the affair she'd had with Levi, but he was still gravely disappointed in her.

Just thinking about it now and replaying every ounce of what had happened that night made her want to scream. The whole idea of it caused her to lose sleep, and her feelings of regret and deep remorse were affecting her marriage. She couldn't remember when she'd slept more than three hours a night, and sometimes all she did was lie in bed with her eyes closed. There were many evenings when she didn't sleep a wink, which was the reason she always drank loads of coffee at work, trying to stay alert. The entire scenario unnerved her, and she constantly hoped and prayed to move on from her past. All she wanted was to be happy with the man she loved — the tall, muscular, handsome man — who, after all this time, still loved her unconditionally and with everything he had in him. If only she could forgive herself and live a normal life, things could be good for her and Levi. They could enjoy the wonderful marriage they'd both dreamed about. They could settle into being the soul mates they'd known they were from the moment they'd first laid eyes on each other.

Levi rested his hand on top of hers. "Baby, are you okay?"

"I'm fine," she said, lying. "I'm good."

Levi gazed at her a few seconds longer, and while she knew he had a pretty good idea of why she was so preoccupied, he didn't let on.

Raven patted her lips with the linen

napkin. "Well, now that we all agree that we need to create a whole new marketing plan, I have something I want to share as well. I've already shared this with my better half here, but Alicia, since you're the church's COO, and Levi, since all the elders report to you, I'm really hoping to get both of your blessings, too."

Alicia raised her eyebrows, wondering what this was all about. She looked at Dillon, trying to read his thoughts, but she couldn't.

"So what's up?" Levi finally said.

"Well, not only have I given this a lot of thought, but I've also been in deep prayer about it. I prayed because I wanted to make sure I was hearing God correctly."

Alicia stared at Raven. "And?"

"He's called me into the ministry. He wants me to serve as co-pastor alongside my husband."

Alicia slightly laughed.

Raven frowned. "Oh, so you think my calling is funny? That it's some kind of joke?"

"No," Alicia said. "I'm just a little shocked is all."

"Well, it's true, and I'm not going to go against what God wants me to do. I'm going to be obedient."

"Wow, well, congratulations," Levi said.

Alicia turned and looked at Levi, who purposely stared at his plate of food, so then she searched her brother's reaction. Dillon sat speechless, but Alicia could tell he had concerns. She had worries, too, because while New Faith was a non-denominational church, Alicia wasn't sure the majority of the congregation would accept a wife being co-pastor. Not every church group was okay with having a woman as senior pastor. But more than anything, Alicia didn't like it because she knew Raven wasn't doing it because God had called her. She was doing it because she knew that being co-pastor would give her the kind of power, prestige, control, and say-so she'd been wanting since the beginning. Raven would even believe she could tell Alicia what and what not to do, even though Alicia was not only COO of New Faith Christian Center, she was COO of New Faith Ministries, Inc., too.

Alicia wasn't sure what it was she'd have to do to stop this crazy idea, but she was going to make sure Raven never became co-pastor or ended up holding any top leadership position in the church. She didn't care what Dillon or anyone else had to say about it. Period.

CHAPTER 3

Dillon pulled the belt of his silk robe tighter with both hands and walked inside his prayer room. He closed the door, took a deep breath, and kneeled in front of the wooden bench. He rested his arms on the purple velvet that covered it and closed his eyes.

"This is the day the Lord hath made, so let us rejoice and be glad in it. Dear Heavenly Father, I come to You right now, thanking You for yet another day and joyful morning. Thanking You for waking me up in my right mind and in good health. Thanking You for my beautiful wife and my awesome church. Lord, I thank You for all the members who have so graciously joined our congregation over the last couple of years, and I thank You for bringing my sister and I so much closer. Thank You, Lord, for my amazing brother-in-law, Levi, who has helped me and the church financially in ways that we couldn't have made it without. Then, Lord, I now come, asking You to direct my path. Show me what we need to do to build up our membership. Tell me what we need to do to grow our church family so that it increases well into the thousands. I also ask that You would help my sister, Alicia, because while she rarely talks about it, I know the death of her first husband is still haunting her. She's very troubled by it, so, Lord, I ask that You give her the kind of peace she needs. Give her what she needs to move on, so that she can enjoy the life she now has with Levi, a man who loves the ground she walks on. Then, Father, I ask that You would change my wife's heart about wanting to become co-pastor. She says that You've called her to do so, and while I realize none of us is supposed to question someone else's faith, I know with all my heart that what she's done is call herself. I know this, because I did the same thing. You never called me, either, but I'm hoping someday that You will, so that I won't have to lie about that anymore. I'm asking You for this blessing, because I'm very good at being a pastor. You gave me the kind of speaking ability that only great ministers tend to have, and I just don't believe You would gift me with those sorts of skills for nothing. I don't believe You would place it in my mind to start a church in the middle of my apartment and then give me more than a thousand members so quickly; not if You didn't want me to be a pastor. Not if You didn't want me to become the most well-known pastor in Mitchell. I just don't believe You would do that and not have your reasons. And my parishioners really love me. They listen to me, they respect me, and they show me the kind of love every pastor hopes for. I realize I still make lots of mistakes and that I struggle with quite a few sins, but in Romans three, twenty-three, it says that we all have sinned and fallen short of Your glory. Then, in first John, chapter one, verse nine, it talks about how if we confess our sins, You are faithful and just and will forgive us for our sins and purify us from all unrighteousness. I know some people believe that if you deliberately continue to sin, you won't be saved. But based on everything I've read in the Bible, I have to believe in the philosophy once saved, always saved. Which to me means that as long as I believe in You and I've accepted You as my personal savior, I'm good. Once I accepted You, I was guaranteed a place in heaven. So, Lord, I'm going to try to do better, but I'm glad to know that when

I fall astray, You still won't leave me. I'll still have You to come to, and You'll still forgive me and welcome me with open arms. I have to say, though, there is something else weighing heavily on my heart, and since You know everything, You already know what it is . . . and I need Your help. To this day, no one here knows that after I left Mitchell three years ago, I became an alcoholic; that after Melissa stole all my money and my dad wouldn't forgive me, I drank to mask all my pain. They don't know that I got so drunk I couldn't keep a job or that I sold Aunt Susan's house and spent every dime of the proceeds on alcohol and living expenses. No one knows that losing her home is the only thing that made me go into treatment . . . and they certainly don't know that, for some reason, over the last three months, ever since I started seeing Porsha, I've had these cravings again. Alcohol nearly ruined my life, and I can't afford to go down that road again. So, dear Lord, I'm asking You to remove that craving from my mind. Remove it from my spirit. Help me to focus on building up my church. Help me to see my dream come to pass of being the wealthiest and most powerful pastor not just in Mitchell, but in the whole state of Illinois. And then if You see fit, help me to become the most well-known pastor in the country. You said in Your Word that You would give me the desires of my heart, so I ask You for these and all other blessings in Your Son Jesus's name. Amen. Amen. Amen."

Dillon breathed deeply, in and out, more than once, and then opened his eyes. He felt better already, and he was glad he'd finally begun praying. He was also happy about his decision to turn the closet of his home office into his own personal prayer room. When he'd first become a minister, he'd never as much as said his prayers before going to bed, but the more he saw folks praying in church and doing it on televised religious broadcasts, he'd known he'd better join them. He'd even studied the idea and process of prayer, and he'd learned how to do it well. Learned how to say the right things in the right way at the right time. He'd learned how to pray for himself, his family, and his parishioners when they needed it. Actually, he'd gone the whole first year of being a minister before adopting this philosophy, and interestingly enough, he had soon started to believe that prayer did work. He still didn't understand, though, why God answered certain prayers but seemed to bypass others. This was the one thing about being a pastor that he didn't like. He wanted things to happen when he wanted them to happen, and he became frustrated when they didn't. He'd once heard his father give a sermon on patience and waiting on God to do things in His own timing. Dillon understood that theory, but he still didn't care for it, and it sometimes made him wonder if it was really God answering some of his prayers or if some of his good fortune was merely based on luck.

Dillon stood up, opened the door, and walked out to his office. When he did, he heard a knock.

"Come in."

Raven opened his door and strolled in. "Good morning, sweetie," she said, hugging and kissing him.

"Good morning to you, baby. Did you sleep well?"

"Not really. I mean, I did this morning, but I tossed and turned a lot last night."

"Why is that?"

She pulled him over to the two leather chairs positioned in front of his antique wood desk, and they both sat down.

She folded her arms. "Can I be honest?"

"Of course. I wouldn't want you to be anything else."

"Look, sweetie, you know I love you, right?"

"Yes, and I love you, too."

"I know that, but you also love your sister."

"Yeah, that's true, too, but what does that have to do with you and me?"

"Baby, c'mon. You and I have always had a nonverbal, unwritten understanding that your sister doesn't like me. And I certainly don't like her. But that's also why I think she's going to be a problem when it comes to my becoming co-pastor. Didn't you see the look on her face? She completely disapproves, and she even laughed at me."

Dillon tried not to show any emotion one way or the other, and he didn't dare allude to the fact that he didn't want her being co-pastor, either. He loved Raven, but he also didn't want to share the title of senior pastor with her or anyone else. Never in his life had he believed in having two chiefs run anything, and this was the reason he had no assistant pastors. There were, of course, ordained ministers who were members of the church whom he sometimes asked to deliver the sermon for him, but that only happened if he was out of town or ill. They also weren't on payroll. They were compensated for their individual services, but they weren't employees and probably never would be. So, if Raven became co-pastor, it would only be a disaster waiting to happen. She'd want to give all sorts of input and take over the ministry in ways he wasn't willing to allow — ways he would *never* allow — which would only mean huge problems for them as husband and wife. They'd begin arguing like they'd never done before, and life as they'd known it would be over.

"Honey, why aren't you saying anything?" she asked. "I mean, please don't tell me you agree with her."

"I never said that," he told her.

"You know I'm the perfect person to co-pastor with you. I look the part, I can certainly speak the part, and I know how to handle and make business decisions. Most of all, though, the women of New Faith love and respect me. The younger women look up to me, and the older women treat me like I'm their daughter. I have a lot to offer the ministry. Much more than just being the head of the women in the church."

"But, baby, you're good at leading the women. You do it well, and that's why so many women are joining. They're also very active in the church, and that's all because of you and the way you encourage them. You're a great example for them, and I would hate to see you step down from that position. The women would be very disappointed."

"I can do both jobs. I can be co-pastor and still head the women's ministry."

Dillon sighed. "I don't doubt that you can, but if you do both jobs, when will you have time for me? And what about when we decide to have children?"

Dillon didn't necessarily think that any of what he'd just said would be a problem, but he was searching for anything that might change her mind.

"Why aren't you backing me on this?"

"Because I just don't know if it's the right thing for you or for our marriage. Let alone for the church."

"Wow," she said, standing up. "I don't believe this. My own husband, who's supposed to be committed to me, doesn't support me?"

Dillon got to his feet and held her hand. "Baby, you know that's not true. I do support you, and you know how much you mean to me."

Raven jerked her hand away from his. "If you love me, you sure have a funny way of showing it. It's almost like we've been living some sort of façade these last couple of years. If you weren't going to be all in when it comes to our marriage, why did you marry me?"

"Why are you so upset?"

"Because I really want this, and I know God wants it, too."

"Okay, look," he said. "I just don't think it's good for a husband and wife to work that closely. Working at the same church is fine, but not sharing the same position."

"Wait a minute," she said, squinting her eyes. "Is this because of my past? The way I used to gamble and because I took money from your dad's church? Is it that you don't trust me to be co-pastor? You think I'm going to steal money from our ministry?"

Dillon would be lying if he said her past didn't concern him or give him pause, but he would never admit it to her.

"Look, why don't we talk about this later on, at dinner."

"Why can't we talk about it now? Why can't you just let me be who God wants me to be?"

Dillon wasn't sure what else he could say at this point, because nothing he suggested was making a difference.

"You know what?" she said. "I don't even want to talk to you right now."

Dillon grabbed her arm and pulled her toward him, but when he tried to hug her, she yanked away from him again.

"Why are you acting like this?" he asked.

"Just leave me alone!" she yelled. "Don't say another word to me."

Dillon watched his wife as she stormed out of his office, and he wasn't sure how this was all going to play out. He hoped this disagreement of theirs wasn't going to turn into some huge fiasco, but either way, he wasn't giving in. No matter what Raven said, she wasn't going to be co-pastor. Regardless of how angry she got, it simply wouldn't happen.

CHAPTER 4

Dillon lay next to Porsha Harrington trying to catch his breath, and she lay her head on his chest. He wrapped his arm around her and closed his eyes. He'd told himself that he wouldn't see her today, especially after having such a major falling-out with Raven, but in all honesty, his troubles with Raven had made him want to be with Porsha that much more. He was to the point where he thought about Porsha all the time, and he regularly daydreamed about making love to her. He'd done the same thing yesterday when he'd seen her at church. If only she wasn't so good to him. If only she didn't know how to make him feel even better than his own wife could. A few years ago, when he'd slept with his brother's wife, Racquel, he'd decided that she was the best he'd ever had, but Porsha was the new reigning successor. She did things to him that no woman had done, and she didn't seem to have to work hard at it. She acted as though making love was a special gift she'd been given, and no one else could do it the way she could.

It was strange how when Dillon had first taken notice of her, he'd been more interested in the fact that her father had passed away late last year and had left her a few million dollars. Needless to say, Dillon was willing to do anything when it came to getting as much financial help as possible to grow his church membership. He was also thinking ahead to the day they would build or move into a much larger location. So when he'd realized how attracted Porsha was to him, something she'd made known more than a year ago, he'd finally contacted her. He'd then gone to her home in Hoffman Estates, which was a little less than an hour from Mitchell. Actually, she'd once lived in Mitchell herself, but when her father's affairs had been settled, she'd purchased a home closer to Chicago. Still, she hadn't stopped attending New Faith, and she drove there every Sunday without fail. She was a dedicated member who gave generously to the church and its overall ministry — sometimes five and ten thousand dollars at a time — and she'd silently made it clear that if Dillon spent the right amount of time with her, she would continue doing so very willingly.

Dillon had debated getting involved with her, but then he'd remembered what Alicia had told him about her second husband, a man by the name of JT Valentine. She'd told him stories about how one of JT's mistresses had been very wealthy, and the reason he'd slept with her was so she would give him large sums of money. Dillon had never met JT, and he certainly wasn't happy about the way JT had treated his sister, but he'd never forgotten what Alicia had shared with him. He'd known from the minute she'd told him that story that in order to have a successful ministry, he would eventually have to do a few things that weren't so noble. The goal, however, had been that he wouldn't have to do these kinds of things for very long. That is, until he'd slept with Porsha for the first time and realized he couldn't stop. He just didn't want to.

Porsha caressed Dillon's chest, which was damp from all the sweating he'd been doing, and he gently rubbed the side of her arm.

"I wish you never had to leave," she said.

"I wish I didn't, either, but it is what it is."

"But it doesn't have to be. I mean, don't I

make you happy?"

Dillon opened his eyes, leaned his head back, and looked at her. "Of course you do. Girl, you absolutely drive me wild, and I love being with you."

"Then leave her, baby. Do it now, before too much time passes. You've only been married for two years, and it'll be a lot easier getting out now than it will be sometime down the road."

Dillon heard what she was saying, but he didn't respond. He'd known that ultimately Porsha would want more than what he was giving her behind closed doors — mistresses always did — but it was just that he'd been hoping she wouldn't start talking about it this soon. She hadn't before today, and he wondered where all this was coming from.

"And let me ask you something else," she said matter-of-factly. "You're thirty-two, right? The same age as me?"

"Yeah, but what does that matter?" he asked.

"It doesn't, but I just want to know why you married a woman who's five years older than you. I mean, the woman will be forty in three years."

"Age has never been an issue for us. It's never been a problem for me, ever. If a woman is younger, the same age, or older, the only thing that matters is how well I connect with her."

"Do you love her?"

"Why all the questions? Because it's not like you've been asking things like this before."

"I don't know. I guess I'm just curious. And my feelings for you are getting stronger all the time . . . I think I'm in love with you."

Dillon pulled her closer to him again so he wouldn't have to look at her. Not because he didn't want to acknowledge what she was saying, but because he was starting to wonder if he felt the same way about her, too. He didn't know if he was simply in love with the way they *made* love to each other or if he was falling in love with her emotionally. He also didn't know if it was possible to be in love with two women at the same time, because no matter how often he slept with Porsha, he still loved Raven.

"Can I ask you something else?" she asked.

"Go ahead."

"Doesn't it bother you that your wife is a criminal who served time in prison?"

"No, it doesn't. Everyone makes mistakes."

"That might be true, but she stole a lot of money from your dad's church, and people who steal almost always do it again."

"I think we should talk about something else."

"That's fine, but I just hope you know you can't trust her. And you should divorce her while you have the chance."

Dillon slipped his arm away from her and sat up. "Look, I'm not saying I don't care about you, because I do. But not once have I lied to you about my wife and the way I feel about her. I love her, and to some degree, I even feel sorry for her because of the gambling problem she had. Worse, when she was a child, she was tossed around between multiple foster homes. She was even abused at one of them."

"I know all about that. She's given a testimony about it too many times to count. But eventually she was placed in a good home, she got a great education, and she was named CFO at your dad's church at a pretty young age. So, regardless of her child-hood, Raven is now an adult who is married and responsible for her own actions."

"Okay, wait. It's clear we don't agree, and from this point on, we're not talking about my wife. It's disrespectful."

"Really? But sneaking away from her and making love to me isn't?"

Dillon sat on the side of the bed and

looked back at her, but he didn't respond — partly because he truly didn't think it was right for a man to discuss his wife with another woman, and partly because she was right about what she'd said: He was in fact sneaking away from Raven to be with her. And it bothered him. It made him uneasy because normally when a man made the decision to step out on his wife, he did it as a result of his being miserable at home or no longer wanting to be married. But that wasn't the case with Dillon. He loved Raven on a level he'd never loved any woman, but he also loved being with Porsha. So much so that he couldn't imagine not seeing Porsha or making love to her the way he had been over these last three months.

Porsha sat up and leaned back against a couple of pillows. "So you don't have anything to say?"

"Like what?"

"I don't know. Anything. Tell me that you hear what I'm saying, because eventually I'm going to need more than what you're giving me. I won't hide around like some low-rate side chick. I want you all to myself, and I can't help the way I feel. And, baby," she said, moving closer to him and caressing his back, "you know how happy I can make you. You know I'll be the kind of first

52

lady New Faith deserves. And I'll support the church in every way possible."

Dillon did hear what she was saying, especially the last sentence she'd spoken. She had proven how much she didn't mind giving to the church financially, and he certainly didn't want to stifle her generosity. So he chose his words very carefully.

"You have to give me some time," he said. "You can't just expect me to go to my wife and ask her for a divorce for no reason. I do want to be with you, and I appreciate all that you're doing for the church, but if divorcing my wife is the only way you and I can be together, we'll just have to end things."

"You know I don't want that," she told him. "I just want to know that you hear me, and that you're going to create some sort of exit strategy. I also realize that I'm sort of wrong for expecting you to leave your wife so soon, when you and I haven't been together for very long. But it's just that I so know in my heart that we're supposed to be man and wife. I wish we'd met before you got married, but since we didn't, we'll have to figure out a long-range plan. So I'll tell you what. I'm going to be patient. I'm going to let you do what you need to do, but at some point we're going to have to talk about this again."

Dillon didn't like this because no matter what she said, he wasn't planning to leave Raven. At the same time, he also wasn't planning to give up Porsha. He wasn't sure how everything was going to work out, but somehow it would. Not only because he wanted it to, but because it had to.

CHAPTER 5

Alicia bit into her chicken sandwich and ate a couple of kettle potato chips. Levi had grilled various kinds of meat, and they were now sitting next to each other inside their four-season gazebo, having lunch.

"This is really good," she said. "So tender and juicy."

Levi smiled. "Why, thank you very much, my beautiful wife. You know I'm the grill master."

"Yeah, okay, grill master," she said, laughing. "Whatever you say."

"I am, and you know I am."

"Like I said, whatever . . . you . . . say."

Levi bit into his cheeseburger and drank some raspberry lemonade.

Alicia looked at Levi and shook her head.

"What's wrong?" he asked.

"I know we just talked about this last night and again this morning, but I still can't get over it. Raven actually wants to become co-pastor."

"Well, if I were you, I wouldn't worry about it. Because I don't believe Dillon wants that anyway."

"Even if he doesn't, I still know who Raven is. She's sneaky, manipulative, and deceitful, and there's no telling what she'll say or do to get Dillon to give her what she wants. Dillon really loves her, so what if he decides it's better to keep his wife happy?"

"I doubt that'll happen. I also doubt that the elder board will even consider voting in favor of Raven."

"Have you forgotten that Dillon founded NFCC and the parent ministry? So, technically, he can veto any decision the board agrees on, even if they vote on something unanimously."

"I understand that, but to date, Dillon has never done that."

"Well, even though I love my brother, I also know that there's a first time for everything. When Dillon first reached out to me saying that he'd started his own church, I was happy for him and glad he and I could finally become close. He ended up being the only family I had when that situation with Phillip happened. But when you decided to sow thousands of dollars into the ministry, we should have created a set of bylaws and had an attorney draw up new legal documents."

"He'd already incorporated by then."

"Still, we should have made sure that you or I or both of us had some sort of say-so when it comes to crucial decision making. My brother is very different than he used to be. He's much kinder and has a lot more compassion for people than he did before, but this whole Raven drama could change everything."

"Yeah, but regardless of how much he loves Raven, he's not naïve. And I just don't see him sharing his position with her. It's just not who he is or something he's ever talked about."

"I've never heard him talk about it, either, but this is the first time Raven has made her intentions known, and I promise you, she won't stop until she gets what she wants."

"Well, it's not like we can say anything unless she becomes more serious about this."

"As far as I'm concerned, she did that yesterday."

Levi didn't comment any further, but if Alicia had it her way she could talk about this particular topic all afternoon.

They sat quietly, still enjoying their food, but when Levi finished his last bite, he wiped his hands with a napkin and looked at Alicia. "You know, Raven is actually the least of my worries."

"Why is that?"

"You and I have our own problems to deal with."

Alicia was stunned by his comments but waited to hear what he had to say.

"I'm really worried about you. I'm worried about us."

Alicia didn't have to wonder anymore what he was talking about, because she knew where this conversation was heading. "I keep telling you everything's fine."

"That's what you say, but you know that's not true. On most nights, you barely sleep at all, and I have no idea how you function. But worse than that, you're starting to distance yourself from me again, and baby, I don't like it. You did the same thing right after Phillip died and the only difference then was that instead of not sleeping, you slept all the time. You were extremely depressed, and you hardly even went out of the house."

"I know, but I haven't been distant because I'm depressed. I'm really busy at work right now. Much busier than usual."

Levi ignored her response. "When are you finally going to decide to forgive yourself and mean it?"

"It's not as simple as that, but I'm trying. Baby, a man died, and it's all because of the way I lied and how selfish I was. I should have told him that it was you I loved, and that I couldn't marry him again."

"I hear that, and I agree, but what's done is done. I'm just as guilty as you, but we can't change what happened. We have to move on with our lives because if we don't, we'll never be completely happy."

"But I am happy."

"Only to a certain extent. You're happy for a while, and then you start withdrawing from me the way you've been doing for more than a couple of months now. It's been a roller coaster ride ever since we got married, and it's really starting to bother me. I've tried to be patient, but I think we need counseling."

Alicia frowned. "Why?"

"Because this has gone on long enough. I thought prayer and loving you as much as possible would be enough, but it's not."

"It *is* enough," she said, resting her hand on the side of his face. "Baby, you know I love you with all my heart. I've loved you since the first time we met, and that same love grew even stronger once we reconnected."

"That might be true, sweetheart, but we don't spend quality time together. Not to mention, when we're making love, it's almost like you're not even there."

"Only because I've been a bit on the tired side lately. And it's like I told you, I'm a little overwhelmed at work. I have a lot going on with all the meetings and preparation for upcoming projects. I'm also working with staff members in every department for the rest of church operations. Then, on top of that, I've been stressing over writing and submitting the synopsis for my next novel to my publisher. I should have done that a long time ago, but all my responsibilities at the church won't allow me to."

"I know you're busy, but I also think something else is bothering you."

"What?"

"You miss seeing and talking to your dad the way you used to."

"I do, but there's nothing I can do about that. When my family made the decision not to genuinely accept you as my husband, they also made the decision not to have a close relationship with me. My dad has preached many sermons about how when a man and a woman get married, they become one. He's always said that a man's wife and a woman's husband must always come before family and friends, yet he isn't happy about you and me getting married."

"I agree, but I still wish you and your dad were close again. Forget that he doesn't want anything to do with me. I'm fine with that. But you, on the other hand, have been a daddy's girl all your life, so I know deep down you're heartbroken over this. More than you're willing to admit."

Alicia's eyes filled with tears, and she swallowed hard, trying to pretend her strained relationship with her father wasn't affecting her to the extent Levi was describing. But truth was, she sometimes thought about nothing else. She couldn't believe so much had happened so fast, and that she'd lost almost everything that had mattered to her. All because she hadn't been faithful to Phillip either of the times she'd been married to him.

Alicia thought about all the skeletons from her past, but then tried pushing each of them from her mind. She worked hard not to obsess over any of them, but there were times, like now, when she was forced to think about Phillip's death. She also thought about how much she missed her dad and brother, Matthew. But more disturbing were the other insane thoughts that consumed her.

The first time this had happened was the night Phillip had died, and that kind of irrational thinking had tormented her ever since. She didn't think she was capable of hurting herself, but for the last few months, a voice had begun speaking to her. She didn't hear it daily and sometimes not even weekly, but it was becoming louder all the time. First it had convinced her that Phillip's death was her fault and only her fault . . . that he would still be alive if it hadn't been for her . . . that she'd still be close with the family she loved if she hadn't committed such a terrible sin as adultery. And the voice told her lots of other horrifying things, too, except now, it told her that she no longer deserved to live and that the only way to make things right on Phillip's behalf was to kill herself. She didn't want to believe the voice, but it was bold and it sounded as though it knew what was best. It seemed to give the kind of logical advice she wouldn't be able to keep ignoring. Not even if she wanted to.

CHAPTER 6

Dillon watched as the twelve lead elders of the church filed into the main conference room, just down the hallway from his study. It was Tuesday morning and time for their weekly staff meeting, and as Dillon observed them chatting and taking their seats, he felt proud. They were all very loyal to Dillon and the church, and Dillon compensated them nicely. Many of the men would have done their best even if they weren't being paid, but Dillon had learned as a teenager that when you rewarded people financially, they tended to work a lot harder. They were a little more dedicated and consistent. So, unlike he'd seen in some churches, he'd decided his elders would be paid great salaries. The elders were full-time employees who worked Tuesday through Friday and also on Saturday when they were needed. He also made sure Levi was paid exceptionally well, what with him being elder of the addiction ministry as well as chairman of the entire board; something that was the least Dillon could offer him, given how much time and money Levi had invested into the church overall.

Everyone quieted down and Levi said, "This meeting is officially called to order, and while our main topic for today is an upcoming marketing campaign, I think we should discuss any new business or specific issues going on within our individual ministries."

"I'll start," Elder Robert Freeman proclaimed.

Dillon almost frowned, but he didn't. What else was new? When did Elder Freeman *not* want to discuss his ministry before anyone else could share anything about theirs? He was elder of the men's ministry, but there were also eleven other ministries that were just as important: prayer, marriage, singles, funeral/loss and grief, conflict resolution, illness and shut-in, addiction, children's, teen, hospitality, and finance. There was also the women's ministry, but because Raven was the overseer, it was considered a separate entity from those that the twelve elders were responsible for.

Elder Freeman was sixtysomething and a good man in general, but Dillon was starting to regret his decision to appoint him as one of the leaders of the church. Sometimes he was way too vocal, and he acted as though he knew everything. He also offered his opinion whether it was asked for or not.

Dillon interrupted him. "That's fine, Elder Freeman, but if you don't mind, I'd like Elder Payne to go first today. He's already shared with me a little of what's happening with one of our married couples, and I'd like us all to give our input."

Elder Freeman sighed and leaned back in his chair more forcefully than normal. He wasn't happy, but Dillon didn't care. Elder Freeman was part of the leadership, yet there were times when Dillon had to subtly remind him who was actually in charge at New Faith.

"Why don't you go ahead," Levi told Elder Payne.

Elder Payne folded his arms. "Well, to put it plainly, the couple Pastor Black is referring to has been married for forty years, but they're contemplating divorce."

"Wow," Elder Vincent Barnett said. Vincent was Dillon's best friend and confidant, and while he was elder of the singles ministry, even he obviously couldn't understand how any husband and wife could be married for all those years and now want to end everything.

"I know," Elder Payne said. "It's shocking and heartbreaking. But this is the deal: The wife has had two affairs, and the most recent was just two months ago."

A couple of the other elders laughed under their breath, and soon the rest of them had half smiles on their faces.

"How old are these folks?" Elder Freeman asked. "Because I'm guessing they're as old as I am."

Elder Payne nodded. "They are. Somewhere in their middle sixties."

"What a shame," Levi said, and most of the other elders mumbled in agreement.

"The devil is always busy," Dillon said. "But my hope is that we can try to help these people. They've been married four decades, and I'd hate to see anyone throw all that away."

"Well, why is her old behind still sleeping around in the first place?" Elder Freeman wanted to know.

"She says she doesn't know," Elder Payne answered. "But she's extremely remorseful and apologetic. She's also begging her husband to give her another chance and says she'll never do anything like this again."

Elder Freeman pursed his lips. "Yeah, right. When did she have the first affair?"

"Years ago."

"Hmmph. I wonder if two affairs is all she's really had. How do we know she's telling the truth?"

"We don't," Dillon said, "but it's not our job to decide that one way or the other. Our job is to try to help save their marriage."

Elder Freeman shook his head, dismissing Dillon's comment.

"I agree," Levi said. "So if anyone has some suggestions for Elder Payne, let's hear them. Or actually, Elder Payne, why don't you tell us how you've advised them thus far."

"I've been praying with them, and I've also given them the name of a Christian marriage counselor who is one of the best in the area. The wife has begun seeing her, but the husband refuses to go. And sadly, I can't say that I blame him. I know God wants us to forgive, but if my own wife stepped out on me, not once but twice, it would be very hard to trust her again."

Elder Freeman rested his arms on the table. "Well, if it were me advising them, I'd tell them both to get over it and move on. Stay together no matter what, because God doesn't like divorce. When they got married, they took lifetime vows. End of story."

Dillon squinted his eyes. "But that's just

it, Elder Freeman; you're *not* the one advising them. Elder Payne is."

The room fell silent, and Dillon hated having to put Elder Freeman in his place in front of all the others. If only he would just shut up sometimes and allow the other men to say a few words. As it was, the younger elders hadn't commented, likely because they couldn't see where their opinions would even matter.

Elder Freeman twiddled his thumbs, but never as much as looked at Dillon.

"Maybe we should ask Lady Black to get involved," one of the younger elders finally said. "She oversees the women's ministry, so maybe she and some of the other ladies can meet with the wife, and then, Pastor, it might be good for you and Lady Black to meet with them together."

"I think you're right," Dillon said, remembering how great of a Christian counselor his dad was. Dillon had lots of ill feelings toward Curtis, but he couldn't deny how good his father was when it came to helping his members who had marital problems. If he and his dad had been on better terms, he'd call and ask him what he should do, but Dillon would never give him the benefit of knowing he needed him for anything.

They discussed the troubled couple for a

few minutes more, but when the fact that the wife had had two affairs came up again, Dillon looked at Levi and thought about his sister Alicia. She'd had two affairs on Phillip as well, and she'd had both with Levi. In their case, tragedy had even struck, and this was likely the reason Levi wasn't saying much anymore.

But then Elder Payne asked for his opinion. "So what do you think, Elder Cunningham?"

At first Levi hesitated, but then he said, "Well, it's no secret to any of you that I can relate to all of this. I'm ashamed of what my wife and I did, and I certainly don't condone infidelity. My wife's husband divorced her the first time we had an affair, and then you all know what happened when she married him a second time, and he found out we were seeing each other again. It was a total disaster, and I'll go to my grave regretting the terrible choices we made. Still, I think the couple in question should fight for their marriage. They should give it their all. I realize how hurt the husband is and that when people hurt you and betray you, it's hard to forgive them and even harder to trust them again, but I believe it can be done. Especially with prayer, open communication, and making sure God is the center of the marriage from this point on."

"Amen," Elder Freeman chimed in. "That's all I was trying to say. God wants married people to work out their differences. No matter how serious they are. That is, unless physical abuse is involved. Even mental abuse can be unacceptable, too, depending on how severe it is. But anything else . . . I say it can be fixed."

Dillon wondered if Elder Freeman would ever change. Giving input was good, but why did he always have to have the last word? Make it seem that he'd already said what needed to be done, and anything the rest of them suggested meant nothing?

Levi turned the page of his legal-size notepad. "The next order of business is the new marketing campaign. Pastor Black, why don't you tell us what the overall theme will be."

Dillon leaned forward. "Well, as you know, we've already been outlining a few ideas, but our main goal will be to introduce all twelve of your ministries to the city of Mitchell and the overall community. What I want is for New Faith Christian Center and New Faith Ministries, Inc., to be known as the church organization that goes out of its way to help people. Not just in one or two areas of their lives, but in all areas. I also want to portray the twelve of you who lead the ministries as twelve men who can, in many ways, be compared to Jesus's twelve disciples."

Dillon waited for a few nods of approval, but when no one as much as blinked, he hurried to explain what he meant.

"Don't get me wrong, I'm certainly not trying to equate myself to Jesus, but because I did in fact select every last one of you, I do believe you represent His disciples."

This last comment made Elder Freeman lean forward, too. "Okay, that's all fine and well, but I think we need to be very careful when it comes to comparing ourselves to Jesus and his twelve apostles. Because if we aren't, this campaign of ours might start to sound more like blasphemy."

Dillon frowned and laughed out loud. "As usual, Elder Freeman, you're taking things way too seriously. I mean, way, way too seriously."

"I just like to do things the right way. Making sure we don't disrespect God and His Word."

Dillon raised his eyebrows but held his temper. They discussed a few more points of the marketing plan, along with a couple of other pieces of business, but thankfully, Elder Freeman kept quiet.

When the meeting adjourned, everyone walked out, but Dillon stopped Levi.

"Hey, man, you got a minute?"

"Of course," Levi said, closing the conference room door and sitting back down. "What's up?"

"I know I've said this many times before, but today is one of those days where I just want to thank you again. You know, for everything you've done to help build up the ministry. We certainly wouldn't be where we are without your support."

"It's no problem, and you're quite welcome. I was glad to do it."

"You're like a brother to me, and you've made a world of difference here."

"All I knew was that when I got out of prison, I wasn't going back. I also knew that I was going to live for God and not find myself pulled back into the life. Selling drugs made me a lot of money, more than most people make their whole lives, but it was wrong. That's why I wanted to make sure every dime was put to good use. Before I met you, I was going to open a restaurant, but investing in God's work has been a lot more rewarding. The church has grown tremendously, and I'm glad to be a part of it."

"I'm glad you are, too, and you already

72

know how happy I am that my sister and I worked out our differences. We couldn't stand each other, but what the devil meant for bad, God had a much bigger plan for."

"Amen to that."

"The other thing I wanted to talk to you about is the marketing campaign. I want you to play an even larger role than you have been when it comes to promoting the church. Particularly when it comes to our twelve ministries. We have a lot of people in the city struggling with addiction, and what I want is for you to share how you were once a drug dealer who did prison time, yet now you've turned your life over to God and will help anyone any way you can. I know this will mean becoming even more transparent about your past than you have been, so we'll only do it if you're okay with it."

"It's true that I will always be ashamed of the life I led, but I'm not ashamed of the way I've turned it around. So whatever you need me to do, I will."

"I really appreciate that."

"Although, I have to say, while I'm fine with helping anyone I can, I'm starting to think that your sister and I are the ones who need help the most."

"How so?"

"You know I love Alicia with every breath

I take, but for the first time since we got married, I'm not so sure we can survive the whole Phillip situation. I believe she loves me completely, but since Phillip died things haven't been the same. There's been a slight disconnect between us. We've never been able to get back to where we were."

"I'm sorry to hear that. Have you talked to her about it?"

"I have, as recently as yesterday. But she won't admit that the problem is as bad as it is. She doesn't see that her guilt is affecting her more and more . . . and that it's starting to wear on our marriage in a pretty harsh way."

"Do you want me to talk to her?"

"Do you mind? She's not going to be happy that I told you anything, but I don't care about that. I just want us to get help. I've been trying to handle this on my own and praying things would get better, but they're not."

"I've been praying for God to give her peace as well, because I can tell Phillip's death still haunts her. I'll make sure to talk to her today, though."

"Thank you for that. I hate putting you in the middle of this, but . . ."

"Don't say another word. Consider it already done."

CHAPTER 7

When Dillon heard a knock at his door, he knew it was Alicia. "Come in."

"Hey," she said, walking into his office. Hers was only a few doors down, and Dillon had called her ten minutes ago, asking if they could have a quick chat.

"Have a seat," he said.

Alicia sat down in the supple wood-framed leather chair in front of his desk.

"So what's going on?"

"Well, first of all, I wanted to update you on our elder board meeting this morning. I brought up a new idea in terms of how we should market, and I really think it could work."

"That's good to hear."

"Yeah, well, I thought it was good, too, but I'm not so sure all the elders agree. Especially Elder Freeman."

"Why do you say that?"

"What I want is for us to promote the idea

of our twelve elders as being similar to Jesus's disciples. But of course, Elder Freeman took it the wrong way. He suggested I was comparing *myself* to Jesus."

Alicia laughed a little. "You don't think he really thought that, do you?"

"Yeah, I'm sad to say he did."

"Did you explain what you meant?"

"I tried to, but you know how Elder Freeman is. Once he gets something in his head, that's the end of it."

"Well, I think promoting all twelve of our primary ministries is a good thing, and it wouldn't hurt to pro mote our women's ministry as well. There are a lot of women in our community who are hurting in many ways, and we could really help them a great deal."

"I agree, and I'll talk to Raven about that tonight."

"Yeah, better you than me," Alicia said.

Whether Alicia realized it or not, Dillon had always known that there wasn't a love fest going on between her and Raven, but he'd never said anything to her. As a matter of fact, until yesterday, Raven had never gone as far as saying anything to him about Alicia.

"Why do you say that?" he asked.

"Well, for one thing, I don't think she was

too happy about the way I reacted to her news on Sunday."

"What? About her becoming co-pastor?"

"That would be it."

"She's been talking privately about it for a while, but now she's at a point where she wants to move forward with it."

"And you agree with her?"

The old Dillon hadn't shown much loyalty to anyone, but for some reason, he'd always felt that he owed a certain level of devotion to his wife. He wasn't perfect by any stretch of the imagination, but he did love Raven and he tried to respect her the way a husband should — that is, with the exception of the affair he was having with Porsha.

Still, he felt compelled to be honest with Alicia. "To tell you the truth, I don't."

Alicia didn't seem shocked. "Did you tell her that?"

"I did, and she wasn't happy. We had a big argument about it."

"I just don't think it's a good idea. Maybe somewhere down the road the church will be ready for a female pastor, but not now. Not when we're trying to grow the membership."

"You're right, but I don't see Raven backing down from this. She wants to be co-pastor, and she doesn't see a reason why she can't."

"Look, I don't want to speak against Raven, because she's your wife, but if you allow her to become co-pastor, you're headed for a lot of heartache. Both with your home life and the way you run the church. Raven is strong, smart, and independent, which is all great, but it also means she's going to want a certain amount of control. Something I don't see you being okay with."

Dillon sighed. He knew Alicia was right, but he also didn't like what all this would mean for his marriage. He and Raven loved each other and had gotten along fine. Until now.

"I'll just have to deal with this the best way I can," he said. "Try to get her to see that becoming co-pastor isn't a good idea."

"I'm sorry I don't feel differently about this, but I have to say, I don't see any of the elders voting yes to it, either. Not even Levi."

"I just wish heading up the women's ministry was enough for her. She does an amazing job, and there's so much more to be done with the ladies who attend New Faith."

Alicia crossed her legs. "I don't understand why it's not. Our stepmom has done great things with their women's ministry for years, and I don't think I've ever heard her as much as mention anything about being co-pastor."

Charlotte wasn't Dillon's favorite person, but Alicia was right about her. She wanted to run things and certainly enjoyed having a noticeable amount of power — churchwise and statuswise — but she didn't want to stand side by side with their dad.

"Maybe you could ask her to talk to Raven," Dillon said, laughing.

"Well, it's actually not a bad idea. Maybe Charlotte could talk some sense into her — that is, if Raven hadn't betrayed our dad."

Dillon shook his head. "After all this time, I still can't believe how close you are with her."

"When she and Daddy first got married I could take her or leave her, but as I got older, she and I got to know each other a whole lot better. Then when Matthew and I became close, Charlotte treated me more and more like a daughter than a stepdaughter. Plus, she's only eleven years older than me, and I think that's how we became good friends."

"I guess, Sis, but to me she's treacherous. That's why I nicknamed her Charlotte the Harlot as soon as I met her."

Alicia shook her head, laughing. "You just need to give her a chance."

"I doubt it, because it's not like she can stand me, either. And then after I did what I did to Dad and Matthew before I left Mitchell . . ."

"I know, but anything is possible. Look at you and me. Who would have guessed that we could connect and have the relationship we have now?"

"That's very true, but I don't think Charlotte, Matthew, or even Dad for that matter, will ever fully forgive me."

"Well, not being around them is the hardest thing I've ever had to do. Charlotte and I still talk pretty regularly, because she gave Levi and me her blessing a long time ago. But Daddy and Matthew just won't do it. With Daddy, I'm not as shocked because he loved Phillip like a son, but Matthew was my heart. He always loved me and saw me as the big sister he looked up to for everything. And I miss that. I miss him. I miss everything."

Dillon heard all that his sister was saying and he understood how she felt, but what she didn't know was that he wanted the same things. He was very good at pretending that he didn't care whether he saw his dad or not, but he did care. And he thought about his brother, Matthew, a lot, too. Curtina was the baby of the family, and while he'd never seen her as anything more than a spoiled brat, he sometimes wondered what it would be like to have a baby sister to love and dote on.

He still couldn't admit his feelings to Alicia even now, though. "I hate that you're not as close to all of them as you used to be, but who knows. Maybe they'll eventually come around. Especially once they continue to see how honest and genuine Levi is. They may not know it or want to believe it, but Levi really does love God. You can tell that just from being around him."

"He's a great guy, and I couldn't love a man more."

Dillon looked at her, and he could tell she knew something was wrong.

"What is it?" she asked.

"Well, I hope you don't get upset, but Levi confided something to me."

Alicia scrunched her forehead. "When?"

"Right after our meeting."

Alicia stared at him emotionless, but Dillon could tell that she wasn't all that happy about what he'd just told her.

"What did he say?"

"He's worried about you and your marriage."

"Wow, and he decided to bring our problems to you? Although, I don't see what problems we have in the first place."

"I don't think he saw it like that. He loves you, and he knows I would never repeat your business to anyone."

"He still shouldn't have bothered you with this. Especially since we're fine."

"I know, Sis, but Levi doesn't think so. He says the whole Phillip issue is really bothering you."

"He's exaggerating. I do feel bad about what happened, and it's only common sense that I blame myself for it, but I'm good."

"Maybe you should talk to a professional or join a support group."

"Look, Brother," Alicia said, standing up and trying to appear normal, happy, and confident. "I know you mean well, and I appreciate that, but I really am okay. There's nothing for you to worry about. I promise."

"All I want is the best for you. I know when we first met, we didn't hit it off very well, but now that we have I can't help but worry. You're the only family I have a relationship with, and as your big brother it's my job to look out for you."

Alicia laughed. "You're only two years

older than me, remember?"

"I know you think this is funny, but I'm serious. If you need help, I'm here for you."

"For the last time, I'm good. Really. Now, I'll see you later, okay?"

Dillon nodded but then sighed when she left his office. She didn't seem like herself, and while she'd tried to cover it up, she'd seemed almost depressed. But at least he'd tried to talk to her the way he'd told Levi he would, and he'd let her know he was in her corner. Dillon and Alicia were siblings for life, and he would do anything he could for her. He could only do that, though, if she let him.

CHAPTER 8

Alicia paced back and forth, wringing her hands, while her heart raced faster and faster. How dare Levi go to Dillon behind her back. She couldn't wait to confront him, something she'd desperately been wanting to do ever since learning from her brother that Levi had told their business. She'd left Dillon's office hours ago, yet she hadn't pondered about much else, and she wouldn't be content until she told Levi what she thought of him.

At first she'd had a mind to question him right there at the church, but it wouldn't have been fair to the other staff members. So instead, she'd held her tongue and feigned a smile for the rest of the day. Now, though, she waited for Levi in fury.

She paced for another twenty minutes, and finally Levi walked in. Alicia rushed into the kitchen toward him. He seemed startled, but lay his black briefcase on the granite island in silence.

"Why, Levi?" she asked.

"Why what?"

"Oh, so now you're going to play dumb, I see. You know exactly what I'm talking about. Why'd you tell our business to Dillon?"

"Look, baby, I apologize, but I didn't know what else to do. I tried talking to you, but you don't think anything is wrong."

"Because there isn't."

Levi sat down in one of the counter-height brown chairs.

Alicia walked closer to him. "What you and I discuss is between us and no one else. So I hope this makes your first and last time doing something like this."

"I understand why you're upset, but I'm not going to just accept what's going on. You have some real issues, and it's affecting our marriage."

"Maybe *you* have issues, but I'm fine."

"Isn't that the same kind of thing your friend Melanie used to say when you accused her of being anorexic? She didn't even know she had a problem until she got sick enough and almost died."

Alicia's heart pounded harder. "Excuse me? I just know you're not comparing my situation with Melanie's."

"I am, because you're in denial."

"Why are you talking to me this way?" she asked. "And why are you betraying me like this?"

"Baby, how in the world am I betraying you? Because I went to your brother, who loves you? Because I'm trying to get you to see that when you tried to tell your best friend she had a problem, she wouldn't hear it?"

"That's exactly what I mean. All this time, you've been a loving, loyal husband, and now, out of nowhere, you've turned into a traitor?"

Levi looked at her like she was crazy, but what he didn't know was that she was just getting started.

"I gave up everything for you! You hear me? Everything! My parents, my brother, my baby sister, my entire reputation. When Phillip died and word got out that he and I had tussled over a gun because of you, even some of my readers sent me nasty email messages. Then others were posting so many awful comments on my social media pages, I had to suspend every one of them."

"I'm really sorry you feel that way, but this is part of the reason I think you need to see someone."

"Like who?"

"A psychologist. Someone who specializes in what you're dealing with and can help you."

"Well, isn't that a coincidence. Dillon suggested the same thing this afternoon, and now I know why. You told him to. You filled his head with so many lies that now he thinks I'm unstable. Maybe even insane."

"That's just not true, baby. I never told him anything like that."

"You're such a liar."

"Honey, what's wrong with you? Why are you so angry and being so mean?"

"Because you betrayed me. You went behind my back like it was nothing. For the whole year we've been married, you've professed your undying love for me, but now the real Levi is coming out, I guess."

Levi stood up and walked over to her. But when he tried to hold her she snatched away from him.

"Don't touch me."

Then the voice in her head told her much more. *If you trust this fool, you'll regret it for the rest of your life. Can't you see what he's up to? All he's doing is trying to turn Dillon against you. The only family you have left.*

"Baby, why are you so worked up?" he asked. "And all because I told your brother I was worried about you?"

Alicia tried to ignore the voice in her head, but it spoke again. *You know he's lying, right? He's not worried about you. He's just trying to destroy you. Cause problems between you and your brother, because he's jealous of the close relationship you and Dillon now have. No matter what he says, he can't be trusted. He also doesn't love you. He doesn't care a thing about you.*

Alicia pressed the sides of her head, trying to gain clarity. Then she looked at Levi. "You never should have done that. Whatever problems you have with *me* are between you and *me*. Period."

"Okay, look. I'm really sorry, and I'll never discuss you or us with anyone again."

"Good."

He's still lying. He's going to tell even more people about you than just Dillon. He's just waiting for the right opportunity, and then you won't have any family members who care about you.

Alicia shook her head and closed her eyes. She fought against the voice, pushing it far out of her mind because no matter how angry she was with Levi, she knew he loved her and that he would never try to harm her. He also loved Dillon.

She sat down across from where Levi had been sitting, and he walked around and hugged her again. She laid her head against his chest and burst into tears.

"Baby, you know I'm here for you, and the only reason I think you should see someone is so you can feel better. You're dealing with the loss of your former husband and the loss of your family, and that's a lot for anyone. And then to hear you talk about what happened on social media with some of your readers . . . Is that why you stopped writing? Is that why it's taking you so long to send your publisher the synopsis for your next book?"

"Partly," she said, sniffling. "I'm busy running the ministry, but after I lost so many readers I just didn't feel motivated anymore. It didn't seem like it was worth it."

"Gosh, baby, I'm so, so sorry, and we have to find a way to get you back on track. You loved writing too much to just give it up like that."

"If your readers don't support you, writing books is pointless. The greatest joy of being an author is talking to your readers in person at events and communicating with them online. I mean, don't get me wrong, the majority of my readers were very kind and supportive when Phillip died, but it was the few who basically said they hated me that caused me so much pain."

"I know you don't think you need to see anyone, but baby, won't you at least try? For you and for us. I'll even go with you."

Alicia heard that awful voice chiming in again, but she tried to ignore it. Until she couldn't.

Don't be a fool. Levi isn't the man you think he is. He never was, but you just weren't able to see it until now. He's been tricking you and pretending all along, and he's never really loved you. He only acted as though he did because he wanted to take you from Phillip. He also wanted Phillip to die, and that's why he gave you that ultimatum. Remember when he told you it was either Phillip or him? And guess what else? He also doesn't love God the way he keeps claiming to everyone. He's only putting up a front to get what he wants, and if you stay with him he'll destroy you. Get real, Alicia. Because how can a criminal stop being a criminal and all of a sudden find Jesus?

"No," Alicia screamed, pushing Levi away from her as hard as she could.

He stumbled and frowned at her. "What in the world is wrong with you?"

She got up from the chair. "You just leave me alone. You hear me?"

"Baby, why are you acting like this?"

Alicia squinted her eyes at him. "You think

you're slick, but I know what you're up to. You say you love me, but now you're sneaking around behind my back."

"But I told you why I went to Dillon. I didn't know what else to do, and I'm worried about you."

"Well, don't, because it's like I keep telling you . . . I'm fine. And I've always been able to take care of myself."

Levi seemed stunned and like he didn't know what else to say, and Alicia was glad because she didn't want to hear any more of his lies. She'd been fooled by his deception for far too long.

Alicia stared at him, rolled her eyes in disgust, and left the room.

But as she backed away, the voice in her head got louder.

Good for you. You did the right thing by walking away from him. Levi is a snake that can't be trusted, and if you're not careful, he's going to betray you again . . . and again . . . and again. Just you wait and see, and the next time it'll be much worse than just his going to your brother behind your back.

Alicia pressed either side of her head again and went upstairs to their bedroom. All she wanted was for the voice to stop. She wanted it to stop torturing her. And, thank-

fully, it did. It was gone, and Alicia prayed
it would never return.

CHAPTER 9

Normally, Dillon never arrived at the church before nine a.m., and especially not on Wednesdays, because he knew he had to teach Bible study in the evening. But this was one Wednesday morning he hadn't been able to wait to leave the house. Two days had passed since he and Raven had gotten into it over her desire to become co-pastor, and sadly, she still wasn't speaking to him. She was angrier than he'd realized, and last night she'd gone as far as sleeping in one of the guest bedrooms.

Dillon had always loved the fact that he and Raven rarely disagreed about anything, and that they never had to raise their voices. But now she had gone from yelling at him to tossing him the silent treatment. She wanted to be co-pastor, and she didn't want to take no for an answer.

Dillon had even tried talking to her this morning before leaving, but she'd pretended he was invisible. He'd told her how sorry he was, but she'd barely blinked, and this was when he'd left and driven to the church.

He couldn't help trying once more to make things up to her, though, so he picked up his office phone and called her. It rang multiple times until her voice mail came on, so Dillon pressed the button on the base of his phone to get another dial tone. Then he tried her again. He did this two additional times, until she answered.

"Why do you keep calling me over and over like some child?" she spat.

"Because we need to talk. You're upset, and we can't go on like this."

"You should've thought about that before you gouged a knife in my back."

"Baby, please. You know that's not true. We just have a difference of opinion is all."

"Well, if you don't support me on this, don't expect me to support you, either. Not with anything."

"But you know how some of the members feel about female pastors, right? Even when some of the female ministers have given sermons, not everyone has been happy about it."

"What does that matter to you? You're my husband, and you're supposed to have my back. It's supposed to be you and me against the world."

"I do, but why would you want us to take a chance on turning people off? What if people start leaving the church, when our goal right now is to bring in more?"

"That's not going to happen."

"How can you be so sure?"

"Because this is what God wants. I told you that already. Becoming co-pastor isn't my decision, it's His."

"Why don't we wait until sometime next year?"

"Why? What difference will that make?"

"We'll be finished with the marketing campaign by then, and I expect that a lot more people will have joined New Faith. We'll be in a better position to make changes and hopefully not lose as many people."

Dillon didn't believe a word he'd just said, but he was trying to buy more time before simply telling her that this was never going to happen.

"Baby," she said, softening her tone for some reason, "can't you at least allow me to go before the elder board? Maybe they'd be more open to it than you think."

Dillon had been hoping she wouldn't suggest that, but maybe explaining her desire to the board in person was exactly what needed to happen. They would never go for it, and once she realized that, maybe she would move on.

"Let me talk to Levi," he said. "But I'm sure it won't be a problem."

"Thank you," she said, seemingly content. "All I need is a chance to talk to them and let them know how good this will be for the church. How great it will be for the ministry."

"I agree," he lied.

"Do you think I'll be able to come to the meeting right away next week?"

Dillon closed his eyes, wishing she'd stop pushing so hard. "I don't see why not."

"Although, I think we both know that even if they all vote no, you still have the right to make me co-pastor. You founded this church, and you can do anything you want."

"Yeah, but you know I've never had to do that. And I don't want to start. The elders of this church are very loyal to me, and making demands and vetoing the majority's decision will only cause problems."

"Well, I'm just saying. You can do whatever you want. But maybe that won't be necessary, because I really believe they'll be fine with it. They've always given me free rein with the way I run the women's ministry, so it's not like they don't trust my judgment."

Dillon knew full well that one thing had

nothing to do with the other, but he kept quiet. He wanted to make his case and try to change her mind, but he decided it wasn't worth it. She was speaking to him again, and it was better to leave well enough alone.

Dillon leaned back in his chair. "So are we good?"

"We're very good," she said with joy in her voice. "And, baby, thank you."

"You're welcome. But hey, I need to get going. I'll see you this afternoon when you get here, okay?"

"See you then. Bye, baby."

Dillon set the phone on its base and relaxed even further in his chair. What a day, and already he couldn't wait until next Tuesday so Raven could address the elder board. They'd never go along with her plans, and this would all be over. She wouldn't be happy, but by then, he'd have thought up something else to appease her.

Now, though, as he sat quietly, he reminisced on how far he'd come. How powerful he was within the church and Mitchell's community. But it wasn't enough. It was a nice start, but he wouldn't be satisfied until he was bigger and better than his dad. He wouldn't feel as though he'd arrived until his congregation was larger than Curtis

Black's. This was Dillon's number one goal in life, and he was willing to do whatever he had to. Sure, increasing the membership was going to help him get there, but he didn't want to wait years for it to happen. He wanted new members, and more than that, he wanted his *dad's* parishioners. He wanted folks to leave Deliverance Outreach in droves and follow him.

Dillon tossed a number of ideas around in his head but then became furious. His dad was a monster. Dillon had just told this story to his congregation for the umpteenth time on Sunday, but now he thought about it again. His dad had actually disowned him when he was a newborn baby and caused his mom to commit suicide. It was that particular thought that always turned Dillon's anger to sorrow. If only Dillon had gotten to know his mom. If only she'd lived until he'd been old enough to spend time with her and remember it. Because as it was now, he had no memories of her at all. His aunt, Susan, had told him everything she could about her, but it hadn't been the same. Dillon almost wanted to cry, but instead his pain turned to rage and he wanted revenge again. Well before moving back to Atlanta, he'd worked hard to scandalize his father's name, but his plan had failed — thanks to that scatterbrained chick, Melissa, he'd been engaged to.

Dillon hit his desk with his fist but then heard a knock at his door. He took a deep breath, trying to gain some composure.

"Come in."

When the door opened, his friend Vincent walked in. "Hey, you got a few minutes?"

"Of course, what's up?"

Vincent closed the door and took a seat. "Nothing really, just thought I'd stop by before my day gets started . . . and to ask you a very important question."

"What's that?"

"Was it as good as always?"

"Was *what* as good as always?"

Vincent smiled slyly. "Man, come on now. You know exactly what I mean. I'm talking about your girl Porsha. Because I know you went and bedded down that sweet thing . . . just like you do every Monday afternoon."

"Man, that was two days ago, and you're just asking me about that?"

"Shoot, better late than never. Now give up the four-one-one."

"Not much to tell, except the girl is still something else. And it's like I keep saying: Hands down, she's the best I've ever had."

"I hear you, but you'd better hope Raven never finds out about her."

"Isn't that the truth? But I don't see how she ever will. Unless you or Porsha get crazy in the head and decide to blab everything to her."

"Man, please. I think you know me much better than that, and I can't see Porsha saying anything, either. Not when you're givin' her all that good lovin'."

"Yeah, well, you know how some of these side chicks can get. They become bold and want to be out front and center. They want you to divorce your wife and marry them. As a matter of fact, Porsha has already mentioned that very thing. Says she'll be patient, but I'm not sure for how long."

Vincent frowned. "You wouldn't actually divorce Raven for her, would you?"

"Of course not, but I do have to make Porsha *think* I would. Gotta keep her happy and convinced, though, that I can't even consider leaving Raven for at least another year. I've already explained to her that all a divorce would do right now is ruin any chance we have of growing the membership. It'll destroy the ministry completely."

"I just hope she listens to you," Vincent told him.

"She will. I made things very clear to her on Monday."

"That's good to hear. You keep her in her

place, and there won't be any drama."

"Exactly."

"But man, I gotta tell you," Vincent said, "it's this very kind of thing that makes me not want to ever get married. Dating is more than a notion itself, but that whole ball-and-chain action seems like more trouble than it's worth."

Dillon shook his head. "You're terrible, and I'm glad you don't say those kinds of things to the young single men at this church. Especially the ones who attend your ministry meetings."

"Course not. I tell them all the time that it's better to marry than to burn. I teach lessons from First Corinthians seven regularly."

"Good. None of us is perfect, but I want it to always be known that here at New Faith, we teach and encourage only what the Bible says."

"No doubt. So what else is up?"

"Well, before you knocked on my door, I was thinking hard about my dad, man."

"Have you spoken to him?"

"No, not in a while, but lately I've been getting more and more pissed off at him. He really did my mom wrong. He did us both wrong."

Vincent rubbed the bottom of his chin.

"Look, man, you don't have to convince me of anything. I know that's your dad, and I don't mean any disrespect, but that fool should've been brought down a long time ago. Your mom is dead because of him, and who would do something that dirty? Have a friend submit a DNA sample, just so you can deny your own child?"

"I feel the same way, and that's why I won't be satisfied until we take his members from him. When I get done, my dad won't even be able to pay the electric bill over at Deliverance. He won't have more than a hundred people left."

"Sounds like a great idea to me," Vincent said.

"We just have to give folks a reason to want to leave there."

"Well, I've already given you the best idea possible."

"I know, but I'm just not sure about that. I was hoping we wouldn't have to go that far."

"Well, it's your call, and I'll do whatever you say. Anything you need, I got you."

"I appreciate that, man. You've been my ride-or-die for the last three years, and I'll never be able to thank you enough. Still can't believe you moved all the way here from Atlanta just so you could help build the ministry. Especially since you don't have any family in Illinois."

"It wasn't a problem, and I'm here for you no matter what."

"I love my wife, my sister, and Levi big time, but with this, I need to do things my way. And I have to do it without either of them knowing about it."

"I agree. They're all for growing the church, but they'd never go along with trying to ruin your father. Raven might be okay with it, but not Alicia and Levi."

"That's why this has to remain between you and me. I don't have a real plan yet, but I will."

"You'll come up with something," Vincent said. "Just like always."

CHAPTER 10

Alicia flipped through multiple pages of New Faith's latest financial report, mostly reviewing month-to-date tithing and offering deposits and overall expenditures. She would be meeting with Lynette Reynolds, New Faith's CFO, later this afternoon, but she was glad to see that things were looking pretty good. Actually, they were looking exceptional, as the current numbers were much better than what Lynette had projected at the end of last year. The church and the overall ministry were taking in much more than they were paying out, which was great news for the upcoming marketing campaign. It would take thousands to do the kind of campaign Dillon had in mind, and thankfully, they'd have no problem paying for it. There were also noticeable funds sitting in the building fund account, and this would make all the difference when it was time to either expand at their current location or move to a larger church altogether. Alicia would have preferred the former, since they were situated in such a great location, but with the high rate of members joining all the time, buying or building a new church was likely their only option.

Alicia scanned a few more pages and then took a quick look at the numbers from this past Sunday alone. People were not only giving tithes and offerings, but they'd also seemed to increase their contributions toward each of the thirteen special ministries. Interestingly enough, the women's ministry tended to receive more dollars than the twelve that were led by the elders, which said a lot about Raven and her ability to get what she asked for. This was great when it came to certain areas of business relating to the church, but it was that same charm and intelligence of hers that might push Dillon to support her desire to become co-pastor. Alicia sure hoped it wouldn't, though, because what a disaster that would be. There was just no way it could work, so Alicia prayed Dillon wouldn't let it happen.

Alicia glanced over at her desk calendar and saw that it was July 1. Within seconds, her spirits dropped, because they were only three days away from the Fourth. Since she'd been a child, this had been one of her favorite holidays, but not anymore. Not since she'd married Levi and they hadn't been able to spend it with her family. In the past, she'd sometimes spent holidays with her mom and stepdad and sometimes with her dad and stepmom, and she'd had the time of her life either way. If only they could love and accept Levi the way they were supposed to, she could still be close with all of them. She and Levi did spend time with his mom on holidays, along with some of his other relatives, but it wasn't the same.

She hated this, but no matter how she tried to weigh things, she just couldn't allow them to treat Levi like he was the enemy. It was wrong, and this was the reason she'd stood her ground for so long. But nonetheless, her mom was heavily on her mind and she couldn't help calling her.

Tanya was a counselor, so she dialed her mother's office number and waited.

"Hi, sweetheart," Tanya said.

"Hey, Mom, how are you?"

"Everything's great. What about you?"

"We're good. Just thought I'd take a break and see what you were up to."

After a bit of silence Tanya finally said, "It's good to hear your voice."

There was another pause, and Alicia could

tell the conversation was just as awkward for her mom as it was for her.

Alicia waited a little longer and then said, "I know you're probably working, so did I catch you at a bad time?"

"No, not at all. I have a few minutes."

"Good. So what are you and Dad James doing for the Fourth?"

"We're going away for the weekend. Heading down to New Orleans for the Essence Festival. I thought I mentioned that to you a couple of months ago."

"Actually, you did. I'd forgotten, though," she said, thinking how the reason she hadn't remembered was because she and her mom talked a lot less than they used to. Before her marriage to Levi, she and her mom had sometimes chatted on the phone two to three times per day, but now, they were lucky if they spoke twice a month.

"We've never gone, so we're really excited about it," Tanya said. "Been wanting to get there for years."

"Mel and I went last summer, and it was a really great time," Alicia said, referring to her best friend, Melanie Richardson. "One of the best events we've ever traveled to."

"That's what I've always heard."

When her mom had first mentioned it to her, Alicia had wondered how two people her mom's and stepdad's ages would even be able to enjoy a music festival. But then she'd realized that there were so many keynote speakers, panels, and old-school singers, anyone could enjoy themselves.

Alicia relaxed farther back in her chair. "It'll be a lot of fun."

"I believe it will, and hey, how is Levi?"

Alicia was a bit taken aback, because no one in her family ever asked about her husband. Whether they spoke to her by phone or accidentally saw her out in public, they acted as though she were single and lived alone.

"He's fine."

"That's good. Please tell him I said hello."

Alicia wasn't sure how to respond, mostly because she was still too shocked that her mom was asking about her son-in-law.

"Honey, what's wrong?"

"I guess I'm just a little surprised that you're asking about him."

"I know, and I'm sorry for feeling the way I have all this time. But I've also been praying about it and doing a lot of soul-searching, and I realize that it's just not right for us to shun Levi or make things hard for you. We may not like the way the two of you got together or the affair you had, but what's done is done and we all have to move on. I've been asking God for direction, and I know I was wrong."

Tears filled Alicia's eyes. "Oh my God, Mom. You have no idea how long I've wanted to hear you say those words. I miss our conversations and visits, and it's been so hard pretending that none of this bothered me. The hardest thing in the world is being married to someone that none of your family members love, or even like for that matter."

"I can only imagine, sweetheart, and I hope you can forgive us. Your dad James feels the same way, and I know he'll be calling you later. I've been meaning to call you the last couple of days to apologize, but I just couldn't get the nerve up to do it. I was too embarrassed," she said, sniffling. "It was too hard to admit that I'd distanced myself from my only child and best friend, all because things didn't turn out the way we wanted. So I'm really glad you called me today instead. It was all in God's plan, and there's something else I want you to know. Regardless of how we felt about Phillip's death and your marriage to Levi, we never stopped loving you. You are my baby, and I love you with all my heart."

"I know that, Mom, and I love you, too. You mean everything to me, but this whole thing has taken a huge toll on me, mentally and emotionally," she said, wishing she had the courage to tell her mom about the voice that kept torturing her.

"I'm sure it has, and again, I'm very sorry. I also hope your father can eventually find it in his heart to accept Levi, because I know that hurts, too."

"It does, Mom. Daddy has talked about forgiveness in more sermons than I can count, yet he won't forgive Levi and me. He says he has, but he hasn't."

"I know this has been tough, but it's just that your dad loved Phillip so much. He loved him like a son, and he's just being stubborn about it. But you just keep praying for things to turn around, and I'll do the same."

Alicia smiled and wiped her tears. "You have really made my day, Mom."

"I'm glad, because you've certainly made mine."

"I'm so relieved."

"Me too, and hey, I have a session I need to do shortly, so I'm going to have to hang up. But why don't you and Levi plan on coming over for dinner one evening next week when we're back in town?"

"That sounds good. And Mom?"

"Yes?"

"I know I just said this a few minutes ago, but I love you so, so much."

"I love you, too, sweetheart, and I'll make sure to call you tomorrow before we leave."

"Talk to you then. Bye, Mom."

Alicia hung up and wiped the rest of her tears, but the more she thought about her mom and how happy she was right now, the more she cried. Her heart was overjoyed, and she couldn't wait to tell Levi the wonderful news. He would be thrilled to know that his in-laws had decided to accept him and that they were finally inviting him over for dinner.

Alicia was beyond elated . . . until Phillip crossed her mind. However, just as quickly as negative thoughts eased their way in, she dismissed those feelings and thought only about the conversation she'd had with her mom. She hadn't felt this joyful in a long time, and she was grateful. She was ecstatic, and she couldn't have stopped smiling if she wanted to.

CHAPTER 11

Dillon moved to the side of Raven, breathing heavily, and all he could think about was Porsha. Here he'd just made love to his wife, the woman he loved, but she simply couldn't satisfy him the way Porsha did. Raven held her own, there was no refuting that, and there had also been a time when Dillon craved being with her, but ever since sleeping with Porsha the very first time, his feelings had changed. It wasn't something he'd counted on happening, and he wondered what it would mean for him and Raven down the road — how it would affect their future as husband and wife. He'd been thinking that he could handle this — being married and having a plaything on the side — but his feelings and attraction for Porsha had grown faster and more intense than he'd been prepared for. Things were escalating in a number of ways, and he had to find a way to keep them in order. He had to gain some sense of control over what was evolving.

Raven nestled her head against the side of his chest and rested her arm across him. "No matter how many times we make love, it always feels like the first time. You still make my world complete."

Dillon wrapped his arm around her. "I'm glad."

"I hate it when we fight, and I'm so glad you called me this morning. Although, I have to admit, there's nothing better than make-up sex."

"Yeah, I guess not. It's always the best," he said, trying to sound as enthused as she was.

"So are you ready for round two?" she asked.

Dillon laughed. "Whoa, I don't think so. Not yet, anyway."

She drew circles on his chest with her finger. "Well, you'd better *get* ready, mister."

"What's gotten into you?"

"I don't know, but I need more of you tonight. We had a bad couple of days, and I just want to be close to you."

Dillon rubbed her arm and closed his eyes. Only three months ago, he would have felt the same and he'd be raring to make love to her again. But that was pre-Porsha.

"And baby," she said, "thank you again for hearing me and for saying I can attend the elder board meeting next Tuesday. It really means a lot to me."

"You're welcome."

"Was Levi okay with it?"

"I never got to talk to him, but I will tomorrow, and of course it will be fine."

"I'm so excited about this new chapter in my life. I've been through so much over the years, and who would have guessed I'd be a pastor one day?"

Dillon wasn't sure whether to comment or keep quiet, but since he couldn't think of the right thing to say, he chose the latter.

That didn't stop Raven, though. "We're going to be able to do so many great things together, baby. Not only will we take the church to new heights, but we'll be well on our way to go national. We'll be broadcasting on television, just like your dad, in no time. And he only has about five thousand members. Although, the reason he's able to do it is because of all the money they bring in through the ministry. Having a church is great, but the key to having any real success is when you create a ministry and treat it as a corporation. That's when you can begin reaching out to people nationally and worldwide. Money comes in from all across the globe, and the next thing you know, thousands and then millions are contributed."

Dillon opened his eyes, but he still didn't say anything. She'd gained a wealth of knowledge while working for his dad, and she knew exactly how to nurture and build a ministry to the highest levels. She thought everything through and knew exactly what to do and when, and Dillon couldn't take a chance on losing her. He wouldn't go as far as taking her on as co-pastor, but he had to be more careful when it came to his feelings about Porsha. He had to keep Raven happy.

They chatted a few more minutes until Raven's phone rang.

She reached toward the nightstand for her cell. "I wonder who that is . . . Oh, it's Dana." She sat up on the side of the bed, then stood up. "Hey, girl."

Raven slipped on her robe and sat over in one of the chairs. Dillon already knew she was going to be on the phone for a while because when Raven and Dana spoke, it was rarely for less than a couple of hours. They were very close, and Raven also felt indebted to her because Dana had been the only person who'd stayed in touch with her while she was in prison. Dana had even visited her in person and periodically placed money on her books, and Raven did everything she could to make up for it. When they went to breakfast, lunch, or dinner, Raven paid for it. When they went shopping, Raven usually bought Dana something nice, and she was there for her no matter what.

Dillon lay there, listening to them talking about everything and also nothing and enjoying themselves, so he flipped on the television. The first thing he saw was a commercial advertising the Fourth of July fireworks show that would be taking place three days from now. This made him think about Alicia and how excited she'd been earlier today. She'd literally walked down to his office just to tell him about her conversation with her mom. She'd been as giddy as a small child, and Dillon was glad for her. But for some reason, Alicia's news and this commercial made him think about his dad. Why couldn't his father love him and treat him like a son? That's all Dillon had ever wanted, yet his dad continued to ignore him. Not to mention, he was likely in full planning mode for the holiday, preparing to spend it with his three prized possessions: Matthew, Curtina, and Matthew's son, little MJ.

Dillon got to his feet, pulled on his navy-blue silk pajama bottoms, and grabbed his phone. He walked out of the bedroom, through the hallway, and down the stairs. As he went into the family room, he clicked on his Contacts icon and scrolled down to his dad's number. Maybe if he tried calling Curtis one more time, things would be different. Maybe if Dillon reached out to him and apologized — again — for all that he'd done in the past, his dad would adjust his attitude. He might have a change of heart the way Alicia's mom had this afternoon.

Dillon dialed the number and waited.

Curtis answered on the third ring. "Hello?"

"Hey, Dad, how are you?"

"I'm good. You?"

"I'm fine. I hadn't spoken to you in a while, so I thought I'd give you a call."

"It's good to hear your voice," Curtis said, but there was no feeling behind his words, and that irked Dillon.

Still, he kept calm and tried not to take it personally. "So what are you all doing for the Fourth?"

"Not a whole lot. Just hanging around the house mostly."

Dillon paused, hoping his dad would invite him and Raven over. He knew it wasn't logical, even more so when it came to Raven because of all the money she'd stolen, but still Dillon hoped . . . and prayed.

But when his dad fell silent again, he said, "You know, Dad, if you're interested, I would love to have you serve as guest speaker one Sunday."

"My schedule is pretty full right now, but I appreciate the offer."

"What about later this year?"

"I don't think so. My speaking calendar is already in place, and I'm not planning to add on much of anything else."

Dillon knew this was just an excuse, and that if his dad honestly wanted to visit his church he could.

"I wish you'd reconsider."

"It's not likely."

His words were nonchalant and cold all at the same time, and Dillon couldn't take it any longer. He'd been living back in Mitchell for two years, yet his dad still wouldn't let go of the past. He claimed he'd forgiven Dillon, but he treated him like an enemy or worse. He acted as though Dillon weren't even related to him.

Dillon wanted to curse him out and hang up on him, but it was the desperate little boy in him that couldn't give up. He'd made the decision to forget about his dad and move forward with getting revenge on him, but deep down, he just wanted a relationship with him. He *needed* it, and he wanted to be a part of a family. If his dad would accept him back and love him like a son, Dillon was even willing to make amends with Charlotte and move mountains to get along with her if he had to. Whatever it took to make things right with his dad would be worth it.

"Look, Dad, can I ask you something?"

"What is it?"

"When is this going to end? When are you going to genuinely forgive me?"

"I forgave you a long time ago."

"But you couldn't have meant it."

"I only say what I mean, so I'm not sure what the problem is."

"You can't forgive someone, especially your own son, and still hate them."

"First of all, I don't hate anyone. I love everyone just the way God expects us to, but I'm also not a fool. I know very well who I can trust, and who can never be trusted."

"But I'm not the same person. I did some awful things, but I've turned my life around. I haven't hurt anyone since I moved back here. I became a pastor, and I've worked hard to live by God's Word."

"Good. That's what you're *supposed* to do."

Curtis was trying Dillon's patience. "But

that still doesn't change the way you feel?"

"You're my son, but you're not right. When you schemed behind my back with Mariah," he said, referring to his second ex-wife, "and had me beaten nearly to death, I understood why. You blamed me for the death of your mom, and you hated me for not being a father to you. And I forgave you. But then, after I did all I could to try to build a relationship with you, including giving you a half million dollars, you still tried to cause a public scandal and blackmail me. And don't get me started about the way you slept with your own brother's wife. I'm certainly not some innocent saint, because Lord knows I've done enough dirt to last a lifetime, but when a man sleeps with his brother's wife, it doesn't get much lower than that."

"So that's what this is about? Matthew, and what I did to him? Your precious little golden boy?"

"Call him whatever you want, but Matthew would never hurt anyone the way you have. He's a kind young man with a huge heart, and he doesn't have a deceptive bone in his body. He's nothing like the way I used to be and nothing like the way you are now."

"Wow. So this is how it's always going to be with you and me?"

"I don't see how it can be any different. As my child, I love you, but I can't allow you to hurt anyone else in this family. Some people live by the three strikes rule, but with you, two times was enough. You showed me who you were and what you were capable of."

"I'm sorry you feel that way, but I'm glad I know where we stand. I'm glad you admitted that you want nothing to do with me ever again."

Curtis didn't respond.

Dillon almost hung up without saying good-bye, but he changed his mind. "You take care, Dad."

"You, too."

Dillon removed his phone from his ear, staring straight ahead. His body felt numb, and though he was hurt, he now had full clarity. His father had written him off and mentally erased him from the family for good. This wasn't what Dillon had hoped for, but he knew he had no choice but to accept it. His dad was very wrong about one thing, though. He claimed he knew who Dillon was and what he was capable of, but sadly, he had no idea. He didn't have a clue, and Dillon would prove it to him soon enough. The amount of pain Dillon was planning to unleash would make national news. It would bring his father to his knees, and this made Dillon smile. It also made him laugh a little.

CHAPTER 12

Alicia held her head back, and the soothing hot water sprayed across the front of her body. She'd finally slept a little better last night thanks to the call she'd made to her mom, but she still felt tired, and a good shower always made her feel more refreshed. It was said that a person should take a warm shower at bedtime to relax and a cold one in the morning to wake up, but Alicia had found that taking a hotter-than-normal shower anytime was what she loved. She wasn't sure why, but she'd always been that way. So much so that when she and Levi showered together, he immediately cooled down the temperature because it was too much for him.

Alicia slowly rotated her body, allowing the water to stream across her back, and smiled. She still couldn't get over how quickly things with her mom had changed. The two of them had always been close, and when Alicia had spoken to her yesterday, it had felt as though they'd never drifted apart. She'd been able to feel her mother's love, smile, and tears right through the phone, and even now, she wanted to cry again. Not because she was sad, but because she was so excited she could burst. A heavy burden had been lifted from her, and she couldn't wait for her and Levi to have dinner with her mom and James. She also couldn't stop thinking about the warm smile on Levi's face when she'd told him, because this was something he'd wanted for a long time as well. He didn't talk about it as much anymore, but in the beginning, he'd blamed himself for the breakdown of Alicia's relationship with her family. Alicia had told him otherwise, but he'd still felt bad about it.

Now, if only her dad could surrender his disapproval. If only he could recognize how wrong he was for alienating his own daughter and her husband. Yes, she'd had an affair with Levi behind Phillip's back both times she'd been married to him, but she and Levi weren't perfect. More important, neither was her dad, and if anyone were to review his list of sins, they'd be reading and thinking for a very long time. Her dad had done a lot, and he'd done some pretty vicious and cruel things to people. Today he was a good man, but Alicia remembered all the way back to when she'd been a small child and her parents were married. No one knew it, but her father had gone as far as putting his hands on her mom. He'd threatened and blackmailed people in the church to get what he wanted, and he'd slept around on all three of his wives: Tanya, Mariah, and Charlotte. Then there was this whole thing with Dillon and how the situation had played out with his mom. So Alicia couldn't understand how her father could judge anyone. It just didn't make sense, but all she could think was that he somehow had a problem with forgiving his own children who had hurt him, even though he regularly forgave others.

Alicia turned back around, facing the water again, and with no warning, Phillip's bloody body flashed in her mind. She blinked a couple of times, but the image only became clearer. She then saw herself throwing her vehicle into park on the side of the highway and jumping out of it. She was remembering the night Phillip had found out she was sleeping with Levi again, and he'd forced her to drive toward Chicago at gunpoint. But when Alicia had discovered that he was planning for them to go to Levi's former residence, she'd known he was going to kill both of them. This was when she'd decided her only chance at surviving was to stop the car and try to flag down a passerby on the highway. But in the end, the gun had accidentally gone off.

Alicia's heart beat faster, and she tried to think about something else. But the visions and reality of that night remained in full effect. She saw Phillip's lifeless body over and over again. It was almost as if she were watching a one-scene movie, and soon she burst into tears and leaned her head against the ceramic wall.

"Dear God, please help me," she whispered. "Please release me from my sins. I'm so sorry for what happened."

You still don't get it, do you?, the voice said. *No one can help you, not even God. You killed one of His own. A man who loved Him, honored Him, and taught His Word. You hurt Phillip two different times, and he had a nervous breakdown because of it. He lost it, and now he's dead. And it's all your fault. It will always be your fault, and you know what you need to do.*

Alicia began hyperventilating and trying to catch her breath. But the voice never let up.

Okay, what you need to do is just breathe. Take deep breaths, but do it slowly.

Alicia listened and breathed in and out.

That's better. Now, try to calm yourself down, because getting upset won't change anything. It won't change what the truth is. You made a mistake, a man is dead, but what's done is done. All the crying for the next decade won't bring him back, and there's only one way to end the tears and guilt. It's time you realize that so you can end all your misery. You say you love God, but God doesn't want any of His children to suffer. Right?

Alicia nodded yes.

Then you know what you have to do. It's time to make things easier for your family. All they want is for someone to pay for Phillip's death. They don't like that an innocent man died, yet the person responsible is walking around scot-free. They just want you to do the right thing. It's the only way they can truly love you again and find peace. It's all up to you, though.

Alicia grabbed the top of her head and cried loudly. "No, please don't do this. Please just leave me alone. I'm begging you."

She cried so hard her chest heaved in and out, and then she dropped to the floor of the shower. The water drenched her hair, but she just sat there curled in a ball.

"Baby, what is going on in here?" Levi asked, opening the glass door and turning off the water. He helped Alicia to her feet. "Baby, what's wrong? Why are you crying?"

Alicia held on to him, still weeping uncontrollably as he walked her out of the shower. He grabbed a large bath towel and wrapped it around her. When she settled down some, he dried her hair and then her body.

He then escorted her into the bedroom and sat her on the bed until he was able to pull one of her robes from the closet. He helped her put it on and then sat down beside her and hugged her.

Alicia leaned her head against him and started crying again.

"Baby, what happened? And please don't tell me 'nothing,' because I know something's wrong."

"I'm sorry," she whimpered. "I'm so sorry."

"Sorry for what?"

"Causing you so many problems. I know I haven't been myself, but I'm okay."

"No, you're not, and it's time you get some help."

"I'm fine."

Levi turned her face upward and looked at her. "Then why were you sitting on the floor of the shower, nearly hysterical?"

She hesitated, but went ahead and told him the truth. Not about the voice, though. "I thought about Phillip and how he died. I saw his body and all the blood, and I couldn't handle it. But I'm not going to think about that anymore. I'm going to pray harder than I have been."

"Prayer is good, but I think you need to talk to someone. I told you that before, but now it's time you call someone to make an appointment. If you don't do it, I will."

"That's really not necessary."

Levi removed his arm from around her. "Why do you insist on doing this? Pretending that everything is okay, when you're clearly about to have a nervous breakdown?"

Alicia grabbed his arm with both hands. "Baby, I know it seems like that, but it's really me who's causing this. I think about things, and I make them worse than they really are. I'm completely aware of everything that's going on. I'm not losing my mind."

"I didn't say you were, but anyone can have a nervous breakdown. You don't have to be crazy for that to happen. And I wish you'd stop making excuses," he said matter-of-factly.

Alicia could tell he'd had it with her, so she agreed to what he wanted. "Okay, I'll do it. I'll call Melanie tonight to see if her psychologist can recommend someone."

"Maybe you can see the same person."

"Her doctor specializes in eating disorders, but I need a grief therapist."

"Well, just as long as you see someone. That's all I want."

"I will. I promise."

"I hope you're telling the truth, baby, because this is serious. This problem you have is tearing you apart, and when you're hurting I'm hurting."

"I know, and I'm sorry. I'm going to take care of this, okay?"

Levi didn't seem fully convinced, but when she kissed him he finally wrapped his perfectly chiseled arms around her and kissed her back. She felt his tense body relaxing more and more, and she knew when he laid her down on the bed and untied her robe that they were good.

She loved this man, and she wanted them to be happy. And they would be. He thought she needed to see a shrink, but he was wrong about that. She just needed to focus on the positive aspects of her life and stop thinking about Phillip and her dad. It was time she forgave herself. That way she could begin healing and truly forget what happened, once and for all.

CHAPTER 13

Dillon drove his black S-Class Mercedes out of the subdivision and waved at one of their female neighbors. Her husband was CEO at one of the top manufacturing companies in the city, and she was a stay-at-home mom. Dillon had never said more than a few words to her, but he always laughed when he saw her because he could tell she wanted him. Her husband was nearly three hundred pounds, not much to look at, and had to be at least sixty, yet she wasn't more than thirty-five. Even Raven had decided the woman had only married the man for money and status, and Dillon agreed. She wasn't Dillon's type, though, so Mr. Overweight CEO didn't have a thing to worry about when it came to his wife; not where Dillon was concerned, anyway.

He continued down the street, heading to the church, and turned right at the first stoplight. When he was a child, he'd longed to have a luxury car, and he hadn't cared which brand. Mercedes, Lexus, Audi, BMW, or Cadillac — he'd loved them all, and he'd told himself that when he became an adult, he'd have one or another. This hadn't happened, though, until he'd moved to Mitchell and met his dad. *And* his dad had given him all that money. It had been a dream come true, and one of the first things Dillon had done was buy himself a black Cadillac Escalade just like Curtis's.

Dillon shook his head, wondering why everything always resorted back to that demon he called his father. Why couldn't he just wipe Curtis from his mind, the same as his dad was doing with him? It was so tiring and frustrating, and Dillon wished he could punch someone. Right now, anyone would do, except he thought about how silly it was to worry about something he couldn't control, something he couldn't change no matter how much he wanted to. It was then that he thought about multiple ways to ruin his dad, and he smiled. He considered one idea after another, but he wouldn't settle on anything until he knew for sure what would work. He'd tried to get him before and had failed, but not this time. All he had to do from here on out was plan things step by step while also considering the consequences.

He turned on SiriusXM radio, which was already set on the Heart & Soul channel. This was his favorite R&B music station, but sometimes he listened to The Heat if that's what he was in the mood for. The Heat aired the kind of gangsta rap music most pastors probably didn't listen to, and he was sure many in his congregation, including some elders, wouldn't understand, either — well, except maybe Vincent, of course. But Dillon liked what he liked. He also wasn't a fan of gospel music, the way some would have expected, but he kept that to himself. The reason: He'd once heard his dad say that anyone who didn't like gospel music was either a lukewarm Christian or not a Christian at all. Dillon didn't abhor gospel music, and there were actually a couple of songs he enjoyed, but he couldn't see listening to it daily the way some folks did.

He bobbed his head to one of Charlie Wilson's songs until his phone rang. His administrative assistant's name and number displayed on his dashboard. He pressed the large control down in front of the center console to activate his car speaker.

"Good morning, Miss Brenda, how are you?"

"Good morning, I'm doing well. And what have I told you about calling me Miss Brenda, young man?"

"You know how I feel about that."

"Yeah, and you know I feel, too. I understand and appreciate the way you respect me as your elder, but I still work for you. 'Miss Brenda' doesn't sound all that professional, and I keep trying to tell you that."

Dillon laughed because they'd been going back and forth about this the whole time she'd been with him. It was their own private little joke. "Well, I'm sorry to disobey you, but I can't help it."

"Anyway," Brenda said, dismissing him, "how are you?"

"Can't complain."

"That's for sure. We're all much too blessed for that. But hey, the reason I'm calling is to remind you that I have a doctor's appointment this morning. So I won't be here when you arrive."

"Oh, okay. I didn't remember, but you know it's fine."

"I just didn't want you to wonder where I was, and I also left your updated calendar for today and tomorrow on your desk. I added a couple of phone calls you need to make because two of our members were just admitted to the hospital yesterday."

"I'm sorry to hear that, and thanks for alerting me. But more important, are you okay?"

"Yes, just having my annual checkup."

"Good. Well, I'll see you this afternoon, then?"

"Yes, and maybe even before noon."

"Okay, then."

"Thanks, Pastor."

"You're welcome."

When he pressed the button, he smiled again. Brenda Dawson always made him feel better about everything. At first, he hadn't been all that open to hiring a woman who was old enough to be his mother, but Raven had made it clear that he wouldn't be hiring anyone close to his age. She'd talked about all the stories she'd heard about pastors and their secretaries, and how she wasn't dealing with that kind of nonsense. Now, though, he was glad he'd hired Miss Brenda, who was twenty years his senior, because she treated him like a son. Miss Lana, his dad's administrative assistant, regarded Curtis the same way, and it was interesting how Dillon unintentionally walked in his father's footsteps in many areas.

He sighed when he realized he was thinking about his father again, and flipped through his radio channels. He didn't want to hear the song that was playing, so he searched for something else. When he landed on a Christian talk station, he turned it again. But then he frowned when he thought he'd heard his dad's voice. He was sure he couldn't have, but he turned back to the program to see. He listened to the male host asking another question, and to Dillon's dismay, his father was in fact the guest.

"Well, I think one of the saddest things I see are phony Christians," Curtis said. "And since I used to be one myself, I can spot them a mile away. Even when they seem near perfect."

"That's interesting, and I agree with you," the host said. "It really bothers me when people play with God."

"Yes, and even sadder are men and women who claim they've been called by God to minister when they know they haven't. In many cases, God hasn't told them anything, yet they decide on their own to become ministers and pastors. And they do it just to make money. Or like in my case when I first became a pastor in the Chicago area, I really was called, but I also loved the way my occupation attracted women. Many of them threw themselves at me and were willing to do anything I wanted. Anything to be with a pastor. At the time, I had about three thousand members, but even pastors who have less than a hundred can usually sleep around with as many women as they want. I was young and dumb, but it still doesn't excuse my actions. I made bad choices, and it's the reason I try to mentor and warn other ministers when I can."

"It's great that you're so transparent," the host said. "This is the reason I wanted to have you call in, and if you're willing I'd love to have you back."

"I appreciate that, Jacob. I'd be glad to."

"So do you meet pastors like this all the time?"

"Unfortunately, I do, and I'm ashamed to say that I know one of the young men very well. He lives right here in Mitchell. And in his case, he'll do anything to get what he wants, and he has no moral values. He even once had a fiancée who he treated like an animal, and he slept with his own brother's wife. He's also done things to other family members, yet he has a pretty sizable congregation."

"Hmmm," Jacob said. "That's really too bad."

Dillon nearly missed seeing the red light and slammed on his brakes. His face tightened, and he squinted his eyes. His father was actually on national radio, criticizing him publicly? It was bad enough that Curtis wanted nothing to do with him, but now he was going too far. He hadn't said Dillon's name, but everyone in Mitchell and most people nationwide knew that *the* Reverend Curtis Black had a son who was pastor of a church and that they lived in the same city.

When the light changed, Dillon stepped on the gas, flying down the road in outrage. But the more he drove, the more he slowed his speed . . . and then he smiled again. He *hated* this man, but oh, was his day coming. After this, Dillon would make paying his father back his top priority. He wouldn't be satisfied until the deed was done. His father had overstepped his bounds, and it was time for Dillon to stop him — it was high time for Reverend Curtis Black to see that his son wasn't some punk. Dillon was his firstborn child, and he would make his dad regret the day he ever met him.

CHAPTER 14

The Tuxson, arguably Mitchell's finest restaurant and certainly Alicia's favorite, was filled with local businessmen and businesswomen. It was the go-to place during the lunch hour for anyone looking to impress out-of-town clients and associates. It was also the most elegant place locally for dinner and special occasions.

Alicia walked past the breathtaking waterfall and farther inside the entryway. She saw Melanie standing closer to the maître d' podium.

Melanie noticed her and smiled. "Hey, girl."

Alicia smiled, too, and hugged her. "Hey, Mel. Have you been here long?"

"No, only about five minutes. It's pretty full today, though, so I'm glad I made a reservation. Especially since I have a patient to see at two thirty, and I need to be back by two."

Alicia looked at her silver bangle watch. "It's only a couple of minutes after twelve, so we should be fine. And by the way, what a beautiful suit," she told Melanie. It was navy blue with a peplum jacket and a knee-length skirt.

"Thank you. You know I got it on sale, though, right?"

Alicia laughed. "Yeah, I'm sure you did."

Melanie laughed as well because it was common knowledge that if she had to pay full price for anything, she left it in the store.

After the maître d' checked off their reservation, he seated them in their requested area, overlooking the river. With it being so crowded, Alicia had doubted they'd get a table with a view, but she was happy it had worked out that way.

When the maître d' left, Alicia and Melanie scanned their menus.

"I'm really hungry today," Melanie said.

Alicia looked at her, smiling.

Melanie noticed her staring. "You're a trip, and I already know what you're thinking. How happy you are to hear me say I'm hungry."

"Yep. Can't help it. I remember what it was like just two years ago, and it's so good to see how things have turned around for you."

"They really have, but it's all because of God, family, and friends like you. And, of course, my therapist, Dr. Brogan. She's been a huge blessing, and it's the reason I still see her once a month."

"I didn't realize that. I knew you still saw her, but not that often."

"Sometimes I see her twice a month if I feel like I need it. Because what I learned early on was that even if I didn't have an eating disorder, therapy is still a good thing for me."

"Why do you say that?"

"Because if I'd had someone to talk to about the way my mom treated me as a child, I might not have experienced so much emotional pain. I might've felt better about myself, because a good psychologist could have helped me deal with my mother's verbal abuse. I've also wondered if counseling would have helped Brad and me. As soon as we started arguing all the time, I knew we were in trouble. He worked day and night, we never saw each other, and I began eating less and less."

"I hate that you guys couldn't work things out."

"Yeah, but that's life. Divorces happen all the time."

"I know, but the two of you were so good

together."

"For a good while, but after he had an affair, I just couldn't stay with him. Maybe if he hadn't gotten someone pregnant, I could've lived with it. I don't know, but I do wish we'd gotten counseling before things got so bad."

Alicia thought about her and Levi's marriage and how her issues were causing a strain on it. Worse, she was now lying to him. She'd told him last night and again this morning that she was going to ask Melanie for her doctor's number when she knew she wasn't. She was also keeping things from him, particularly the voice she heard.

A young waitress with long coal-black hair and flawless cocoa skin walked up to their table. "Good afternoon, ladies. My name is Tory, and I'll be taking care of you."

Alicia and Melanie greeted her at the same time. "Good afternoon."

"Would you like to hear our specials for the day?"

Alicia nodded. "Yes, please."

"We have Dijon-crusted Chilean sea bass with new potatoes, red peppers, and zucchini; chargrilled New York strip with twice-baked potato, green beans, and sautéed mushrooms; and finally, free-range chicken breast Florentine with whipped potatoes, wilted spinach, and grilled tomato."

"All three sound great," Melanie said.

Alicia agreed. "They do, and I think I'll have the Chilean sea bass."

Melanie closed her menu. "Me too."

"Sounds good," Tory said, reaching for their menus. "Any drinks or appetizers?"

"Not for me," Alicia said.

"Me either," Melanie answered.

"Okay, then I'll bring your orders out to you as soon as they're ready."

Alicia looked out the window.

"Are you okay?" Melanie asked.

"Uh-huh. Why do you ask?"

"Right before the waitress came over, something changed. For a second you looked a little down."

"It was nothing."

"Alicia, come on now. We've been best friends for how long? So tell me."

"Things have been a little rocky with Levi and me."

"Oh no. You were just saying on the phone this morning that everything was great. Especially now that your mom and James have finally accepted him."

"I know, but this thing with Phillip has really bothered me, and lately it's been worse. So, of course, I haven't spent a lot of time with Levi. I just haven't been myself."

"And you've not said anything? You've been suffering all alone?"

Alicia wished with everything in her that she could tell Melanie about the voice she kept hearing, but she just couldn't will herself to do it. She loved Melanie like a sister, and she trusted her with her life, but she didn't want her to think she was crazy. She didn't want anyone to know about it, and she believed it would eventually go away anyhow. "I didn't want to worry you."

"But you don't mind me worrying you when I have problems?"

Alicia didn't say anything.

"I hid my issues from you and everyone else for years, and look where it got me. Pretending everything is okay only makes things worse. And if you can't tell your best friend that something is wrong, what's the point of having one?"

"I know, and I'm sorry. But I was hoping things would get better."

"What difference does that make? Maybe that's what I should start doing, too."

"What?"

"Not telling you anything."

Alicia laughed. "You crack me up."

"You think it's funny, but I'm serious. Do

you want your marriage to end up like mine?"

"No, but —"

"But nothing," Melanie interrupted her, clearly peeved about the whole thing. "When you have a problem, you get help for it. No excuses. So I suggest you guys go see a marriage counselor as soon as possible."

"Levi said the same thing, but I don't think that's necessary."

"Really? Well, I've given you the best advice I can, but you do what you want."

Alicia frowned. "Why are you so upset?"

"Why? I'm a thirty-year-old nurse practitioner who's divorced, who has an eating disorder and a mother who's never loved her. I'm successful careerwise but I'm emotionally damaged, and I spend every night alone. But imagine how things might have turned out had I stopped pretending everything was perfect. What if I'd gotten help?"

Alicia hadn't looked at things that way. She also didn't know Melanie felt so critical about her life.

Alicia drank a sip of water. "But you do know you'll find someone else, right?"

"Maybe, but I would have rather stayed

married to the man I'd loved for so many years."

"I guess I don't know what to say."

"You don't have to say anything. Just stop being in denial. Stop acting as though it's normal to still be grieving over Phillip after all this time. Stop telling yourself that his death is all your fault and that you and Levi don't have the right to be happy. Because I know that's what you're doing."

She was right, but Alicia let her finish.

"I still struggle with my eating disorder from time to time, but like I said, my therapist is a blessing. And she's also helped me through my divorce pain. She helps me with other stuff, too. Sometimes it can be something as minor as a coworker issue I'm having trouble with. If you ask me, every human being on this earth could benefit from counseling. Either regularly or at certain times in their lives."

"Can you give me her number?" Alicia said. "Maybe she can suggest a good marriage counselor."

"Of course. I'll text it to you."

Alicia had only asked for it so Melanie would stop reaming her left and right. But just like she wouldn't be calling Dr. Brogan regarding the voice she was hearing, she also wouldn't be calling about her marriage. She and Levi were going to be fine, and it wasn't necessary.

"Thanks," Alicia said.

Melanie locked her hands together in her lap. "I'm glad you've come to your senses."

Look how she talks to you, the voice whispered to Alicia out of nowhere. *Remember when she hid all her problems from you? She just reminded you of that herself, so what a hypocrite. Remember before she went into treatment and you tried to talk her into eating, and she criticized you for messing around on Phillip with Levi? Yet she claims to be your best friend. Before it was all said and done, she'd thrown you out of her house and stopped speaking to you. And it wasn't until she was locked away at that treatment facility that she called you. She needed someone to be there for her, but other than that, you never would have heard from her again.*

Alicia closed her eyes and opened them. She did the same thing again.

The waitress set their meals on the table.

Melanie thanked her and then looked at Alicia. "Are you feeling okay?"

"No, I've got a bad headache. Do you have anything I can take?"

Melanie pulled her leather shoulder bag from the back of her chair. "I think so." She pulled out a bottle of ibuprofen and passed it to her.

Alicia poured two gel caps into her hand, swallowed them, and drank the rest of her water.

Melanie picked up her fork. "Have you been getting headaches a lot lately?"

"Not really. Only every now and then."

"Well, if it continues, you should get it checked out."

"It's probably just stress. Both personal and professional."

"Why, what's going on at work?"

"Girl, that sister-in-law of mine has decided she wants to be co-pastor."

"You've got to be kidding."

"No, but I'll tell you the whole story another time."

"What are you guys doing for the Fourth?" Melanie asked.

Alicia ate some of her fish. "Going over to my mother-in-law's. What about you and your dad?"

"As far as I know, nothing."

"Why don't you come spend the day with us? My mother-in-law would love that. To her, the more people she can cook for, the better."

"Maybe we will."

"I hope so. And hey, I know this is way off the subject, but when are you going to start dating?"

"I don't know. After all this time, I'm still afraid of being hurt again."

"I get that, but at some point I think you should take a chance."

"I guess."

"I'm surprised Brad finally gave up."

"Yeah, well, he had until a couple of days ago."

"And you didn't tell me? Now look who's not sharing news with their best friend."

Melanie grinned. "Definitely not the same thing."

"Maybe not, but I'm still surprised you didn't mention it. What did he say?"

"He wanted to get together and talk, but I don't have anything to say. Some things are better left unsaid, and I just don't want to open old wounds. I shed far too many tears, and I don't ever want to hurt like that again."

Alicia opened her mouth to respond, but closed it when the voice stopped her.

See, this is the reason you need to end things. Otherwise you'll end up more hurt than your girl Melanie here. If you think what Brad did was awful, just you wait. Levi is going to hurt you ten times worse. You hurt Phillip to no end, and you know what the Bible says: We all reap what we sow. So are you going to wait for that? Wait to be hurt in a way you'll never recover from? It's not like your family cares about you anyway. I mean, let's face it, even though your mom claimed all was forgiven, you know she doesn't mean it. She said she was sorry, but you know she was lying. Everyone around you lies and says whatever you want to hear. So why not do yourself a favor and get this over with? Why don't you go home and pull that gun from your desk drawer?

CHAPTER 15

Hours had passed, yet Dillon was still livid over the way his dad had slandered him on the radio. He had a mind to leave his own church and drive straight over to Curtis's. What he wouldn't give to confront his father face-to-face, beat him down, and have him begging for mercy. Dillon hated how easily his father could torment him, and he just wanted to move beyond that. Why did he even care what his father said or thought about him in the first place? Because it wasn't like he helped Dillon with anything. Dillon took care of himself, and he made things happen on his own. Plus, Dillon had a church to worry about. He had members who loved and depended on him, and he didn't have time to focus on his dad's foolishness.

He sat thinking about his aunt, Susan, and how he wished she were still here. Before Raven and Alicia had come into his life, she'd been the only person who had truly loved him. She'd raised him as her own son, and she'd given him everything she could. She hadn't been wealthy like his dad, but she'd worked hard and done her very best to provide for Dillon. Her passing still broke his spirit sometimes because, sadly, he hadn't spoken to her much before she'd died; all because he'd been chasing after a man who didn't want him. When he'd discovered who his dad was and where he lived, Dillon had packed up everything he owned and moved to Mitchell. His aunt had hated to see him go, and she had begged him not to expect too much from his father. But he hadn't listened to her. He'd ignored her warning, and he'd been sure his father would become the loving man he'd hoped for. Then when it hadn't happened, it had been too late to return to Atlanta to spend time with his aunt. She'd passed away, and the next time he'd seen her she was in her casket.

Dillon wasn't a weak man, but he still shed tears over his aunt because he had so many regrets. He'd walked out on her like some teenager from Bell Buckle, Tennessee, who couldn't wait to get wild at his first Mardi Gras. He'd been naïve, and he'd paid a high price for it.

If only he could have one drink — just one — to ease his pain. He wanted to so badly, but what if he couldn't quit? What if his alcoholism reared its ugly head again and took total control?

Dillon's phone rang, and when he saw that it was Alicia he answered it.

"Hey, Sis, what's up?"

"Well, if it's okay with you, I'm taking the rest of the day off."

"Really? And since when do you need my permission to do that?"

"I know you've told me that before, but don't I always respect you as the founder of New Faith? I get that you're my brother, but that doesn't change anything as far as work. Especially since the church is closed tomorrow for our floating holiday."

"Yeah, well if *you're* taking off you must have a very good reason. Because you don't take off nearly enough, if you ask me."

"I'm cooking for my husband, and spending the entire evening with him."

"Good for you. He needs that, and he deserves it."

"I'm getting ready to make a lot of other changes, too. Life is much too short, and I've been letting my past control my future."

"You're right, and I need to do the same thing."

"Are you speaking literally? Because you sound like you're talking about something specific."

"Well, I won't go into a lot of details, but I accidentally heard your dad doing a satellite interview today."

"Oh, so now he's *my* dad?"

"He definitely isn't acting like mine. He said some awful things about me to the host, and to be honest, I still can't believe it."

"What did he say? And he mentioned your name?"

"No, but he didn't have to. He talked about phony Christians and gave an example of a pastor who'd slept with his brother's wife and had treated his former fiancée pretty badly. He then admitted that he knew the person very well."

"Oh my goodness. Why would Daddy do something like that? I know he doesn't have much to do with us, but it's unlike him to speak against his children so publicly."

"You mean it's unlike him to speak against you, Matthew, and Curtina. I'm a totally different story."

"I don't think so."

"Yeah, well, he definitely doesn't care about me the way he cares about all of you. I know that for a fact."

"He doesn't have much to do with me, either, though."

"But he still loves you, and that won't ever change. I remember the way he always looked at the three of you. Like he would die for you in a second. He would give up everything to protect you. I used to sit and watch how you guys interacted with him, and it made me sad because I knew he would never feel that way about me."

"Gosh, D, I don't know what to say, but I'm really sorry."

"It's just the way it is, and I even called him last night."

"Really? Why?"

"I just wanted to talk to him. I guess, deep down, I was hoping he would be glad to hear from me. But like always, he was cold and uninterested. Then, when I pushed him to tell me why he acted like this, he said I was a bad person that he would never trust again. He even went as far as saying that Matthew would never hurt people the way I have. He's compared me to him many times before, so I'm done."

"This really makes me sad."

"I'm sorry. I didn't mean to bring you down."

"It's not your fault, but I just keep hoping that we'll all be a family again. I know that sounds like some fairy tale, but I can't help the way I feel."

"Well, I doubt that will ever happen. Maybe it will for you, but your dad is through with me just like I'm through with him."

Alicia didn't say anything else, so Dillon changed the subject.

"But hey, don't you worry about me. These are my issues, and you just hurry home so you can take care of Levi."

"Are you okay?"

"I will be."

"If you want to talk about this some more, I can drop by the church. I was on my way to the grocery store, but that can wait."

"No, don't you even think about it. I'll be fine. I've been doing okay all along, and today was just a temporary setback."

"Okay, then. You guys are still coming to my mother-in-law's on Saturday, though, right?"

"Yep. Wouldn't miss it. You know how I feel about *my* Mrs. Cunningham."

Alicia laughed. "Yeah, and she loves *her* pastor, too. I know you'd rather spend the holiday with Miss Brenda, too, though."

"I would, but she's leaving for Dallas tomorrow to go see her daughters and grandchildren."

"I'm so glad you have her in your life."

"So am I. I never thought I'd find someone who cared about me the way my aunt, Susan, did, but Miss Brenda is the best."

"Which is a huge blessing."

"It is. Anyway, you guys have a good time tonight," he said.

"We will. See you this weekend. Love you."

"Love you, too, Sis."

Dillon set his phone down, and thankfully, he felt better than he had before Alicia had called. Now, though, he thought about Porsha and contemplated sneaking over to Hoffman Estates to be with her. He'd had a rough, stressful day, and he needed her to calm his nerves. He longed for her to give him the kind of affection only she knew how to give. He wasn't in an uproar the way he'd been before speaking to his sister, but he still needed something to help clear his thinking; something that would take his mind off his dad and the rest of his troubles. Hoffman Estates wasn't even a full hour away, so he could get there in no time. He would, of course, have to think of a good story to tell Raven, but lying wasn't hard for him. He'd actually been doing just that every Monday afternoon anyway, and since this was the day Raven usually shopped, she never questioned what he told her. She typically stayed gone for hours, and that gave him plenty of time to do what he wanted.

Still, he couldn't become careless, which meant he had to think of the kind of lie that made sense. That way he could enjoy his time with Porsha and still find peace with Raven when he got home. But as quickly as he settled on his plan, an immense urge to drink riled up inside of him. It was much stronger than it had been a little while ago, and he was struggling to conquer it. Maybe he actually could have one drink and then walk away with no problem. It had been two years since he'd drunk anything with alcohol, so maybe he was cured. While in treatment, he'd been told that alcoholism was a disease that never left you, and that sober alcoholics were alcoholics in recovery. Dillon didn't want to believe that, but all the literature he'd read taught that same theory. Still, not everyone was the same. For instance, some people who'd been sober for years attended twelve-step meetings multiple times a week, while others never went at all. So it truly did depend on the person, and Dillon wondered if maybe his one-year bout with alcohol had been a one-time thing. It wasn't like he needed a fifth or even a pint of liquor, anyhow; he only wanted one drink — just one and not a single ounce more than that.

CHAPTER 16

Alicia pulled a box of Saran wrap from the drawer, opened it, and tore off a sizable piece of plastic. She covered the large ceramic bowl of salad that she'd just made, which consisted of butter lettuce, carrots, cucumbers, cherry tomatoes, and shredded cheese. Then she set it in the refrigerator next to the spinach, cheese, and ground turkey lasagna she'd prepared not long ago. Levi wouldn't be home for another two hours, so she wouldn't place it in the oven until about sixty minutes beforehand. That way she could take it out right before he got there.

After having lunch with Melanie, she'd gone to the grocery store, and she was glad she'd taken the afternoon off. When she'd called Dillon, she'd been telling the truth about wanting to cook dinner and spend the evening with Levi, but what she hadn't told him was that the voice in her head had mentally wiped her out. It had been speaking to her a little more often as of late, but this was the first time in months that it had told her to physically go pull out a gun — the one she'd purchased right after Phillip's death. This was the same gun Levi didn't know about and would never approve of because of his felony status.

When the voice had mentioned the gun, though, Alicia had wanted to scream and tear out of the restaurant, but she couldn't let Melanie see her like that. As it was, Levi had seen her react in the worst possible way when she'd broken down in the shower, and she could tell he'd thought she was disturbed. Sadly, she was starting to think the same thing, too.

Alicia went into her home office and sat down in front of her computer. Two years ago, when she'd heard the voice in her head the first few times, she'd Googled "What does it mean when you hear voices?" But after reading multiple articles and learning that severe trauma and tragic loss could cause brief psychotic disorder, she hadn't worried so much. *Brief* had been the word that had made her feel better about everything. She also hadn't been able to cope with any of what had happened, and not coping with a major stress incident or loss of a loved one was another cause of brief psychotic disorder. She'd assumed that this was only a temporary situation, but when the voice had periodically shown up again, she'd wondered if something worse was going on. This was when she'd done more research and had discovered that ongoing symptoms might mean she had a form of psychosis, or worse, schizophrenia. As she'd read line after line of no less than twenty articles, she'd become more and more ashamed and terrified. Because there was no way she could take another round of public humiliation and scandal. If anyone found out that Reverend Curtis Black's daughter was insane, her life would be over. She would never be able to walk outside her house again without being judged and ridiculed, she would lose her position as chief operating officer at the church, and Levi would, slowly but surely, decide to leave her.

She'd decided that the best thing for her to do was to work harder at controlling her thoughts. She'd even begun exercising seven days a week to clear her mind and meditating more than usual. She'd done all sorts of things to try to help herself, and for a while, she'd been successful. Until these last couple of months, not even Levi had suspected that she might have a form of mental illness. He'd mentioned how he thought she might be depressed, but that had been it. Now, though, thanks to what happened yesterday, he suspected something was wrong and wanted her to see a doctor. But she couldn't do that. She couldn't take the chance of being diagnosed with anything relating to psychotic behavior. If she did, it wouldn't be long before everyone found out and they'd keep their distance from her. They'd be afraid of what she might do to them, and she'd be forced to walk around with a stigma she couldn't live with. Her name and face would forever mean *crazy,* and she wasn't doing that to herself. She wouldn't bring shame to Levi, her parents, her siblings, or her little nephew. They'd all been through far too much, and she refused to burden them with something new. She'd already caused them enough pain to last a century, so she would deal with this problem of hers on her own.

The first item on her list of changes was to think positively. The second was to remind herself daily that she wasn't the Creator and that even though she'd made many bad choices, she couldn't control anyone's fate. Which meant she wouldn't continue to blame herself for Phillip's death.

Then, on the way home from the grocery store, she'd made a conscious effort to forgive herself. She'd spoken the words out loud and prayed like never before. She had a new attitude, and she was going to deal with this thing head on. She would beat Satan at his own game, because she now believed that it was his voice she'd been hearing. Her dad used to talk about how powerful and cunning Satan was, and how he was always on the lookout for his next victim. Whether a person had been diagnosed with a mental illness or not, the enemy could use the person's own mind to destroy them.

Alicia remembered the time her father had taught Bible study one night, and the topic had been "Temptation and the Tricks of the Devil." It still stuck in her mind, because that particular Bible study had taken place shortly after Levi had been released from prison and Alicia had begun having another affair with him. She'd also been set to marry Phillip again in three months, and her father's words had unnerved her. Her dad had shared a number of scriptures relating to temptation, but he'd also recited a scripture about Satan that she would never forget. It was First Peter 5:8, which said, "Be sober-minded; be watchful. Your adversary the devil prowls around like a roaring lion, seeking someone to devour." This verse would stay with her forever because that very same afternoon before she'd gone to Bible study, a voice had told her that maybe being with the man she was most attracted to was the right thing to do. The voice had been referring to Levi, even though Alicia was engaged to Phillip. Then, in the middle of Bible study, it had spoken to her again. *Everyone deserves to be happy. Follow your heart. Do what makes you feel good. Call Levi and tell him you want to see him.*

There was no doubt that this had been Satan whispering to her all along, but the voice she'd been hearing since Phillip's death sounded different. Satan had changed it on her, and it wasn't until now, at this very moment, that she realized it was him again. He'd altered the tone of his voice to fool her into believing that this had nothing to do with him and everything to do with her losing her mind.

But she was finally onto him, and she would stay conscious of it. She would stand on another profound scripture her dad had taught her, too, Ephesians 6:10–11, which said, "Finally, be strong in the Lord and in the strength of his might. Put on the whole armor of God, that you may be able to stand against the schemes of the devil."

For a second, Alicia reminisced about her dad and how much she'd learned from him. She recalled all the happy times they'd shared and how he was the first man to genuinely love her. He was also the first man she'd loved unconditionally. She missed him so very much, and suddenly, she felt her spirits dropping. Sadness and utter melancholy crept their way inside of her, and she wanted to open her lower right-hand drawer to pull out her handgun. But instead, she closed her eyes and declared, "Satan, I rebuke you in the name of Jesus. I reject and renounce everything about you."

Then she quoted Ephesians 6:10–11 again. "Finally, be strong in the Lord and in the strength of his might. Put on the whole armor of God, that you may be able to stand against the schemes of the devil."

She repeated the scripture two more times and seemed to feel better. She wasn't sure how long Satan would continue taunting her, but she wouldn't go down without a fight. She couldn't. Not when she had, in fact, listened to him earlier. On her way to the grocery store, he'd reminded her about the gun again, and she'd almost driven straight home to get it. Thank God, though, she hadn't. She'd started to believe everything the enemy had said to her, but in her heart, she'd known she didn't want to die. So, yes, she would fight for as long as she had to. She wouldn't stop for anyone.

As soon as Levi walked inside the house, Alicia smiled at him. He'd just come from the garage, and she was excited to see him. An old-school love song CD that one of the members of the church had made for them played in the background. Right now, "Sparkle" by Cameo was on.

She walked over to him. "Hey, baby."

"Hey yourself," he said, grabbing her around her waist and kissing her on the lips. "You sure are in a happy mood."

She held both sides of his face, paying close attention to how gorgeous he still was. "I just don't want to be sad anymore. I want us to get back to the way we used to be."

"I want the same thing. I've never wanted anything else."

"I know, and I'm so sorry that I put you through all this. It's been a long, rough couple of years, but I promise you things are going to be different."

Levi hugged her tightly. "I love you so much, baby. You're my entire world."

She clasped her arms behind his neck. "And you're mine. You always will be."

He pulled away from her slightly, looking toward the stainless-steel oven. "Whatever you're cooking smells really good."

"It's lasagna. I also warmed up some garlic bread, and there's a salad in the refrigerator."

"You haven't taken an afternoon off work since I can remember. And definitely not to cook dinner."

Alicia walked over to the oven and pulled out the lasagna and garlic bread. "Yeah, well, that's going to change, too."

Levi pulled off his navy blazer, hung it on the back of one of the island chairs, and sat down. "Did something happen that I need to know about? Because you were in a totally different frame of mind yesterday. You seemed more upset than ever."

"I took a long look at myself this afternoon and realized I wasn't going out like that. I wasn't going to let the devil ruin my life."

"And Melanie gave you her doctor's number?"

"She did."

"Did you call her for a recommendation?"

"Not yet, but I will."

"You really need to, baby. Right away in the morning. I know you're feeling pretty good about things today, but I still want you to talk to someone just to be safe. Just

168

to make sure nothing more is going on."

Alicia was trying to live the way God wanted her to, so she didn't want to lie to him. But she could tell by the way he was talking and looking at her that she didn't have a choice.

"I'll call her when I get to work."

"You're going in?"

"Yeah, aren't you?"

"The church is closed tomorrow, remember?"

"Oh yeah, that's right."

"I can't believe you forgot."

"I didn't, it just slipped my mind for a minute. I actually mentioned it to Dillon earlier, and that's why I was glad to take the afternoon off. It'll be great to have a long weekend."

"I'm really looking forward to hanging out at my mom's."

"I am, too."

Alicia walked near Levi, heading toward the refrigerator, but he stopped her when Jeffrey Osborne started singing their favorite song, "Love Ballad." He pulled her into his arms, gazing at her. She never took her eyes off him, either, but her eyes also filled with tears. This was their theme song. When they'd gotten married, they hadn't bothered with having a large wedding, but even though they'd gone to the courthouse, Dillon, Raven, and Melanie had thrown them a small dinner party that evening to celebrate. There had only been eleven people there, but Levi had still wanted them to have their first dance, and this was the song he'd chosen. The lyrics talked about never being so much in love before, not caring what people say, and having so much more to their relationship than others could see. The song told their story from beginning to end.

Levi stood up and as they danced to the music and cuddled close, he sang every word to her. Now her tears fell down her cheeks.

They danced until the next track started and then kissed wildly and passionately. The chemistry between them had always been incredible, but Alicia was feeling especially close to Levi tonight. They were in total sync, and the love they shared was as strong as ever. They'd weathered some terrible storms, but it hadn't changed the fact that they were soul mates. They loved each other hard and as though their lives depended on it, and that's what was sustaining their marriage. It had also sustained them as individuals. The formidable bond between them was for keeps, and Alicia thanked God for it.

They kissed long and forcefully until Levi led her down the hallway and into their first-floor master bedroom. They hurried to undress each other and relaxed cozily on the bed. They kissed more deeply now, and Alicia couldn't wait to make love to her husband. She was thrilled about their new beginning, and looking forward to their long future together.

CHAPTER 17

From the time Dillon had left the church, he'd told himself that one drink was all he needed. But as he'd gotten closer to Porsha's, he'd decided that maybe it wasn't such a great idea. Then, just as quickly as he'd made up his mind to forgo it, he'd driven past a bar that was no more than ten miles from Porsha's house. Still, he'd kept going, but the more he thought about his father and the stressful day he'd had, he found himself making a U-turn in the middle of the street and heading back in the direction he'd come from.

Now he sat in the parking lot of Benny's Tavern, debating whether he was doing the right thing. If he went in, it would only be for a few minutes and just to have one drink. He'd told himself those same words over and over, so he wasn't sure why he still hadn't gotten out of his car. Maybe it was because a small part of him did worry that once he started he wouldn't be able to stop. But at the same time, he did believe he was cured. If he hadn't been, he never could have gone two years without drinking at all. He also hadn't attended more than ten AA meetings before leaving Atlanta, and that was only because his inpatient treatment counselor had insisted on it. His counselor had told him that the most successful alcoholics joined AA and attended meetings regularly. He'd also stressed that meetings needed to be a part of Dillon's life from now on. Dillon had heard him, but it hadn't been long before he'd realized he didn't need them. He'd discovered that he could stay sober on his own, and then when he'd become a minister, he'd decided that if he ever got weak, he would simply pray about it. But when he'd moved back to Mitchell and founded New Faith, he'd known for sure he wouldn't be attending any AA meetings — ever again. For one, he didn't want his family to know he'd once had a drinking problem, and secondly, he didn't want his parishioners to know that their pastor had been labeled an alcoholic. There was no way members of any congregation could respect a leader such as that, and it was the reason he'd also never as much as told Raven about it.

Dillon breathed deeply and stepped out of his vehicle. He walked past three rows of cars, and while it was a Thursday night, the parking lot wasn't full. This was likely because it was only six in the evening, because Thursdays at a bar tended to be just as busy as the weekends. His hope had been to leave the church early so he could head over to Porsha's a lot sooner, but Brenda had reminded him about a meeting he had with the president of a local organization. Dillon had wanted to cancel it, but because he had a huge place in his heart for all nonprofits that helped underprivileged children, he'd kept the meeting on his schedule. He hadn't known what he was going to tell Raven, because there was no way he'd be home from Porsha's before ten or eleven o'clock. But to his surprise, Raven had called him, saying that if he didn't mind, she and Dana were running by a couple of shoe stores. After that, they were going to dinner and a movie. Her call had been too good to be true, but she'd mentioned something about Dana having to work the entire holiday weekend, so they were having a girls' night out this evening. Dillon hadn't cared what the reason was and had just been relieved he could still go be with Porsha.

As he pulled open the glass door and walked inside the bar, he glanced at his watch. It was a quarter after six, so if he was in and out of there within the next half hour, he could be at Porsha's by seven. He could spend time with her for a couple of hours, take a shower, and be home by eleven. From the way it had sounded, Raven and Dana were going to the movie theater last, which meant whatever they were seeing probably wouldn't start before nine. If for some reason she got home even a few minutes before him, though, she still might question where he'd been, so he pulled out his phone and texted Vincent the following: "I should be home by eleven."

This was code for *I'll be home by eleven, but if Raven calls you before then tell her I just left your house and I'm stopping by the store on the way home.*

From the time Dillon had begun seeing Porsha, he'd set up that particular text arrangement with Vincent, just in case he needed an alibi. Whenever he got together with Porsha, he sent Vincent that same message, and the only thing that ever changed was the time. He always entered the approximate hour he was planning to arrive home. Then, once he hit Send, he deleted it.

175

Dillon strutted farther inside the bar and looked around. It was a nice establishment, but he hadn't been to a place like this in a long time. Not once since he'd left Atlanta, and he hadn't wanted to. He'd had his moments of wanting to drink, but even then he'd only wanted to buy something from a store.

He walked past a few tables, unbuttoned his classic gray suit jacket, and sat at the bar. ESPN aired on two flat-screen TVs behind it, and there were multiple rows of liquor bottles. Vodka tonic had always been Dillon's go-to cocktail, and tonight would be no different.

A gentleman with a thick salt-and-pepper beard stepped in front of him. "What can I do you for?"

"Vodka tonic."

"You got it."

Dillon glanced around the place, which wasn't huge but wasn't small, either. There were patrons of all ages, and they were mostly men. That is, with the exception of the two thirtysomething-looking women in the corner. One of them smiled at him, and Dillon returned the gesture.

"Here you go," the bartender said. "Enjoy."

Dillon pulled money from his wallet and

set it on the counter. "Thanks."

Back in the day, he would start a running tab because he knew he'd be drinking for a while, but tonight the drink in front of him would be his only one.

He sat there with his hands clasped together on the bar, staring at his glass. Did he really want to do this? After going this long without taking one sip of alcohol? Maybe he should just leave and head over to Porsha's the way he'd planned and call it a day. He had so many reservations, but already just the smell of the vodka that the bartender had prepared for him was drawing him in. The smell was so intoxicating that he could almost taste it.

Still, was it truly worth it? Especially since his out-of-control drinking was the reason he'd lost job after job and lost his aunt Susan's home? He hadn't lost it because of lack of payment, but he'd sold it to get the money and then squandered every dime of it away. She would have been so disappointed in him. But this was all a result of the way his father had rejected him. Curtis had pretended to accept and love him, but he'd never shown it in the right way. He'd never made Dillon a priority over his other children, and for whatever reason, that had been the one thing that had bothered him most. His father had owed him that, and after all this time, he still wouldn't give him the love and respect he deserved . . . and then today, he'd talked about him on national radio as though it were nothing.

Dillon's body heated up with anger, and his heart began to race. It was then that he loosened his tie, lifted the glass to his lips, and took his first drink. He hissed and frowned from the bitter taste and loved it at the same time. He took another gulp of it, and then another . . . until the glass was empty. He hadn't had anything to eat since breakfast, so it didn't take long for the liquor to calm his nerves. This was the reason he'd wanted a good, strong drink in the first place. Being calm was what he needed, and this vodka tonic had done the trick.

He was fine now and ready to leave for Porsha's. Until the woman who'd smiled at him walked over. Dillon turned and looked at her long, flowing black hair and deep-cappuccino skin, and there was an immediate attraction.

"Want some company?" she said.

"Actually, I was just on my way out."

"So soon? You just got here."

"I know, but I have someplace to be."

"Well, that's too bad," she said, eyeing him

up and down.

"Oh yeah? Why is that?"

"I was planning to sit down and keep you company."

Dillon looked over at her table. "It looks like you already have some."

"That's just my sister. She and I decided to meet after work for a drink, but she has to get home to her husband. I, on the other hand, don't have one," she said, looking down at his wedding band.

"I think I'd better go."

"Couldn't you just stay a little while? You know, just to have another drink, maybe."

Dillon wouldn't tell her this, but the more he felt the liquor taking effect, the more he thought about maybe having a second one.

"Come on," she said, touching the top of his hand. "One drink together, and you can leave."

Dillon thought about Porsha and how she was surely wondering why he hadn't arrived at her house yet, but he'd be on his way as soon as he finished his final drink. This one would definitely be his last. He was sure of it.

CHAPTER 18

When the woman slid farther down his body, Dillon shut his eyes, moaning. Just three hours ago, he hadn't even known who *Taylor Thomas* was, but what he did know now was that she certainly knew how to pleasure a man. In more ways than one. So now he lay there, enjoying himself and letting her have her way with him. He'd known by the way she'd strolled up to him at the bar that she was bold, aggressive, and knew what she wanted. She was the kind of woman who didn't ask a lot of questions, didn't require a long introduction, and just simply wanted to have a good time. Dillon had wanted the same thing, so when she'd asked him if he wanted to "go someplace a little quieter to talk," he'd drunk the last of his third drink and walked out with her. She lived about twenty minutes away, and Dillon had followed her to her condo. Interestingly enough, he could tell he was slightly drunk but not in a staggering kind of way, and he'd driven his car with no problems.

The woman continued on her mission, and Dillon wasn't sure how much more he could take. So he pulled her up toward his chest so she could give him the rest of what he'd come there for. She smiled, clearly eager to oblige him, and the more he watched her move, the more excited he became. She was good, and now he knew why he'd been so attracted to her. There was something about the way she looked and the way she smiled that had turned him on, and now she was showcasing all her bedroom skills. She did everything a man could want, and he knew at this very moment that this wouldn't be the last time he saw her.

When they were both fully satiated and quietly relaxing next to each other, Dillon looked over at the clock on Taylor's nightstand. Time had flown by quickly. It was already just after nine p.m., and Dillon would soon need to get dressed.

Taylor turned on her side, facing him. "Did I satisfy you?"

"And then some," he said, staring at the ceiling.

"Same here, and I needed that tonight."

Dillon had no idea what she meant, but

he didn't say anything.

"I'm also sure that by now, you think I'm the tramp of the week."

"No, why do you say that?"

"Please. I don't even know you, yet I walk up to you at a bar and invite you to my home?"

"Yeah, but who am I to judge? I didn't know you, either, but I'm here."

"It's different for men, though. They can get away with that kind of thing."

"Still, I'm not judging you. Some people just like to have a good time. No strings attached."

"True, but this isn't something I normally do. You might not believe me, but I've never picked up a stranger in a bar and then brought him to my home to have sex. For all I know you could be a serial killer."

Dillon laughed. "Yeah, okay. But I can assure you, I'm not. I'm harmless."

Now Taylor laughed. "So you say, and for my sake, I hope you're telling the truth."

"And anyway," he said, looking at her, "maybe you're the one who's a serial killer. I could be dead in no time."

"Nope. Sorry to disappoint you. Just an average woman who found out yesterday that her fiancé has been sleeping with another woman. For more than a year."

"Man, I'm sorry to hear that." Dillon wasn't sure why, but he genuinely felt sorry for her. Maybe it was the alcohol in his system, because he felt her pain.

"I was devastated and humiliated out of this world. I just couldn't believe it."

"I can imagine."

"Anyway, I felt like drinking my problems away, and I asked my sister to meet me at Benny's."

"You go there often?"

"Not really. Only every now and then. I like it because it's always quiet and I never see anyone I know."

It did seem like that kind of place, and that's what Dillon had liked about it also. He couldn't even fathom what would happen if anyone in Mitchell, specifically his congregation, discovered he'd been hanging out at a bar, and worse, drinking hard liquor.

"It's a pretty nice place," he said.

"Was that your first time? Because I've never seen you there before."

"It was."

"You said you lived in Schaumburg, right?"

"Yeah." When Taylor had asked him about that at the bar, it was the first place he thought of. He certainly wasn't going to tell her he lived in Mitchell, but he also had to think of somewhere within a thirty-mile radius to make his lie believable.

"That's not that far, but it's too far to come to a bar you've never been to. And to come by yourself."

"I was in the area for something else and just decided to stop."

"I'm glad you did. I was so tense and stressed, and you made me feel so much better. Better than I was hoping."

Dillon locked his hands behind his head. "Is that right?"

"Yep."

Dillon wasn't sure what it was about her exactly, but he liked Taylor. Any man could see how beautiful and shapely she was, but maybe it was the calm, kind demeanor she exuded. He wouldn't tell her this, but normally, he would see a woman like her — someone who slept with a man she didn't know — as some skank who had no respect for herself. But for reasons he couldn't explain, none of that mattered to him.

"Well, I'm happy to have been of service," he said, smiling.

"I'm sure you are, but I also know you're married."

"That I am."

"When I saw your ring, I almost walked

back to my table."

"But you didn't."

"No, and I'm not proud of it, either. I've never been married, but I won't lie. I would never want to know what it feels like to have my husband messing around on me. Having a fiancé doing it was bad enough."

Dillon didn't see where there was anything he could add to that, so he didn't.

"Can I be honest about something else?"

Dillon looked at her again. "Go ahead."

"You're not going to like it."

This made him nervous, but he didn't react. "Well then, maybe you shouldn't say anything."

"I wouldn't, except I was sort of hoping I could see you again."

"Is it something bad?" he asked.

"No. Although I guess it depends on how you look at it. I don't think it's bad, but you might be upset when you find out that I wasn't completely honest with you."

Dillon was getting a little irritated. What if this woman had AIDS or some other contagious disease? Because it wasn't like they'd used any protection. He never bought condoms, because he didn't have a reason to use them. It wasn't that he was being careless when he slept with Porsha, but he and Porsha had ordered two at-home HIV testing kits, taken their blood samples in front of each other, and mailed them in. They'd purchased the express version, and they'd received their results the next day. Then, as far as Raven, she was his wife. She loved him, and even if she wanted to mess around, he didn't believe she would because she had too much to lose.

Dillon sat up and stacked the two pillows he'd been lying on against the leather headboard. His head felt a bit woozy, but he leaned backward. "So are you going to tell me or what?"

Taylor sat up as well. "You're already upset, aren't you?"

Dillon stared at her, and she was right. He wasn't happy.

She stared at him, too, and then said, "I know your name isn't Marcus."

A nervous wave swept through his stomach. "Really? Then what is it?"

"Dillon Black."

It was actually Dillon Whitfield Black, with no hyphen, but that was the least of his concerns.

He folded his arms. "And who are you?"

"Taylor Thomas."

"No, I mean who *are* you? Did someone have you follow me? Are you trying to set me up?"

"Wait a minute. No, it's nothing like that. I was in the bar before you, remember? So, how could I follow you?"

He couldn't argue with that, and actually, her response gave him a slight sigh of relief. "Then why did you act like you didn't know who I was?"

"Because I knew it would be awkward. Especially when you told me your name was Marcus. If I'd let on that I knew you were Dillon Black, you probably would have left me sitting there."

"Yeah, that's a fact."

"I'm sorry. But if it's any consolation to you, I don't care that you're Curtis Black's son, and I won't make any trouble for you."

Dillon hated being caught off guard, especially in situations like this. He was the pastor of a future megachurch, and he couldn't afford to be involved in any scandals. He needed his reputation to stay clean and on the up-and-up, and he couldn't keep making these kinds of mistakes. He still felt a little tipsy from the alcohol he'd drunk, but he'd been well aware of what he was doing. Nonetheless, had he not decided to take a drink, he never would have stopped at Benny's. He wouldn't have met Taylor, and he would have gone to Porsha's the way he was supposed to.

Dillon swung his legs over the side of the bed and looked back at her. "I really wish you'd told me."

"So does that mean we can't see each other again?"

"Do I have a choice? For all I know you're planning up some sort of blackmail scheme right as we speak. Probably can't wait to tell the world that Curtis Black's pastor son was in a bar drinking. Not to mention sleeping with you."

Taylor crawled across the bed and sat next to him. "I promise you, I'm not. I wouldn't do that, and if you want to know the truth, I could barely breathe when I saw you walk into that bar tonight. You look even better in person than you do in some of those online photos I've seen."

At first Dillon had wanted to ask her what photos she was talking about, but when he'd first met Curtis, he'd gone on a local TV station in Mitchell and exposed his dad as a deadbeat. Dillon had done it for his own personal satisfaction, but because of who his dad was, it hadn't taken long before the tabloids had plastered the news all over social media. Then when he'd returned to Mitchell and founded New Faith, a number of magazines and newspapers had done features on him. They'd all been fascinated with the idea of Dillon founding his own church and following in his famous father's footsteps.

"I think I'd better go."

"Please don't be mad at me," she said. "I know we just met and you have no guarantee that you can trust me, but I'm really not trying to harm you. I like you, and I want to spend more time with you," she explained, taking her hand and turning his face toward her. "I'm serious. I'm not one of those women who will suddenly think she can be your wife."

Dillon half believed her, but he also knew the dangers of starting up too many affairs. As it was, he was sleeping with Porsha and had to keep her as content as possible, but if he kept this thing going with Taylor, he wasn't sure what would happen. What troubled him, though, was that just three days ago, when he'd been with Porsha, he'd thought he might be falling in love with her. But now, after spending only a couple of hours with Taylor, he knew his obsession with Porsha was purely about sex. She made him feel extra good in bed, and he'd confused that with emotional feelings. But as he gazed into Taylor's eyes, he felt a different kind of connection with her. It was almost similar to the way he'd felt about

Raven when he'd first met her, except with Taylor, the sex was perfect, too. She was a mixture of Raven and Porsha all in one.

Taylor caressed his back and then stood in front of him. She leaned his body back on the bed. "I know you don't think you can trust me, but you can."

Dillon wanted to tell her he didn't, but he also didn't want to stop her from what she was getting ready to do.

"I really need to go," he said.

"All I want is to make you feel good again. I want us both to feel good."

Dillon wanted to tell her no, but then she kissed him.

He reluctantly and yet willingly kissed her back, and there were no more words between them.

CHAPTER 19

"Where were you, Dillon?" Porsha yelled.

"I told you, I was home. I couldn't get away like I thought."

"Then why did you call, saying you were already on I-Ninety?"

"Because I was. But then Raven called to see what time I was leaving the church. She was supposed to be going to dinner with a friend of hers and then to the movies, but her friend had to cancel."

"So? What does that have to do with you coming to see me?"

Dillon didn't like her tone. He'd just left Taylor's, and as soon as he'd gotten in the car he'd checked his phone. Porsha had called him ten different times — even though she'd never called him before — so he figured he'd better call her back before he got home. Now he regretted it, though, because the whole time they'd been on the phone, he'd had to make up one lie after another.

"Hello?" she spat.

Dillon adjusted his rearview mirror. "I'm here."

"Then why aren't you saying anything?"

"What was I supposed to tell her, Porsha? She was already home for the rest of the evening, so it wasn't like I could be gone for a ton of hours."

"You do it every week. Sometimes more than once."

"Only when I know Raven will be doing something else."

"Well, the least you could have done was call me or text me."

"I just told you, I couldn't get away."

"Yeah, right. You could have if you'd wanted to, and I don't take kindly to being stood up. If you weren't coming, you should've let me know."

"Look, I'm sorry, okay? It won't happen again."

"Where are you now? Because I can tell you're in the car, driving."

Dillon had known that was going to come up, which was the reason he'd first thought about parking somewhere and turning his car off before calling her. But it was already going on eleven and he needed to get home. After quickly making love to Taylor a second time and then hurrying to shower, he'd still stayed at her house longer than he'd planned to.

"Raven wanted some ice cream, so I'm on my way to a convenience store. That's why I'm calling you."

"I don't like this," she said. "I don't like it at all."

Dillon thought about all the money her father had left her, and while he wished he could forget about that, he couldn't. He needed all the contributions she was willing to give, so that they wouldn't have to lower the budget for their marketing campaign. He, Alicia, Levi, and his CFO, Lynette, were meeting with the firm next week, but Dillon knew they would need no less than two hundred fifty to three hundred thousand dollars. He wanted to roll out something big, and his plan was to have commercials airing so often that whether Mitchell residents watched TV in the morning, afternoon, or evening, they'd still see one or more of them. This didn't count the online and radio advertising they wanted to do or the direct mail campaign. They needed a lot of funding, and the last he'd checked, Lynette had only budgeted about one hundred fifty thousand. He wouldn't tell his staff where the rest of the money had miraculously come from; instead, he would simply let them know that an anonymous donor, someone who believed in their vision, had decided to bless them. But even if he put the marketing campaign aside, he still needed at least another fifty thousand dollars from Porsha to carry out his plan of ruining his father. For days, he'd been trying to figure out how he would go about doing it, and strangely enough, it had been Vincent's original idea that had come to him when he was following Taylor to her condo. The alcohol had given him the ability to think on an uninhibited level, he guessed. For a while now, no matter how many times Vincent had insisted that his idea was the perfect scheme, Dillon had sometimes thought it might be going too far. But not anymore.

"I promise I'll make this up to you," he said.

"I don't want to hear it, Dillon. You stood me up, and I think you and I both know that you'll be spending the entire holiday weekend with your little wifey."

"Yeah, but I'll still see you on Monday like always."

"That's four days from now."

"Sometimes we don't see each other more than once a week anyway."

"I know, and it's not enough."

Dillon shook his head and changed lanes. "Baby, why are you doing this? Didn't you tell me the other day that you understood my situation, and that you were willing to be patient?"

"Doesn't matter. I changed my mind. I won't wait a whole year or more for you to leave that woman."

"Well, what do you expect me to do? Leave her tomorrow?"

"You're trying to be funny, but I'm serious. I'm not stupid. I know you can't just pack up and move out immediately. But I need you moved out and filing for divorce before Christmas. I won't spend the biggest holiday of the year without the man I love, and I'm certainly not going into a new year being treated like a whore. My parents didn't raise me to settle."

"You do realize it's already July, don't you? So how am I supposed to leave my wife and ask for a divorce in five months? And for no reason?"

"The reason is because you've decided to marry me. Or maybe you don't want that. Maybe you only started seeing me because of my father's money."

Dillon raised his eyebrows. What she'd said was true, but he also loved having sex with her. Still, that was neither here nor there. What concerned him was that she'd become terribly demanding and so in love with him, even though they'd only been sleeping together for three months.

"Why don't we talk about this when I see you next week?"

"Why can't we talk about it now? You left me sitting here all night, wondering what happened to you, and now you're trying to rush me off the phone? Your little wifey's ice cream can wait."

Porsha was starting to get on Dillon's nerves. She was sounding more like a crazy woman and nothing like the classy, intelligent person he'd gotten to know. "I know you're upset, but you've got to give me some slack here. Do you want me to rush my divorce and then lose all my members? People don't take kindly to pastors sleeping around on their wives, and if that pastor ends up with his mistress, they definitely don't want anything to do with *her*. If I left Raven and then married you right away, everyone would know I've been seeing you all along."

"Nobody would have to know anything. We can figure out a way to break the news. We can even wait a few months before we start being out together publicly. But I still want you to leave Raven."

There was just no getting through to her, and he was starting to wish he could have another drink. He still felt pretty good, but the vodka he'd drunk earlier hadn't been nearly enough to deal with this kind of drama. Porsha was in rare form, and he could tell that if he didn't find a way to calm her down, she might be trouble.

"I'm going to try my best to see you tomorrow or Sunday."

"How, Dillon?" she asked.

"I don't know. Just let me see if I can work something out. I can't promise anything, but I'll definitely try. And anyway, girl, you're not the only one who was disappointed tonight. I wanted to see you, too. The whole reason I was coming was because I so needed to make love to you. I had a really stressful day, and when that happens, you're the only one who makes me feel better."

"You're just saying that because I'm pissed off."

"No, I'm saying it because I mean it. But I can show you better than I can tell you," he said, slightly laughing.

"Whatever," she said. Her voice was a lot softer, and Dillon breathed easier.

"Now, let me go inside this store and do

what I need to do. I'll call you tomorrow, though, okay?"

"Yeah."

"You love me?" he said. He'd never asked her that before because he didn't want to have to say it back, but desperate times called for desperate lies. He needed that money, and he was willing to say whatever he had to.

"What difference does it make?"

"Do you or don't you?"

She paused and then said, "Why do you think I've been acting such a fool tonight? But the question is, do you love me?"

And there it was. He'd known that question was coming. "I wasn't sure until three days ago, but I do," he said, preparing to pour things on thicker than usual. "And that's what makes my marriage to Raven and my position at the church so difficult. I want nothing more than to be with you, but I can't just move out without consequences."

"I guess I just got upset because you told me you were on your way, and then hours later you still weren't here. All sorts of stuff went through my head, and the last thing I want is to be used. I wouldn't be able to handle that, baby. It just wouldn't be good."

Dillon's call-waiting signal beeped, and

his home number displayed on the screen. He had to deal with the matter at hand and would have to call Raven back. "I wouldn't do that to you. I wouldn't hurt you that way."

"I want to believe you," she said, sounding as though she was crying. That was a little scary.

"You can, and you'll see that soon enough. I haven't always been the best person, but when I started ministering, I changed. It's one of the reasons I know I'll have to divorce Raven, because I can't continue committing adultery. It's wrong, and I know God isn't happy with it."

"I don't want to keep fornicating, either. I want us to do things the right way. So that's why I'm going to keep helping the church financially, and I'm just going to trust you. And I'm sorry I went off on you the way I did."

Dillon grinned. "You had every right to be angry. I would have felt the same way. But hey, I really do need to get inside this store."

"Okay, but baby, I love you."

"I love you, too."

How exhausting was all Dillon could think, and he hoped he wouldn't have to deal with this kind of thing for too much longer.

He dialed his home number.

"Hi, baby," Raven said. "Where are you?"

"I'm just dropping Vincent off at home. We went out and had pizza."

"Oh, that's nice. Are you on your way home?"

Dillon knew he needed a little more time to get there, so he used the lie he'd told Porsha. Except he wouldn't be lying about it now. "Yep, right after I stop and get your favorite ice cream."

"I'm still stuffed from dinner, but if you're getting my dark chocolate that would be great."

"Dark chocolate it is," he said, looking at the time on his dash. He was still twenty minutes away from Mitchell, so once he picked up the ice cream, it would take him an additional twenty minutes to get home. But if Raven asked him what had taken him so long, he would tell her that the first store he'd gone to didn't have dark chocolate, and he'd had to drive to another. It would mean telling yet another lie to another woman, but what else could he do? Tell the truth? Only if he were brainless.

CHAPTER 20

Alicia hugged Levi from behind, and he turned his head around so she could kiss him. The Fourth of July had finally arrived, and they were standing in front of the grill in his mom's backyard. Levi had been working on the meat since early this morning, and there were only a few small items left to cook. The ribs and chicken were done and already simmering in the oven with barbecue sauce slathered over them, and once Levi finished the burgers and bratwursts, they'd be able to eat. Alicia's mother-in-law was in the house finishing up her last couple of side dishes, and some of Levi's family members sat patiently on the deck. They were a little on the loud side, but they were definitely already having fun. Uncle Buck, Levi's mom's older brother, was a seventy-five-year-old jokester and the life of the party. Aunt Tilly, his wife, still wore high heels even to family cookouts and joked just as much as he did. Their youngest two children, Kane and Kawana, who were boy and girl twins who Uncle Buck and Aunt Tilly had conceived when they were in their forties, were as nice as could be as long as you didn't cross them. Otherwise another side of their personalities showed up, and if you disrespected one twin, they made it known that you'd automatically disrespected both of them. They also each had one gold tooth in the top front row of their mouths . . . just like Uncle Buck and Aunt Tilly. They were all good people, though, and they loved Alicia. She, of course, loved them, too.

Melanie and her dad walked from the kitchen through the patio doors. Alicia had thought she'd heard her mother-in-law speaking to someone, but she hadn't been sure.

Alicia smiled and walked up on the deck. "Hey, Mel," she said, hugging her.

"Hey, hey."

"I'm so glad you came, Mr. Johnson," Alicia said, embracing him. "How are you?"

"I'm doing well, and I've lost a little weight, too," he said, laughing.

Alicia chuckled. "I see, and good for you."

Mr. Johnson had been overweight for a while, but after having a heart attack and then surgery, he'd finally made the decision to go on a diet. He'd been losing a little here and there the whole time, and it showed. This was all after separating from Melanie's mom and divorcing her, and he seemed so much happier.

"Thank you, my dear, for having us," he said.

"You're quite welcome. We're glad you could make it."

Alicia turned toward one of the patio tables. "Let me introduce you to some of Levi's family members, and then you can have a seat. Uncle Buck, Aunt Tilly, Kane, and Kawana, this is my best friend, Melanie, and her dad, Mr. Johnson."

"Nice to meet all of you," Mr. Johnson said. "And you all can just call me Andrew."

"Yes, very nice to meet you," Melanie added.

Uncle Buck smiled. "It's great meetin' you two also, and we're glad you came."

"Why don't you two sit down here at our table," Aunt Tilly said.

Mr. Johnson pulled back a chair. "Don't mind if I do."

"Hey, how's everybody doing?" Dillon said when he and Raven walked outside. Dillon had on a white short-sleeve polo shirt and khaki shorts, and yes, both were made by Ralph Lauren, but Raven had on a white floor-length sleeveless dress made by Diane von Furstenberg. Alicia knew quality clothing, which was the reason she recognized it, but who wore a five-hundred-dollar dress to a backyard cookout? Raven also had a Louis Vuitton cross-body bag hung over her shoulder and waist — and she didn't own any purse that wasn't made by Louis, Chanel, or Gucci.

"Hey, Brother," Alicia said, hugging him, and then looked at her sister-in-law. "Hi, Raven."

Raven forced her usual phony smile. "Good to see you. Thanks for having us."

Dillon and Raven spoke to everyone, and Dillon walked down to the grass by Levi.

"What's up?" Dillon said. "I see you're cooking up a storm out here."

"Trying to. Thanks for coming."

"We wouldn't want to be anywhere else."

Alicia watched Raven, who was still standing on the deck. She definitely didn't want to be there, and she certainly wouldn't want to sit with the Cunninghams. They didn't have enough education, money, or expensive clothing to meet Raven's standards, and she seemed uncomfortable. She was acting as though she were better than them already.

"Have a seat, Raven," Alicia said.

Raven looked at Melanie and her dad and Levi's family, and quickly sat down at the other table, which was still empty. Alicia wanted to laugh, but she didn't want to start anything.

"So you're the pastor's wife, I hear," Uncle Buck said to Raven.

Raven nodded her head. "Yes, I am."

"We don't do much churchgoing, but my sister tells me that your husband is a dynamic speaker. She loves her some Pastor Dillon."

Raven forced another fake smile. "That's always nice to hear."

Aunt Tilly laughed. "And he's a fine young thing, too. Bet he keeps you reeeeal happy, don't he . . . if you know what I mean."

Aunt Tilly and Uncle Buck cracked up laughing even louder, and Kane, Kawana, and Mr. Johnson laughed right along with them. Melanie knew how Raven was, though, and tried not to smile.

Alicia could tell Raven wanted to crawl under the deck.

Levi and Dillon were still down by the grill, but they'd heard what Aunt Tilly said.

"You all leave Lady Raven alone," Levi said.

Kawana scrunched her eyebrows. " 'Lady'? That's what they call you at the church?"

Raven didn't look at her but said, "Some members do, and others call me Lady Black."

"But we can just call you Raven, right?" Kane wanted to know. "We don't need to go bein' all formal on the Fourth of July, do we? This ain't the royal palace or nothin' like that. This is just the commonfolk side of town."

The Cunninghams and Mr. Johnson laughed out loud again. They knew Raven was as uppity as they came, and they were having a ball with her.

Finally, Raven pulled out her smartphone and ignored all of them.

Ironically, Alicia's phone rang, and she picked it up from the ledge of the deck. She smiled when she saw her mom's number.

"Hey, Mom."

"Hi, sweetheart. How are you? Happy Fourth."

"I'm good, and Happy Fourth to you."

"Are you all getting ready to eat?"

"Almost."

"Wonderful, and please make sure you tell your mother-in-law I said hello."

"I will. So how's New Orleans?"

"Well, remember when I called you yesterday and told you we were going to the concert tonight?"

"Uh-huh."

"Well, honey, your mom and stepdad went last night, too. And talk about a good time."

"You two are partying hard."

Tanya laughed. "We definitely are. Can't wait to come back next year, either."

"I knew you guys would have a great time."

"Maybe you and Levi can come with us."

Alicia swallowed the lump in her throat. She wouldn't cry in front of all these people, but she was so happy she definitely wanted to. "That will be the best trip, Mom."

"I know. Your dad James and I were talking about it earlier. He wants to speak to you, but if Levi is close by, let me say hello to him first."

Now tears filled her eyes, and Melanie looked at her.

Alicia walked over to her husband and brother. "Hold on a second, Mom," she said, holding the phone out to Levi.

"Who's that?" he asked.

"My mom."

Levi smiled at her and took the phone. "Hello?"

Dillon smiled at Alicia, too, and then hugged her. "I know you've wanted this for a long time, and I'm so happy for you. I'm happy for both of you."

Tears fell from Alicia's eyes, and when Dillon released her, Melanie walked over.

"Didn't I tell you this would happen?" Melanie said, embracing her.

"You did, but I was starting to lose hope."

"God always comes through in His own timing, and while we don't know why He chose now, you can believe He has His reasons."

When Levi finished talking to Tanya, he gave the phone back to Alicia, and she chatted with James for a few minutes. When she hung up, she went inside the house to see if her mother-in-law needed any help. As she entered the kitchen, she hugged Darrell and D.C., Levi's two closest childhood friends, and they stepped outside where Levi was.

"Hey, Mom, you sure I can't help you with anything?" Alicia said.

"Now, young lady, you know how I am about my cooking. I always appreciate the offer, but I like to handle all my dishes on my own."

Levi's mom owned one of the best family-style restaurants in town, and she was very particular about everything she prepared. She wanted everything to be perfect, so when she hosted dinners, parties, or cookouts at her home, she told everyone they didn't have to bring anything. She did trust Levi with grilling the meat, but only because she was the one who'd taught him how to do it so well.

"I know how you do," Alicia said, "but I still wanted to ask again. I hate not helping you."

"It's fine, really. You can help me carry some of it out, though, if you don't mind."

"Not at all. Oh, and my mom just told me to tell you hello."

"When you talk to her again, tell her I said hello back. Levi told me the great news."

"We still can't believe it. She even asked to speak to him a few minutes ago."

Treva Cunningham walked around the small island and hugged her daughter-in-law. "Praise God. I know these last couple of years haven't been easy for you and Levi, but I'm glad everything worked out. I always knew it would."

Alicia teared up again, still hugging her mother-in-law. "Thank you for not judging me, and for being a mother to me when I needed it most. I love you, and I won't ever forget it."

Treva pulled away from her. "Sweetheart, you don't ever have to thank me for something like that. When you married my son, you became my daughter. And that's that, you hear me?"

Alicia nodded, and they hugged again.

Not every woman could say she had a mother-in-law who loved her unconditionally — or even liked her for that matter — but Alicia could, and she thanked God for her husband and his mother. These last two years, she wasn't sure what she would have done without them. They'd been there for her in every way possible. They'd been her angels from heaven for sure.

CHAPTER 21

They were all sitting on Sister Cunningham's deck, eating everything imaginable: potato salad, seven-layer salad, cucumber-and-tomato salad, macaroni and cheese, baked beans with ground beef, and all the different meats Levi had grilled. The only thing was, Dillon felt like jumping out of his skin. He'd put on a happy face and had acted as normal as he possibly could, but from the time he'd gotten up this morning, he'd wanted a drink. He literally hadn't been able to stop thinking about it, and he was afraid of what might happen next. Before they'd left home, he'd snapped at Raven for no reason, and he'd had to apologize to her. But since they'd arrived at the cookout, he'd put on the best front he knew how because more than once, he'd thought about giving some bogus excuse and leaving.

He didn't understand why this was happening, though, because he'd only had three drinks on Thursday night at Benny's and then three beers yesterday afternoon. Raven had gone shopping again, and though he'd told himself that he wouldn't, he'd driven thirty minutes outside of Mitchell to a tiny town. He'd found a liquor store there, bought a six-pack, and had brought it home. He'd drunk one can right away and then had decided to throw the other five cans out. But he'd changed his mind and had drunk a second and a third. He hadn't felt as tipsy as he had on Thursday night, but it had given him enough of a buzz to be satisfied. This was when he'd willed himself to toss the other three cans in the trash out in the garage. He'd gotten rid of them because he'd had flashbacks to his Atlanta fiasco, and he didn't want to slide down that same road again. To say it had been rocky was an understatement, and he didn't want to take a chance on losing everything. He'd lost a lot the first time around, but he had far more to lose here in Mitchell. Plus, he kept telling himself that while he *wanted* alcohol, he didn't *need* it. It was just something he chose to do but didn't have to. He could stop whenever he wanted, and he'd already proven that for two whole years.

Dillon tried to cover up how on edge he

was, but when he glanced across the table at Levi, he could tell Levi thought something was wrong. So Dillon looked elsewhere.

Raven rested her hand across his back and looked at him. "Are you okay, baby?"

"I'm good."

"You seem like you're in deep thought."

"Just thinking about my sermon for tomorrow."

Dillon had gotten so good at lying that he didn't even have to think about it. Lies rolled off his tongue with no effort.

"You already wrote it, though, right?"

"Yeah, for the most part."

"You'll be fine," she said. "You always do a great job, no matter what."

Levi's friend D.C., a well-known loan shark, sat across from them. "I don't mean to eavesdrop, but my boy Levi says you were *born* to speak. Keeps telling me I should come hear you."

"You should," Dillon said.

"I haven't been to church in at least a couple of years. As a matter of fact, the last time I went, I attended your dad's church. I've always had mad props for him. Never seen anyone do some of the things he did and then turn everything around for the better. Well, maybe with the exception of

Levi. But what I also love about your dad is that he don't mind talking about it. He don't just tell people what they shouldn't do, he tells you why because he's already done it. But I hear you do the same thing, and that's good."

Dillon ignored the comment about his dad because it was better not to think about him. "Praise and worship begins at nine thirty in the morning, and then we go right into service," Dillon said, smiling.

D.C. smiled back at him. "I don't know about tomorrow, man, but maybe sometime soon."

"Well, just think about it, because we would love to have you."

"I don't know, though," D.C. joked, "next thing you know, you'll have me endin' up just like my boy Levi here. Saved, sanctified, and filled with the Holy Ghost."

Levi rolled his eyes and shook his head. "We can only hope, because Lord knows if anybody needs to be saved, it's you."

D.C. laughed and so did their friend Darrell, who sat on the other side of D.C. Melanie was also sitting next to Darrell, and Alicia sat between Levi and Dillon.

"No, but in all seriousness," D.C. said, "I respect what you're doing, and if you keep going the way you are, you'll be just like your dad. You'll make a huge difference for a lot of people in this community. And now he's building that huge sanctuary right next to the old one. And from what I hear, he's going to turn the old church into a community center. Supposed to be something like a Boys and Girls Club, I think. So I'm telling you, that's a bad man, and you and my girl Alicia are lucky to have a dad like that."

Alicia and Levi looked at each other, and Dillon could tell the community center idea was news to them as well. This was yet one more thing his dad would have that would gain him more members and support from the city. But more important, didn't D.C. know that Curtis wasn't close with Dillon and Alicia? So why would they feel lucky to have him as anything? Dillon thought about letting it go, but he was tired of people keeping the good Reverend Black on some pedestal.

Dillon drank a few sips of his bottled water. "You do know that my father doesn't have anything to do with me, don't you? And after all this time, he still won't accept that my sister and Levi are married. And you say we should feel lucky to have him in our life? No disrespect, but you obviously don't know the same stubborn, unforgiving man we do."

D.C. ate a forkful of potato salad. "No disrespect from here, either. I know you might not be all that close with him, but I was just stating how great he's been for the community. He's done a lot of stuff for a lot of people, and I was just givin' credit where credit is due. Nothing more."

"It's fine," Alicia said, clearly trying to prevent any further conversation on the subject. "We weren't offended."

Dillon was *beyond* offended, and now his father was in his head again, causing him more distress. But he knew his sister was right for defusing the situation. He would never want to cause trouble or disrespect Sister Cunningham's home, anyway.

Raven had been quiet until she glanced toward the other table at Kawana, who'd just whispered something to her brother while looking in their direction.

"Is there a problem?" Raven asked her.

Kawana pointed at herself. "You talkin' to me?"

"You're the only one over there staring at us."

"Well, if you wanna know the truth, I wasn't staring at you and your husband. Just you."

"Well, in case you don't know, staring is rude."

Dillon touched Raven's arm. "Baby, just leave it alone. It's not a big deal."

Raven jerked her arm away. "This ghetto chick is gawking at me, and you're going to sit here and defend her? That's why I didn't want to come over here. I can't stand dealing with ghetto people who don't have any manners."

"Whoa, now wait a minute," Kane said. "Sis, did this female just call you ghetto?"

Kawana dropped her fork on her plate. "And didn't stutter, either. Her words couldn've been more clear."

"Hey, hey, hey," Sister Cunningham said. "You all stop that. We're all family here, and I won't stand for any foolishness. Not at my house."

"That's right," Uncle Buck said. "Kawana and Kane, you two let it go, you hear me?"

Kawana didn't say anything else . . . until a few seconds later. "With your gambling-addict thievin' behind. You might be some bougie first lady today, but we all know you used to be locked up. So, baby, you can call me ghetto and anything else you want, but at least I don't steal from people. And I certainly wouldn't be stupid and low enough to steal from the house of the Lord."

Raven jumped up. "Dillon, let's go."

Kawana got up, too. "Yeah, Pastor, take that trick out of here before she get a beat-down. Comin' up in here with her nose all turned up, actin' like she better than the rest of us. I've been laying for you for the last couple of hours," she told Raven.

Levi went over to the table where his family was sitting. "Kawana, just cut it out, okay? You know you're wrong for this."

Kane didn't say anything, and Dillon was glad Levi's two cousins listened to him.

Raven turned around. "Dillon, did you hear me? Why are you still sitting there?"

Dillon finally stood up. "Sister Cunningham, all of you, I'm really sorry. Levi, Alicia, I'm sorry this happened, so please forgive us."

Raven frowned so hard Dillon thought she would burst a blood vessel. "Why are you apologizing? That woman was staring and whispering about me. Let alone the Lady Raven comment she made when we first got here. So don't you dare apologize to her."

"Let's go," Dillon said, already walking down the steps of the deck. When they'd arrived, they'd come through the house from the front door, but Dillon was so embarrassed he wanted them to get into the car as fast as they could. He couldn't wait to get

Raven home. He'd promised Porsha he would try to come by there, anyway, and that's exactly where he was going. Or maybe he would see if Taylor was home instead. Either way, he wouldn't be dealing with Raven. She knew how important Levi was to him and how much he'd done for them and the church, yet she'd showed her behind at his mom's house like Levi didn't matter. Dillon loved his wife, but her arrogant and vain personality was sometimes too much for him. He wanted money and power himself, but he didn't want it so he could look down on people. He wanted those things for his own enjoyment and to make up for all the times when he hadn't had much as a child. Raven, however, seemed to be letting all of their blessings go to her head. The more members they got and the more money the two of them made, the more snobbish she became.

He wasn't going to say a word to her about it, though. Because if he did, he might say something he would regret, and it just wasn't worth it.

CHAPTER 22

Alicia waved good-bye to her mother-in-law. "I can't believe Raven said all those things to Kawana. And then to say she didn't want to come over here, right in front of your mom."

Levi backed his black Escalade out of his mom's driveway. "Kawana shouldn't have made that comment about her being called Lady at the church, though, and then Kane made that joke about the royal palace. I could tell Raven was through from that point on."

"Yeah, but she didn't have to say Kawana was ghetto. Or that she can't stand being around ghetto people. I told you a long time ago that Raven was full of herself, and now she's worse than ever."

"Well, I just hate that it happened, because my mom didn't deserve that."

"I was so embarrassed, and I could tell Dillon was, too. Raven showed us exactly who she is, and that's why we can never let her be co-pastor."

Levi slowed down before turning the corner. "Hey, speaking of Dillon, did you notice anything different about him?"

Alicia slightly twisted her body toward him. "I thought it was just me, but he seemed nervous and kind of anxious at the table. I couldn't put my finger on it, but something seemed wrong."

"I noticed it before we even started eating. It was like his mind would drift off somewhere and like he was a little fidgety."

"He was really upset about Daddy a couple of days ago, so I hope that doesn't have anything to do with it."

Levi looked at her and then back at the road. "Hmmm."

"What?"

"I know I'm probably wrong, but baby, you know I've seen it all. When I was dealing drugs, I only sold coke and prescription drugs, but I met every kind of addict there was. From people who shot dope to chronic alcoholics, you name it."

"You don't think he's doing drugs, do you? Please don't tell me that."

"Baby, I don't know. If he is, he hasn't been doing it for very long, but something just wasn't right."

"Maybe he and Raven had gotten into it before they came to your mom's," Alicia suggested, but she wondered if she even believed her own words. "Or maybe it's like I said, he's still worked up over what he told me about Daddy."

"What, the radio interview?"

"Yeah, remember I told you about it Thursday night?"

Levi looked at her with a sly grin. "I vaguely remember you saying something, but after you wore me out the way you did I was pretty out of it."

"Yeah, whatever."

"I'm serious. You did wear me out, but it was one of the best nights we've had in years. Our lovemaking was as powerful and passionate as it was when we first met. You seem so much more like yourself."

"I feel more like myself, too. I feel good."

"Well, as far as Dillon goes, let's just hope I'm wrong and you're right. Because being a pastor and doing drugs won't work."

Alicia prayed that drugs were the furthest thing from Dillon's mind. He didn't need something like that in his life right now, and neither did she. As it was, she was still working on her own problems, and that was more than enough. She just hoped her brother's issues with their father hadn't pushed him to start doing something he shouldn't. He was progressing so well as a pastor, and their vision for the church was successfully moving in the direction Dillon wanted it to.

Alicia and Levi rode along in silence, listening to a smooth jazz radio station.

Levi held her hand, and Alicia loved how he still sent chills through her body when he touched her. Sometimes just looking at him, even when he didn't know she was, made her heart flutter like a teenager in love for the first time.

They continued on their way, but when they were about five minutes from home, Alicia's phone rang. When she pulled it out of her purse, she got nervous and excited all at the same time. Her dad's house number displayed on her screen.

"Oh my God."

"What?"

"This is from my dad's house."

"Well, answer it."

"Hello?"

"Hey, Alicia," Charlotte said.

It wasn't that Alicia wasn't happy to hear from her stepmom, because she was. It was just that Charlotte usually phoned her from her cell, so Alicia had been hoping this was her dad.

Alicia smiled. "Hey, how are you?"

"Good. I just wanted to call to say happy Fourth of July to you and Levi."

"Thank you," she said, looking at Levi. "Charlotte says happy Fourth of July."

"Tell her I said happy Fourth."

Alicia relayed Levi's message.

"So did you guys go to your mother-in-law's as planned?" Charlotte asked.

"We did. We're just on our way home from there now. Did you guys enjoy the day also?"

"We did, but it still wasn't the same without you. I miss having you over here for the holidays. We all miss you."

"Well, maybe most of you, anyway."

"No matter what your dad says or does, trust me when I tell you he misses you. He never wanted to stop seeing you, but I don't blame you for standing your ground about your husband. I would do the same thing if someone treated your dad that way."

At that very moment, Alicia wished she could hear his voice.

"Mommy, who is that on the phone?" Alicia heard Curtina say.

"It's your sister."

"Ooooh, let me speak to Licia, Mommy. Please let me speak to her."

"Okay, okay. Alicia, here's your baby sister. Goodness."

"Hi, Licia," nine-year-old Curtina said.

"Hi, sweetie. How are you?"

"I'm fine. How are you?"

"I'm fine, too."

"And how is Levi? Is he with you?"

"He's doing well, and yes, we're on our way home."

"Did you go to his mommy's house?"

"Yep."

"Did you eat a lot of food?"

"Unfortunately, we did. We ate too much. What about you?"

"Yeah, we ate too much, too. Especially Daddy. And now he's lying down in the family room already asleep. Can you come over, Licia? I miss you sooooo much."

Alicia's hand shook, and she burst into tears.

"Licia, what's wrong?" Curtina asked. "Why are you crying?"

"Baby, what's wrong?" Levi said.

Charlotte got back on the phone. "Honey, what's the matter?"

"I hate the way things are with all of us."

"I know," Charlotte agreed, "and we have to find a way to fix this."

"I don't know how."

"Well, we'll figure out something, because it's time to move on from two years ago."

Alicia sniffled. "Thank you for always caring about me."

"We love you, and don't you ever forget that. I'll call you tomorrow or Monday, okay? And maybe we can set up a day for me to bring over Curtina and little MJ."

"Sounds good. And hey, where's Matt and MJ, anyway?"

"After we ate, Matt took MJ to see his other grandparents."

"Well, tell him I said hello. I know he's still not speaking to me all that much, but I still love him."

"He loves you, too. He just can't handle that you and Dillon are as close as you are, but he's going to have to get over that."

Alicia knew Dillon had slept with Matthew's wife and that Matthew wouldn't be happy about her forgiving Dillon. But she'd never imagined that Matthew would be upset with her for this long. He didn't understand how she could have anything to do with Dillon, and he saw Alicia as a traitor.

"Well, it was good talking to you," Alicia said.

"You, too. See you soon."

Alicia ended the call and leaned her head against the passenger window. Levi grabbed her hand again, but he didn't say anything. There wasn't much he could say at this point. Not much anyone could do at all, when her father wasn't willing to accept Levi, and she wasn't willing to be around a father who couldn't accept her husband. So they were at a standstill. They'd been at one for all this time, and she didn't see how it would ever change.

CHAPTER 23

After pulling into the driveway, Dillon had waited for Raven to get out, and when she didn't, he'd gotten out of the car, marched around to the passenger side, and opened her door. She'd still sat there, pleading with him to tell her what she'd done so wrong, but he'd told her to get out and go in the house. When she'd refused, he'd waited until she had. After that, he'd gotten back in his vehicle and driven off. He'd left her standing and watching him, and he hadn't had any sympathy.

He'd needed to get away from her. Run from an environment that wouldn't allow him to do what he wanted in peace. So he'd started on his way toward either Porsha's or Taylor's place, he hadn't known which yet, but he'd also stopped at a liquor store. He'd promised himself that, at the very least, he wouldn't purchase anything hard, especially since he had to drive, but he did buy a cold six-pack of beer. He hadn't drunk anything while driving, but he had traveled down a long, two-lane country road and parked in a secluded area. This was where he'd drunk two cans, tossed the empties away, and placed the other four in his trunk. Before leaving Mitchell, he'd purchased a bag of ice and a small cooler, too. That way, if for some reason he was stopped by the police and they searched his car, they wouldn't find any broken seals.

Now, though, he lay next to Porsha feeling good again. He'd leaned more toward calling and going to see Taylor, which was where he actually wanted to be, but he knew he needed to make things up to Porsha from the other night. She'd been more upset than ever, and she'd been talking in ways he hadn't counted on. She'd sounded almost desperate, like she didn't know what she would do without him. It didn't make sense to him, but he still needed her help. What she gave monthly to New Faith Christian Center was commendable and very helpful, but at some point, he would have to figure out the right way to ask her for a lump sum. It would be in the six figures, and he'd have to offer her a good reason to do it. He'd have to keep giving her the kind of attention she wanted and the sex she swore she couldn't go without.

Porsha turned toward Dillon, the side of her face resting against her hands on the pillow. "Thank you for coming to spend time with me. I never thought I'd be able to see you on the holiday. I thought you would be with Raven."

Dillon lay on his back with his eyes closed, not saying anything.

"And I don't think you've ever made love to me the way you did just now. It was so intense. It's always great, but today it was the best ever."

Dillon still didn't respond.

"Baby, why aren't you saying anything?"

"I'm sorry, but if it's okay with you, I just want to lie here quietly. Let's just enjoy the moment."

Porsha nestled closer to him and did as he asked.

But the truth was, Dillon wasn't enjoying anything right now, because he had a lot on his mind. For one, he couldn't stop thinking about the way he'd turned on Raven and how angry he'd gotten at her. Yes, he hadn't liked the way she'd acted at Sister Cunningham's, but she still hadn't done enough for him to stop speaking to her. He hadn't uttered one word to her the entire ride home, and then he'd barely glanced at her when he'd left her standing in the driveway. In that moment, she was the last person he'd wanted to be around, and he was starting to wonder if his desire to drink had anything to do with it. Surely drinking a little vodka and a couple of beers wasn't enough to alter his mind and feelings to such an erratic level.

He just didn't know, though, because he hadn't begun to feel so out of sorts or anxious until the day he'd taken his first drink. But this all went back to his father and that hurtful radio talk show rant of his. Two days had passed, yet Dillon was still consumed by it. He'd thought about it on and off, day and night, and no matter how much he'd tried to say, "Forget my dad, I'm moving on," he couldn't. It just seemed that the only way to do that would be to hit him where it hurt. Dillon wished there was another way, but even God brought vengeance on the wicked.

Dillon remembered years ago when he'd heard his dad quote the scripture: "Vengeance is mine; I will repay, saith the Lord." Back then Dillon had rarely picked up a Bible, let alone read one, so he hadn't even known what book of the Bible it was in. Today, though, he knew it came from Romans 12:19, and once when he'd been sitting at his dad's church, listening to him, the words of this scripture had crossed his mind. It just seemed fitting because it defined how Dillon had the right to pay back anyone who hurt him. This was also the reason he couldn't let his former fiancée, Melissa, get away with what she'd done, either. He'd thought he would start making plans to take care of her soon, but now he knew he had to gear all his thoughts, plans, and energies toward his dad. As for Melissa, he'd gone three years allowing her to think she'd gotten away with her dirty deed, so waiting another year or two to punish her wouldn't make a difference. Actually, it would make his revenge that much sweeter, because the more time passed, the more comfortable and content she'd become with her new life, and then out of nowhere, Dillon would take everything from her. Her money, her happiness, her reason for even wanting to live. He would leave her be for now, but her day was coming and that gave him comfort.

However, just as quickly as his spirits were lifted, he thought about Raven again. He was sorry for the way he'd acted this afternoon, and he knew he had to correct it. He loved Raven, maybe not as much as he'd been thinking, but he needed her by his side as first lady. He wasn't like a number of pastors he knew who were hired by churches and could be fired at any time; however, he was smart enough to know that the majority of Christians wanted their pastor to be married. Some required it and wouldn't support one who wasn't. They wanted their leader to have a wife because if he didn't, it might encourage too much temptation and he'd end up sleeping around with the many women who approached him. Dillon had even met some pastors who'd told him that not only was being married a requirement written in their employment contracts, it had been included in the bylaws at their respective churches. It was a rule that had to be abided by, and if that pastor separated from his wife for too long or divorced her, it was grounds for dismissal.

Dillon also knew he had to fix things with Raven before the weekend was out, because even though she was looking forward to making an appeal to the elder board on Tuesday, things weren't going to evolve the way she wanted. She wasn't going to be his co-pastor, and that was a fact. He would then have to figure out yet another way to make things up to her and get her thinking about some new goal that would work better for her.

But for now, he was done thinking about Raven, his dad, and anyone else who kept his mind swirling in too many directions. Instead, he was going to make love to Porsha again. Give her what she wanted. Satisfy her in a way that would last until the next time he could see her.

CHAPTER 24

Dillon rehearsed his lies one last time and then stepped out of the car. He'd just arrived home, and he knew he was about to enter a war zone. Raven had called him no less than twenty times, and it was going to take more begging and apologizing than usual to pacify her.

He walked inside, and she never gave him an opportunity to close the door behind him.

She rushed toward him and beat his chest with both her fists. "You must think I'm an idiot! Some desperate wife who won't leave you."

Dillon caught both her arms in midair. "Baby, don't do this. I'm sorry. I know I was wrong, and I apologize."

Raven tried to twist her arms away from him. "Let me go, Dillon. You're just like your father. You have no respect for women, and now you're sleeping with some whore."

Dillon wondered if she'd found out about Porsha or if she was simply speculating. "I would never mess around on you, and you know that."

Raven yanked away from him. "You don't know who you're dealing with. I've loved you and been there for you, and this is the thanks I get? This is the way you treat me?"

"Baby, just listen to me. Please."

"Listen to what? More lies. Where were you, Dillon?"

"I drove over to Chicago."

"For what?"

"I needed to be alone. I was upset, and I just wanted to take a drive."

"Oh my goodness," she said, laughing. "And you think I'm stupid enough to believe that? You drove all the way to Chicago and back just for the sake of doing it?"

"I did. I know it sounds strange, but I had a lot on my mind."

"Well, even if you went all the way downtown that should've only taken you three hours round trip. You've been gone six. Six . . . whole . . . hours."

"I parked for a while and listened to music, and then I got something to eat. But I promise you with everything in me, I wasn't with anybody. I was alone the whole time."

"I'm getting to the point where I can't stand you. First you wouldn't support my calling to become co-pastor, and then you humiliate me in front of all those ghetto people this afternoon. And now you're messing around?"

"But I am supporting your calling, and that's why you're coming to the board meeting on Tuesday."

"Only because I brought it up. If I hadn't suggested it and kept trying to make my point, it never would have happened. You'd have been fine if I'd forgotten about it and given up. You never even cared. You just care about yourself."

"That's not true. I've loved you from the very beginning, and I've always been indebted to you for loving me, helping me with the ministry, and for being loyal. Which is why I would never betray you."

Raven leaned against the granite-top island and folded her arms. "I'm not like your dad's first two wives, and I hope you know that. From what I hear, he disrespected both of them whenever he felt like it, and he did it for a lot longer than I would've taken it. It took them forever before they finally got smart enough to leave him, but Dillon, just as sure as my name is Raven Jones Whitfield Black, I'll become your worst enemy. I'll take half of everything you have, and I won't feel bad about it. I'll do it publicly and very quickly."

She was more furious than he'd imagined. He'd known she'd be upset, and that he'd have to cower and make far-fetched promises, but now she was threatening him.

"What have I done?" he said with tears filling his eyes. He wasn't in the mood for crying, but this disaster here called for tears and anything else he could think of. "I should have told you what happened on Thursday. But instead, I kept it to myself, and I let it make me crazy in the head."

Raven pursed her lips, looking at him as though he were acting. Which he was, but she hadn't left him a choice.

She stood there expressionless, and Dillon dropped down on his knees, weeping. He gazed up at her, pleading with his eyes, but when she raised her eyebrows in disgust, he grabbed her around her hips and laid his head against her. Real tears fell, and he boohooed like a child. "Baby, please don't leave me. I was wrong, but I really let my father get to me this time."

"Dillon, what are you talking about?"

He bellowed some more, and she finally touched the top of his head. "What did your dad do? Tell me."

"He went on national radio saying what an awful person I was. He said I was lying about being called into the ministry, and that I had no moral values. But I had also called him the day before, and I didn't tell you about that, either. He said he would never trust me again, and then he compared me to Matthew. So baby, even though I've always known my dad doesn't love me, that really hurt. I grew up not knowing either of my parents, and I've always felt lost and rejected. Like nobody wants me, and now all that pain is causing me to hurt *you.*"

Dillon kept his head pressed against her, and just as he was wondering if his story and tears were doing the trick, he heard her sniffling.

He moved his head away from hers and saw her crying. Dillon had known she would identify with the last part of his alibi because of the terrible childhood she'd had. She herself still struggled with the memory of being tossed around to so many different foster homes.

"Why didn't you just come to me?" she said. "Why didn't you just tell me what happened?"

Dillon stood up and hugged her. "I couldn't. Because what you also don't know is that when I spoke to my dad, he said that he would never let me hurt any of his family members again. He spoke to me like I wasn't part of his family. Like I was an outsider who had no right to call him."

Raven breathed deeply. "I'm so sorry. I had no idea what you've been going through the last couple of days, and you really should have told me. I'm your wife, and that's what I'm here for."

Mission accomplished. Dillon hated using Raven's feelings about her troubled childhood against her, but it was all he'd had left to make her sympathize with him. He didn't like taking advantage of her pain, but she'd threatened him with too much. She'd sounded serious, and he hadn't known another way to deal with it.

"From now on," she said, "I want you to tell me everything. No matter how bad it is. No matter how hard it might be for you to talk about it. We can't keep things from one another, baby. We have to be honest so we can help each other."

Dillon didn't bother responding and kissed her. Then he grabbed her hair, slightly pulling her head backward so he could kiss her neck. He pushed her against the wall, roughly, and though he felt tears falling from her eyes onto his face, she kissed him back with force and great passion. She was dressed in a full-length silk robe, but he opened it and kissed her chest. She whimpered with pleasure, the same as Taylor had on Thursday — the same as Porsha had only hours ago.

Raven wanted him, he wanted her, and he couldn't wait to have his way with her. He would remind her that no other man could ever make her feel the way he did. This, of course, would be the first time he'd made love to both his wife and another woman in the same evening, but he couldn't worry about that. His job was to satisfy Raven by any means necessary so she wouldn't be suspicious. He had to keep things in order at home so his marital problems wouldn't cause a scandal. He knew the Bible stated that when a man and woman became married, they became one, but for Dillon, New Faith Christian Center and New Faith Ministries, Inc., was his priority. It had been his priority from day one, and it always would be.

Chapter 25

Three days had passed; it was bright and early Tuesday morning, and Dillon and Raven were sitting at the island eating breakfast. Reluctantly, Raven had scrambled some eggs, cooked tiny turkey sausage patties, and made oatmeal. Then she'd toasted a couple of pieces of whole-wheat bread and set a glass pitcher of orange juice on the table. She did this because she knew Dillon liked a full breakfast in the morning, but the only things she ate were a slice of toast and some oatmeal.

Raven spread a large linen napkin across her black sleeveless sheath dress. "I don't mean to complain," she said, "but I can't wait for the day when we can afford to have a full-time cook, seven days a week, and not just someone on the weekends. Cooking is for the birds."

Dillon nodded in agreement, but he never looked up from the newspaper he was reading. It didn't bother him that they didn't have a full-time cook, but as a result of what he'd done to Raven on Saturday, he was still in yes-man mode.

"Gosh," she said. "I don't know why, but I'm already getting nervous."

"Why?" Dillon asked, still reading his paper. "You never have a problem speaking in front of anyone. You'll do fine."

"I guess, but I've never had to present myself for something so important. Telling the elders that I've been called to co-pastor is huge. Do you think they'll want me to speak for a long time or just get to the point?"

"I think you can say whatever you have on your heart. Tell them why you want to be co-pastor and why you'd make a good one."

"What did Levi say?"

Dillon spooned up a helping of oatmeal and looked at her. He wouldn't dare tell her that he hadn't as much as mentioned to Levi that she was coming to the meeting until yesterday. "He was fine with you attending, and I'm sure he's looking forward to hearing you share with them."

"Is there anything I should mention in particular?"

"Not that I can think of. I mean, I wouldn't go telling them you're planning to start some Christian women's pole-dancing class or anything like that," he said, laughing.

Raven pursed her lips. "You're being silly, and, baby, I'm trying to be serious. This is important to me."

"It was only a joke, and it's like I said, just speak from your heart. You've said that God has called you, so I know He'll give you the right words."

"I'm trusting that He will, but I'm still nervous. What if some of the board members are against the idea right out of the gate? What if they say no without giving me a fair chance?"

"None of those men are like that."

"What about Elder Freeman? He questions everything. He even questions you, and you founded New Faith."

"But he's only one man, and majority rules."

Dillon longed for this whole process to be over with, because he was tired of trying to appease her and pretending he wanted her to be co-pastor.

Raven ate some of her toast. "Maybe I should tell them some of my new ideas."

Dillon looked up at her again, wondering what she meant. "Like what?"

"Well, first, I think it's time we start having two services. When the membership finally grows to the number you're projecting, we'll need to have two anyway. We could do the first at eight, and I'm more than willing to deliver the sermon for that one."

Dillon didn't like the idea of her already trying to incorporate something they hadn't done before. He was all for eventually starting a second service, but he would deliver both sermons every Sunday. The only way he wouldn't was if he was ill, out of town, or too exhausted. Still, he told her, "That's a great idea, baby."

"You wouldn't have a problem with it?" she asked.

"Not at all. That would mean less work for me."

"That's what I was thinking. We could still work together, though, just so we can make sure we speak on similar subjects on the same days. I was also thinking that since some people work on Sundays or have other obligations, it might be good for us to start having service on Saturday evening also."

Dillon wasn't interested in holding service on Saturday. To him, this was the one day everyone should be able to enjoy with family and friends. But once again, he agreed with Raven. "I hadn't considered doing anything on Saturday, but I definitely see your point. That's another great idea."

Raven beamed with excitement. "And I have a few others, too, but I'll wait to tell you about those after the elder board gives me the go-ahead."

She went on and on for another twenty minutes, and mostly Dillon nodded, said "uh-huh," or tuned her out altogether. But the good news was that they were just about ready to leave for the church, and once the meeting was over he could begin picking up the pieces — after she learned that the entire board had unanimously voted down her request.

On most days, Dillon and Raven normally arrived at the church at different times, so they drove in separate vehicles. But now they walked side by side down the carpeted hallway. Raven adjusted the single-strand pearls around her neck and stroked her hair back toward her chignon. Then she and Dillon walked into the conference room. Levi and the other eleven elders were already seated, and interestingly enough, Alicia sat at the end of the table. As COO, she rarely attended the weekly elder board meeting. So Dillon knew that Levi had told her about Raven's desire to speak to everyone, and she wanted to be there.

When Dillon closed the door, the chatter among the attendees quieted down, and Dillon took his seat. Normally Levi sat adjacent to him at his right, but today he'd moved down a space, leaving that seat open for Raven.

Levi opened the meeting. "Before we get to the items listed on our weekly agenda, Lady Raven would like to address the board."

Raven smiled and stood up. "Well, I first want to thank all of you for allowing me this opportunity. This is a pretty big day for me because not even a year ago would I have thought I'd be standing here for the reason I've come. God has called me to minister," she said, pausing. "I wasn't sure at first, but I've prayed about it for six months, and the more I prayed, the more he revealed everything to me. So not only has he called me into the ministry, he's called me to become my husband's co-pastor."

Dillon scanned the room, waiting for facial reactions, and of course Elder Freeman didn't let him down. He raised his eyebrows and looked as though Raven had told a funny joke. Dillon waited to see who else might give some indication as to what they thought, but not a single person moved or said a word. At first he was shocked, but then it dawned on him. None of them knew how he felt about his wife becoming co-pastor, and they didn't want to fight against something he might be okay with. They respected him and didn't want to make any unnecessary waves.

Their silence didn't deter Raven, though, and she continued. "I know this likely comes as a huge surprise to all of you, because for a while I was surprised myself. But I finally realized that there was no way I could ignore God's calling on my life. So with that said, what I can promise you is that I will make this ministry my priority, and I will follow God's direction with every decision I need to make. I'll do the same with every sermon I give. The other thing I thought about, too, was that God's calling is in such perfect timing. We're not there yet, but as the church grows larger, we'll be needing a co-pastor. And with my being called now, it means I'll already be in place, and we can focus on the ministry's vision as a whole. We'll be able to do it together."

Raven paused again, but no one said anything. They didn't as much as turn to look at the person sitting next to them on either side. But the one who openly displayed the overall climate of the room was Alicia. She sat texting on her phone, totally ignoring Raven and making it obvious.

"Anyway," Raven went on, "that's my news, and my prayer is that you will support me and approve my becoming co-pastor here at New Faith. Thank you so much."

"Thank you, Lady Raven," Levi said. "We'll discuss everything you've shared with us, and either I or Pastor Black will get back to you very soon."

"That'll be fine, and thanks again. I really appreciate it."

Dillon looked at Raven. "Thanks, baby. I'll see you when we adjourn."

"I have a lunch meeting, but I'll see you as soon as I get back."

When Raven left the room, Dillon purposely didn't say a word. Instead, he waited for Levi to handle everything — just like he'd asked him to yesterday.

Levi leaned back in his chair. "Does anyone have any questions?"

Elder Freeman raised his hand. "I don't mean any disrespect to you, Pastor, but I'm not sure it's good for any pastor to work side by side with his spouse. I mean, working here at the same place in different capacities is one thing, but what if the two of you have an argument or a major dispute at home? You'll still have to work together as pastors like nothing's wrong. What will that do for either of you when you're dealing with church business, attending meetings together, or doing anything else church-related that requires the two of you to interact? Won't it be uncomfortable to not be speaking at home but then have to come here pretending? I mean, I'm no expert on any of this, because I've never worked with my wife, but I'm just wondering."

Normally Dillon would be irritated by the good elder trying to take charge of something, but not today. No, today Dillon *wanted* Elder Freeman, Levi, and anyone else to speak their minds so he didn't have to. That way when he broke the unfortunate news to Raven — that the board was in total disagreement with her becoming co-pastor — she wouldn't be able to blame him.

Levi scanned the room. "Does anyone have anything to add to Elder Freeman's opinion?"

"I tend to agree with him," Vincent said, and Dillon silently thanked him. Dillon had already told him, yesterday, too, that he didn't want Raven being co-pastor.

"Well, let me just say this," Levi began, "and, Pastor, please know that I have nothing against your wife, because I love Raven. But I also don't think this is a good idea. I have a number of reasons that I could share, but in the end, I just don't think it's a good move for the church right now. Not when we have so many other items to focus on."

Dillon was proud of Levi for giving his honest opinion. He'd told Levi yesterday to do just that, because he knew how much the other elders respected him, which also meant that once they learned that Levi didn't agree with Raven being co-pastor, they wouldn't, either.

Alicia locked her hands together and spoke from a COO standpoint. "That's my thinking exactly. Maybe sometime down the road we can reconsider Raven, especially with her saying that God has called her. But I don't even think we can revisit this before the end of next year. The overall business and vision of the church has to be our priority, and we have to stay on track with that. Also, just because I don't think Raven should be named co-pastor doesn't mean she still can't become a minister and even go to seminary school. But again, I think we need to leave things the way they are in terms of who leads the church."

When Levi asked for final comments and no one else spoke up, he called for an official vote. As expected, everyone said no. Dillon couldn't smile externally, but he smiled on the inside. He would still have to deal with much drama later today, but it wouldn't change anything. He was New Faith's founder and only senior pastor — and he would be from now on.

CHAPTER 26

Alicia walked into her office, and Levi followed behind her. She sat on the edge of her desk. Levi sat down in a chair in front of her.

"Wow," Alicia said. "Was that awkward or what?"

"Yeah, but it had to be done. And it was unanimous."

"Well, unanimous or not, Raven isn't going to simply take no for an answer. I could tell from the look on her face that she really wants this. Which means she's going to do everything she can to get Dillon to veto the board's decision. Just wait and see."

"Maybe," Levi said. "But trust me, it won't help."

"How can you be so sure?"

"I just am. Your brother doesn't want that, and he'll never allow it."

"He told you that?"

"Yes, and I'd rather we just leave it at that."

"Well, I hope you're right, because we don't need these kinds of issues. We have too many other things on our plate."

"I agree."

"As a matter of fact, we're meeting with the new marketing firm this afternoon at three."

"I saw the email reminder this morning," he said.

"This company comes highly recommended, so I'm hoping they have lots of great ideas that will coincide with and even enhance our new vision."

"I'm sure they will," Levi said, looking her up and down and smiling.

"What?" she said.

"I really do love you. You know that?"

"I love you, too, but where is all that coming from?"

"I just felt like saying it. I'm happy, and I'm grateful for the way things have shifted around for us. It's been five days since you took the afternoon off and made dinner for me. It was a huge turning point."

"I'm glad you're happy, because that's all I've ever wanted," she said.

"Ever since you talked to your mom, you've seemed so much more at peace."

"I am," she said.

Things were good, but Levi still didn't know about the voice or the gun it kept reminding her about. He also didn't know how hard she'd prayed or how she believed Satan was the one who'd been trying to destroy her. Satan had tried to speak to her again on the Fourth of July, right after she'd broken down on the phone with Curtina, but Alicia had ignored him and he'd left her alone. She hadn't heard a voice of any kind for the last three days, and she'd also gotten a lot more sleep. After hearing from her mom, she'd begun to feel a lot less stressed, and she believed that had made a difference for her. She still had regrets and she missed her dad and other two siblings, but mentally, she was so much better. She felt more equipped to deal with her problems, and she didn't feel as sad or depressed.

"So," Levi said, "did Melanie's doctor suggest someone for you to see?"

"I never called her, but I'm fine now anyway."

"That may be true, but I still want you to see a specialist."

"You worry too much."

"Baby, after what we've been through these last two years, I have reason to. Now, promise me you'll call her."

"I will. Right after our marketing meeting."

He got up and kissed her on the lips. "I hope you're telling the truth this time."

"I told the truth before," she lied. "I just didn't think I needed to call her anymore. But if you insist."

"I do."

"Okay, I hear you."

"I need to get to my office, but I'll see you this afternoon."

"Bye, baby."

"See you," he said.

Alicia smiled, walked around her desk, and sat down. Then she called her mother.

"Hey, Mom."

"Hey. I was just getting ready to call you."

"Really? About what?"

"Just to see how you were doing and also to ask if Thursday will work for you and Levi."

"For dinner?"

"Yes."

"I'm sure it will, but I'll ask him. I don't think he has anything going on, though, and I know I don't."

"Good."

"So what time did you and Dad James get home last night?"

"Our flight out of New Orleans was a little

256

delayed, so by the time we got to O'Hare, grabbed our luggage, and made it over to the parking garage, it was after ten."

"That wasn't too bad, but I know what it's like when you're ready to get home and your flight doesn't leave on time."

"Exactly. No matter how much you enjoy yourself, when it's time to head home, you can't wait to get there."

"That's for sure."

"So did you speak to your dad over the holiday weekend?" Tanya said.

"No. Charlotte called me, and she let me talk to Curtina, but that was it. Why do you ask?"

"I spoke to him right before we left, and I told him he should call you. I didn't tell you because I didn't want to get your hopes up."

"Well, he didn't. Charlotte told me she was going to talk to him, too, but I'm not expecting his feelings to change."

"You don't think so?"

"No, because let's be honest, Mom, you and Daddy didn't end your relationship with me. I ended it with both of you because you wouldn't accept Levi. So if I were to call Daddy and never talk about Levi or go visit him and never bring Levi with me, he would like nothing more than that. He would be fine. But I wouldn't."

"I told him that we were all wrong, and that I apologized to you."

"And what did he say?"

"Not a lot. Mostly he was just quiet. But I know he misses you."

"I doubt it."

"He does, and the reason I know that is because he said it. Not talking to you or seeing you is tearing him apart."

"Then why won't he accept that I have a husband?"

"I don't think it's so much that he doesn't like Levi as a person, because he liked Levi before you met him. Even when Levi was a drug dealer, he gave money to the church and went to your father for advice. But you already know all that."

"Well, if he doesn't dislike Levi, then why won't he have anything to do with him?"

"Because he somehow believes Levi is the reason Phillip is dead. I felt the same way, but it's like I told him, we were wrong and it's not our place to judge Levi."

"No, it's not. Especially when I was the one who was married to Phillip, and I was the one who chose to have an affair on him."

"I'm going to talk to your dad again."

"I appreciate it, Mom, but I'm not sure it'll help."

"Let's hope it does."

"We'll see."

"Okay, well I need to get going, but text me and let me know what Levi says about dinner."

"I will. I love you, Mom."

"I love you more."

Alicia set her phone on her desk and signed into the email account she posted on her website for readers. She'd been so busy that she hadn't checked it in a while. Every now and then someone expressed their dislike for one of her books or characters, but the majority of the messages were very thoughtful and kind.

She read through a few of them, responding to each one. When she opened another, however, her smile vanished. It was from a reader who'd recently read an old article about Phillip's death.

Dear Alicia,

I know it's been a while since your husband died, but because something similar just happened to my brother I couldn't help writing you. Like Phillip, my brother was a wonderful minister who everyone loved, but like you, my sister-in-law was never satisfied. My brother practically worshiped the ground she walked on, yet she just couldn't stop looking for something better. So, of course, she finally found a man who she claimed she was in love with. Let her tell it, he was her soul mate. At first, she hid it from my brother for as long as she could, but then she came up with what she thought was some big bright idea. She said she deserved to be happy, and she was going to be. Even if it hurt my brother. So she slept around with her man and then told my brother she wanted a divorce.

Well, needless to say, he was more hurt than any of us could have imagined. He begged her to change her mind, but when she wouldn't, he became deeply depressed. She still moved out anyway, and filed for divorce. She even had the nerve to move in with the no-good she was sleeping with, even though her divorce from my brother wasn't final. But her moving in with another man while she was still married to my brother was the biggest mistake she could have made. My brother became more depressed, but then his depression turned to rage. He got so angry that the next thing we knew, he'd purchased a gun and gone over to the man's house. He shot the man first, then his wife, and then himself. Most of us still can't believe this happened, and I don't have to tell you how much we hate my dead sister-in-law. She ruined my brother's life, and now because of her selfish behavior, she's ruined our family's as well. I know this isn't your fault and that you had nothing to do with my brother's death, but somehow you were the first person I thought of today. Maybe it's because I'd read all your books — before you caused your husband's death — and I couldn't believe someone I had admired so much could do something so cruel. And evil. Like you, all my sister-in-law had to do was not marry my brother, and she could have slept around with whomever she wanted. And the same goes for you, too. You had a choice, but you chose to get married and have an affair. Now thanks to you and my sister-in-law, two innocent men are dead.

I guess the only difference, though, is that while my sister-in-law got what was coming to her, you're still walking around scot-free. You've gone on with your life, business as usual I'm sure. You're probably still enjoying your life as an author and famous pastor's daughter. I wouldn't know, though, because after you betrayed your husband and caused his death, I stopped reading your books and I also unfollowed all your social media accounts. I was completely sickened when I found out what you did, but somehow now that the same kind of thing has happened to my brother, I like you even less. I think what angers me most is that you got away with what you did. You weren't punished for anything, and for that, you should be ashamed of yourself. If I were you, I wouldn't even be able to look at myself in the mirror without becoming disgusted. Women like you should be thrown under the jail, or better yet, thrown six feet under. Right now, I'd be satisfied with either one, just as long as you paid for what you did in at least some way. Although, if I had to guess, the guilt has probably been eating away at you for years, and you're not very happy. If that's true, then good.

Signed,

An angry, hurt, and hugely

disgusted FORMER

reader of yours

Alicia sat back in her chair, dumbfounded. But soon her heart began to race, and she felt hot. Then she pictured Phillip's body lying on the ground on that awful night he'd died. She remembered how deranged he'd become and how he'd pointed a loaded gun at her head. She also replayed some of what he'd said to her: "I did everything I could to make you happy. Everything." "Why couldn't you just be faithful to me? Why did you have to turn into a worthless tramp?"

"Oh God, what did I do?" Alicia said out loud.

You know exactly what you did, the voice told her. *You slept around on your husband, and now he's dead. He loved you, and he tried to give you everything, but it never mattered. All he wanted was for you to be faithful, but you wanted Levi. You slept with another man and broke Phillip's heart, and now he's gone.*

Tears flowed down Alicia's face, and she felt like she was cracking up. But then she remembered what she'd done the last few days and how it had helped her. She closed her eyes. "Satan, I rebuke you in the name of Jesus. I reject and renounce everything about you. Satan, I rebuke you in the name of Jesus. I reject and renounce everything about you. Satan, I rebuke you in the name of Jesus. I reject and renounce everything about you."

Alicia felt her nerves somewhat settling

down, but she wondered when this was going to stop. She'd been doing so well until today, and why on earth would anyone send her such a scathing email? Yes, the situation had been similar, but why was this woman contacting Alicia about her brother's death? Alicia didn't even know these people.

She closed her eyes again. "Lord, please help me. Please give me what I need to overcome this. Please help me find peace. In Jesus's name, Amen."

When she opened her eyes, she waited for a few minutes, and thankfully, the voice no longer spoke to her. But when another twenty minutes passed, it whispered to her again.

You'll never be happy. Phillip is dead and so are those people that lady wrote to you about. So the only way to fix this is for you to go get your gun and end all of this. But deep down, I think you already know that. You've known it since the very night Phillip died.

Chapter 27

"Hey, baby," Raven said, strutting into Dillon's office, smiling at him.

"So how was your lunch meeting?"

She took a seat in one of the chairs sitting in front of his desk. "It was good. I met with my three favorite first-lady friends. We hadn't gotten together in a while."

"I love that the four of you connect the way you do from time to time."

Dillon was trying his best to talk about anything he could, hoping to delay the conversation he didn't want to have.

"It's always a great get-together, and you know I wanted to share my news with them. But I figured I would wait until we announce it to our congregation. Enough about my friends, though. What happened after I left the meeting? I'm dying to hear what everyone had to say."

Dillon sighed. "Well, I've spent the last couple of hours trying to figure out how to

265

tell you."

Raven frowned. "How to tell me what?"

"They all voted no. Every single one of them."

"No way. Why would they do that? Especially with them knowing how much you support me on this. You did tell them that, right?"

"I didn't have a chance. As soon as you left, they discussed it, took a vote, and that was that."

"And you didn't speak up for me? You let them vote against me right to your face? Please tell me you didn't."

Dillon got up, walked around his desk, and sat down next to her. "Baby, I know you really wanted this, but I can't cause problems with my elders. Not when I need them to help build up the membership. I need them to help us get to a point where you and I will never have to want for anything. And I know that's what you've been wanting, too."

Raven seemed stunned. "Oh . . . my . . . God. I don't believe this. You still betrayed me after all. Even though you agreed to let me come speak to the board."

"I didn't betray you, but my hands were tied. I'm caught in the middle, and I need you to understand that. You'll be co-pastor soon enough, though," he said, reaching for any lie or false guarantee he could muster. "But now isn't the right time."

"Please. You must think I'm some naïve child. Or that I don't have a brain in my head."

"Baby, that's not true. This is a church, but it's also no different than running a business, and we have to handle things a certain way."

Raven stared at him as though she wanted to murder him. "You never wanted me to be co-pastor. You think all this is yours, but if it weren't for me, this church wouldn't be nearly where it is today. Levi may have invested all the dollars, but it was my knowledge and good judgment that made all the difference."

"And I always give you credit for everything you've done. Always, baby."

Raven stared at him again, her eyes colder than before. "You have to fix this."

"How?"

"Well, for one thing you can easily get Vincent to change his vote. The man is your best friend. And Levi loves you like a brother, so I know you can change his mind, too. You can make this happen if you want."

"And I will, but not until some time passes."

"How much time, Dillon?"

"Maybe a year at the most. Hopefully sooner."

"That's too long. And what am I supposed to do in the meantime? Huh?"

"The same as you've always been doing: being the best first lady you can be."

Raven tightened her face in disgust, and then there was a knock at the door.

"Come in," Dillon said.

Alicia opened the door. "Oh, I'm sorry. I didn't know you were in here, Raven."

Alicia looked upset and as though she'd been crying, and that concerned Dillon. Something wasn't right.

"No," Raven said. "I'm glad you're here because I have a question for you. Were you in on this with your brother the whole time?"

Alicia frowned. "Excuse me? What are you talking about?"

"Alicia, please don't try to insult my intelligence. I know you think you're better than me. You've always thought you were better than everyone. But sweetheart, I don't care who your daddy is, and from now on, I don't care about you being my sister-in-law, either. I knew you were going to try to stop me from being pastor. I knew it the moment you laughed at me at dinner two

Sundays ago. And then I saw you texting on your phone when I was addressing the board this morning. You were making sure all the elders knew how you felt."

Alicia raised her hand. "Raven, you know what? I don't even have time for this. Dillon, can you just call me when you're free?"

"I will."

Raven got up. "No, you can talk to him now, because I'm done here. But I will say this. It would seem to me that instead of always putting your nose in my business, you'd be somewhere praying about what you did. You whored around on your husband, and now he's dead. Yet you've got the nerve to be worrying about what I'm doing? Please."

Raven strutted back out in the same manner she'd come in and slammed the door behind her.

Alicia looked at Dillon. "She took it a lot worse than I thought."

"Tell me about it, but you have a seat. What's wrong?"

"Nothing, I just wanted to make sure you had the latest financial report from Lynette, and here's the revised marketing plan we created on our end," she said, passing it to him. "The firm will be bringing copies of what they've put together, but I also wanted us to have ours on hand, just in case they miss something we really want to include."

"Sounds good, but are you sure you're okay? Your eyes look swollen."

"I'm fine," she said. "Just a busy day."

Dillon didn't believe her, but he didn't press her any further.

When Alicia left, he thought about the catastrophe that would be waiting for him at home this evening, and he already dreaded it. He then thought about his dad for no reason, but quickly pushed him out of his mind. That was only for a few seconds, though, because it wasn't long before his dad crossed his mind again. Dillon wished he could just forget about the man. Erase him from his life for good. Technically, Curtis wasn't in his life, but he was still Dillon's father, and not having a loving father-son relationship bothered Dillon. He didn't know why a grown man his age couldn't just move on. Why he couldn't get beyond needing to get revenge on him. If only his father would wake up one day and let bygones be bygones, Dillon wouldn't have to hurt him.

Dillon wished, once again, that he could have a drink. On Sunday after church when Raven had taken a nap, he'd drunk two of the beers from his trunk. Then he'd drunk the other two on Monday before heading back over to Porsha's. He was surprised that neither Raven nor Porsha had noticed that he chewed gum a lot more. He even kept mouthwash in his car and offices now. He'd also been popping Altoids whenever he thought about it.

He knew he'd said he would only have the one drink at Benny's, but drinking made him feel good, and he liked it.

Still, he knew it wasn't good for him, so he took a deep breath. "Lord, give me strength. Keep me from tipping down that awful path again. Help me to stay clean and sober."

Dillon kept his eyes shut, hoping his prayer would be answered. But at the same time, he just wanted to have one drink one last time — just one more, and that would finally be it. So he pulled the flask of vodka from his desk and took a nice, long swig. The bite of it was as strong as ever, and it eased into his bloodstream very quickly. He leaned back in his chair and enjoyed it.

CHAPTER 28

Alicia slowly opened her eyes, but they still felt heavy. She blinked a few times, trying to bring them into focus, and looked at the digital clock on her nightstand. It was eight a.m. Could she really have slept fourteen hours straight? She couldn't have. So she lay there thinking back to the day before. She actually had to think pretty hard, but then she remembered. Some woman had sent her that blistering email, and she'd been devastated. She'd felt like she was having a nervous breakdown, and then that voice had begun haunting her again. It had pushed her a lot further toward the edge than it had in the past, but when she'd begun renouncing the devil and praying for peace, it had gone away. However, it had started up again, whispering only every now and then. She'd sat at her desk, telling herself that the voice wasn't real and that it was only Satan trying to trick her, but the whispers had soon gotten to be too much — especially when she'd started wondering if going home to get her gun was, in fact, her only option.

She'd seriously considered it, but this terrifying moment had also made her decide to tell someone. Levi had been the first person she'd thought of, but then she'd changed her mind. The reason: She didn't want her husband thinking he was married to a lunatic. She just couldn't live with him looking at her as though she belonged in an insane asylum and constantly monitoring her every move. So she'd decided, instead, to go to Dillon. However, when she'd arrived at her brother's office, his annoying wife had been there, and that had changed everything. Raven had obviously gone off on Dillon, and she'd made sure to give Alicia a piece of her mind, too. Raven had eventually stormed out of Dillon's office, but by then, Alicia had lost the courage to tell him that something wasn't right with her. He'd asked her what was wrong, but she'd blown his question off and just given him information for their marketing meeting. That in itself had been a struggle, because throughout the entire meeting, the voice had kept whispering to her. Even now, she wondered how she'd made it through the whole two hours without screaming at the top of her lungs. She'd felt the same way last week when she'd had lunch with Melanie, and that was the reason she'd left the church yesterday as soon as the meeting had adjourned. She'd then gone straight to the pharmacy and purchased the strongest over-the-counter sleep aid she could find, as it had been the only thing she could think to do to silence the voice.

Right after Phillip had passed, her primary care physician had prescribed her a couple of sleep medications, too, but both of them had caused her to have nightmares. At first, she'd thought she could handle them, especially since she was finally sleeping more than two or three hours at a time, but soon those nightmares had started to feel too real. She remembered once trying to wake up from one of them and not being able to. When she had, her body had felt like lead and almost as if she were paralyzed. So she figured this time, she'd try something a lot less potent that hopefully had fewer side effects.

Alicia wondered if Levi was already gone, although he rarely left before nine. She, however, had decided last night that she was taking the day off to get proper rest.

Alicia lay there, thinking how good it felt

to sleep for so many hours, but she wondered if the dose she'd taken was a bit too strong for her. She hadn't thought so when she'd purchased the medication, but now that she was awake, she still felt as though she could drop back off in a second. All she'd have to do was close her eyes.

But as she slowly shut them, Levi walked into the bedroom.

He sat down beside her. "You awake?"

"Not really."

"Are you okay? You barely even moved last night."

"I'm fine. I took a sleeping pill."

"You went to the doctor?"

"No, just bought something at the drugstore."

"Well, it must be pretty strong."

"Yeah, I was thinking the same thing."

"Well, you'd better get up, because it's getting pretty late."

"I'm not going in. I just need to rest today."

"Are you sure there's not something else going on?"

"No, I'm just tired of not sleeping. I'm exhausted, and it's really starting to catch up with me."

"Did you call Melanie's doctor?"

"No, but I promise I will today. As soon

as I get up."

Levi frowned. "Why do you keep saying that and then not doing it? That really upsets me."

"Baby, do we have to do this now? I'm really sleepy."

"I understand that, but you need to talk to someone. I should have insisted on that two years ago, and now I'm sorry I didn't."

Alicia heard him but closed her eyes again.

"Baby, are you listening to me?" Levi asked.

"Yes."

"Well, if you don't make an appointment with someone today, I'm doing it for you. I told you that before, but I'm serious this time."

"Okay," she whispered, feeling herself falling back to sleep.

"I'll call you later," he said, kissing her on the cheek. "I love you."

"I love you, too."

It was so puzzling to Alicia how the voice tended to come and go, but thankfully she hadn't heard it today. After Levi had left for the church this morning, she'd slept until noon and then had eventually gotten herself up and into the shower. She'd been in bed eighteen hours, but she finally felt wide awake and not like she wanted to go back to sleep. Maybe she needed to take half a pill tonight instead of a whole one, because she certainly didn't want to miss another day of work tomorrow.

Now, though, she thought about Levi's threat of calling a doctor himself, so she sat down in her home office and dialed Melanie's therapist.

"Dr. Brogan's office," the woman said.

"Uh, yes. I'm a friend of Melanie Richardson's, and she referred me to Dr. Brogan."

"Sure, how can I help you?"

"I was hoping that Dr. Brogan could refer me to a counselor who might be able to help me."

"Of course. Dr. Brogan is with a patient now, but if you'll tell me what type of problem you're having, I can give her a message. She may have me call you back or she'll call you back herself."

Alicia didn't like the idea of having to give her name and number to the receptionist. For all she knew, the woman might recognize it. "I was really hoping to speak to Dr. Brogan directly, so could you just ask her to call me?"

The woman paused. "And you said Melanie Richardson referred you?"

"Yes."

"And your name?"

"Alicia."

"Last name?"

"Just Alicia."

"A number where you can be reached?"

Alicia gave her the number to her cell.

"I think that's all I need, and I'll be sure to give Dr. Brogan your information."

"Do you think she'll be calling this afternoon?"

"More than likely. She has a couple of back-to-back appointments, but she should still be able to get back to you."

"I really appreciate your help."

"No problem."

Alicia hung up the phone and signed on to her computer. She Googled "What does it mean when you hear voices?" the same as she'd done two years ago. She wasn't sure what she thought might be different, but she was hoping for some other explanation besides psychosis and schizophrenia.

Alicia closed her eyes with sadness. Just the idea of possibly having a mental illness broke her heart. On the one hand, she truly did believe the voice was only a trick from Satan, but on the other, she wondered if there was something clinically wrong with her, too.

She clicked on one of the website links

that displayed. She read through it, clicked out of it, and then pulled up another. She read through that one very quickly and pulled up another. And another. But they all basically stated the same thing: Hearing voices was usually a sign of psychosis or schizophrenia. She did see one diagnosis called psychotic depression, and hearing voices was a symptom of that also. The only thing, though, was that some of the other symptoms didn't apply, such as getting angry for no apparent reason, not wanting to be around others, and sleeping in the day and staying awake at night. But then as she thought back to when Phillip had died, she had in fact felt all of the above. She hadn't wanted to go anywhere or talk to anyone, and she couldn't sleep. The article also talked about how a person with psychotic depression could feel worthless or a voice might be telling them that they were no good. It was the next line she read, though, that made her grab her chest.

They may have strange or irrational ideas. For example, a person with psychotic depression might think they've done something bad that they really didn't do or that they've been possessed by the devil.

Alicia didn't believe she was possessed by the devil — or was she? She did think it was the devil's voice that kept speaking to her, but not that he had control of her mind and body. But what if her thoughts about anything relating to the devil were merely irrational thoughts, and the voice she was hearing was a result of psychotic depression? If that were true, what was she going to do? Because she couldn't live with that kind of diagnosis. She'd thought about it and had settled on that decision more than once. Having a physical illness was one thing, but being crazy was something different. Although, maybe she could find a counselor or doctor on her own and not tell anyone about it. Because as she read further down the article, it sounded as though there were a number of treatment options, some of which included specific medications that could eliminate psychosis completely, as long as a person didn't stop taking them.

But what local doctor would she be able to call who didn't know her father? Or didn't know *her*, even? What psychiatrist in the state of Illinois, or in the country for that matter, hadn't heard of the infamous Black family and their drama? It was true that doctors were supposed to keep all patient information confidential, but nowadays there was no telling what people might do for a certain amount of money. Especially when a pastor or anything relating to a church was involved. Some media outlets were willing to pay thousands for the right kind of story, and she couldn't go through that.

This was the reason that even though she now heard her phone ringing, she didn't answer it. She hadn't been expecting Dr. Brogan to call back so soon, but Alicia recognized the number on her screen. It was the same one she'd called not long ago. The phone rang and then went to voice mail, but whether the doctor had left a message for Alicia or not, Alicia wouldn't be calling her back. She was also glad she hadn't given the receptionist her last name.

CHAPTER 29

Dillon knocked on Raven's office door at the church.

"Yes?"

"It's me."

"Go away."

Elder Freeman walked past, eyeing Dillon with curiosity, but he didn't say anything.

Dillon thought about leaving and going back to his own office, but he opened Raven's door and walked inside.

"Didn't I tell you to go away? Now, get out."

Dillon hurried to close the door and went over and sat in front of her desk. "Baby, we really need to talk."

Raven shot him a dirty look and flipped through some documents on her desk.

Unlike Dillon had expected, when he'd arrived home yesterday evening, Raven hadn't yelled, screamed, or started even the smallest argument. Strangely, she hadn't said anything to him, and he couldn't understand why. Her silence was sort of making him nervous because she'd gone from being outraged to acting as though the board had voted in her favor. She'd seemed calm and quiet, and it wasn't making any sense.

"Baby, I wish you'd talk to me," he told her.

She still didn't look at him, but said, "About what?"

"Anything."

"There's nothing to say."

"But I know you're upset about what happened yesterday, and I just want you to know I understand."

Raven flipped through more paperwork, ignoring him.

"Things won't always be this way," he explained.

"Meaning what?"

"The board feeling that it's not the right time to hire you as co-pastor."

"Is that right?"

"Baby, can't you at least look at me when you say something?"

Raven still ignored him.

"Look, I know you really wanted this, but everything is for a reason, and I believe it'll happen in God's timing."

Raven scanned a sheet of paper with her finger, as though she was reading it line by line.

Dillon wasn't sure what else to say at this point, but then said, "You want to go out for dinner this evening?"

"No."

"Why?"

"Because I don't."

"Baby, come on. Let's go out to a nice restaurant and try to get past this."

Raven sighed loudly and finally looked at him. "Dillon, why won't you leave me alone?"

"Because I love you, and I care about the way you feel."

"If you cared so much, you would have vetoed the board's decision."

"But I already explained why I couldn't do that."

"Well, I'd really appreciate it if you would leave. I have work to do."

Dillon got up and strolled around her desk. Then he leaned down to kiss her, but she tilted her head away from him.

"Oh, so now you don't even want me to touch you?"

"What I want is for you to stop talking to me. I want you to leave my office."

Dillon stood there for a few seconds and

finally stepped back.

"Oh, and by the way," she said, "you have new sleeping quarters. So feel free to choose whichever guest bedroom you want. All I care is that you won't be sleeping with me."

Dillon frowned. "Now, baby, you know I'm not doing that."

"You don't have a choice."

"This is crazy. All because I couldn't force the elders to do what you wanted?"

"No, it's because you never even tried. You never wanted me to be co-pastor, and I feel used."

"How?"

"You know how. I taught you everything you know about running a ministry, and this is how you repay me?"

Dillon was tired of going over the same thing. He was tired of talking about this topic, period. "I've included you in everything. And any rewards I reap, you reap the same benefits."

"Yeah, all except when it comes to being pastor. You want to run New Faith like some dictatorship, but if you think I'm going to sit back and play second fiddle, you've got another thing coming. When I told you the other day that I would take half of everything, I meant it."

"You know what? I'll see you later."

"Fine, but like I said, you're sleeping in a guest bedroom."

Dillon tossed her an irritated look and walked out. Now he wished he'd gone to get himself another drink last night, because if he had, maybe he wouldn't need one so badly now. But after finishing the last of what was left in his flask, he'd told himself it was better to go straight home to talk to Raven. Then when she wouldn't respond to him, he'd changed into a T-shirt and a pair of shorts. Actually, as he thought back on things, it was probably good that she hadn't wanted anything to do with him, because he had felt a little drunk and last night might have ended up being a night when his gum and mouthwash wouldn't have masked his drinking. Nonetheless, he'd relaxed at home watching a baseball game and had fallen asleep on the sofa. He'd actually enjoyed doing nothing, what with his always being busy with the church. But had he known things were going to become this bad between him and Raven, he would have gone out last night and enjoyed himself in a different way. He might've even driven over to Benny's and then called Taylor. He'd purposely not contacted her because he'd thought it better to focus on Porsha for the time being, but he hadn't been able to get

Taylor out of his head. There was something special about her, and he was going to call her as soon as he got back to his office.

But just as he passed by his administrative assistant's office, she stopped him.

"Hey, Pastor," Brenda said. "You got a minute?"

Dillon walked inside. "Of course. What's goin' on?"

"Can you close the door?"

Dillon did as she asked, but he didn't like the look he saw on her face. "Is everything okay?"

"Well, it depends on how you look at it, I guess."

He sat down. "What's wrong?"

"Remember when I told you I had a doctor's appointment last week?"

"Yes."

"Well, I owe you an apology. I owe God one, too, because I wasn't being honest."

"What do you mean?"

"I lied."

"About what?"

"The reason I was going. When you asked me if everything was okay, I told you it was and that this was just for my annual physical. But that wasn't true."

Dillon's heart dropped. "Then what was your appointment for?"

"To discuss my test results with my doctor."

"What kind?"

"For ovarian cancer."

Dillon gazed at her in silence, but he immediately thought about his aunt, Susan. She'd died from pancreatic cancer within days of being diagnosed.

"What stage?"

"Well, that's why I said whether I'm okay or not depends on how you look at it. I do have cancer, but it's only in the second stage. That's not great, but it's also a lot better than third or fourth. My chances of survival are a lot better than they could be."

Dillon shook his head with disappointment. "I'm so sorry, Miss Brenda, and I hate hearing this."

"Well, you know how strong my faith in God is, and I'm not claiming anything terminal. Death isn't even on my mind, and I don't want it to be on yours, either. But I still thought it was only right that I told you, because I'll be having surgery to remove my ovaries next week and then chemo."

Dillon felt his whole body tense up. "Is there anything I can do for you? Just say the word, and it's done."

"Pray for me. Pray for my strength, healing, and peace with this."

"I'll be praying daily. You know you mean the world to me, and I love you like a mother."

"I know that, and you're nothing less than my son," she said. "And then there's something else."

"Whatever you need."

"This is more for you than it is for me."

Dillon lowered his eyebrows. "Not sure I understand."

"I want you to get rid of all the malice you have in your heart for your dad. I've tried not to say anything, but I can tell by the way you respond whenever anyone brings up his name or his church. I've watched you in meetings, and I've sometimes overheard you saying things to your wife, your sister, Elder Barnett, and a few others."

Dillon was ashamed. Not for the way he felt about his father, but because he hadn't known Miss Brenda had been paying attention to anything he said about him, which meant he must have stressed his feelings and opinions about his dad out loud more than he realized.

"I wish things were different, but my dad has made it very clear that he wants nothing to do with me."

"I understand that, but son, he has good

reason. I'm not saying any father should cut off a son completely, but you did some pretty awful things before you left Mitchell."

"Yeah, and I've apologized over and over and he still hates me."

"I don't think he hates you. I just think he's hurt, and he doesn't trust you."

Dillon thought about the last conversation he'd had with his dad, and how he'd talked about the trust issue. Curtis hadn't said anything about being hurt, though, and in all honesty, Dillon didn't think anyone could hurt Curtis Black. As far as Dillon was concerned, any man who could deny his own newborn baby didn't even have a heart.

"Well, I'm tired, Miss Brenda. I tried to talk to him, and I even called him last week, but that was it for me. I'm not going to keep begging someone who doesn't want a relationship with his own son. I just won't keep belittling myself that way."

"Son, I hear you, but that's what we call pride. I know your dad was wrong for not claiming you, but when you first came to Mitchell you did some terrible things. Yet your dad forgave you, and he was willing to make a new start with you."

"Not really. He gave me a large sum of money, but he never gave me his time or the kind of love he gave his other children. I was always treated differently than them, and I shed a lot of tears over it. That's what pushed me to try to blackmail him. I just wanted him to hurt like I did."

"Doing things tit for tat never works. It doesn't get us anywhere, and I just think both of you went about things the wrong way. Your dad is stubborn, and you're just like him. So I'm asking you to please not give up on him. Please call him, or better yet, go see him. Pour your heart out to him and let him know that you forgive him for everything he's done to you, and that you're sorry for everything you did to him. And then, son, you have to pray about this as well. You can't just pray about your problems every now and then, you have to pray about them all the time. The Bible says to pray without ceasing, and that really does make a difference. Just last month, you taught one of our Bible study lessons from Philippians four, six. 'Be careful for nothing; but in everything by prayer and supplication with thanksgiving let your requests be made known unto God.' Remember?"

Tears filled Dillon's eyes. "I'm just so tired. I just want to forget about my dad and go on with my life."

"Well, you say that, but I can tell from the

look in your eyes that you're constantly thinking of ways to get back at him. Even when you're quiet, it still shows. You're letting your pain control your thinking, and son, hear me when I tell you this . . . no good can come from that."

Dillon wasn't sure how she knew what he'd been planning, but she did. She'd always been a wise woman; it was part of the reason he loved her and went to her for advice, but he didn't understand how she knew he spent every day of his life figuring out the perfect plot against his dad.

"Everything is going to be fine. Eventually I'll get over all this and that will be that."

"I wish you would hear me on this. You need to go to your dad in person. Talk to him, and then if he still doesn't change the way he feels, you'll know you tried everything. You won't have any regrets, and if nothing else, you'll finally have some sense of closure."

Dillon didn't want to tell her no, but he didn't want to say he would go to his father, either.

"Promise me you'll at least think about it," she said, smiling. "You asked me if there was anything you could do for me, right?"

Now Dillon smiled. "Isn't that kind of thing called a guilt trip?"

"Yeah, exactly. But just do it, all right?"

"I'll think about it."

"Good. That's all I'm asking. That's all anyone can expect."

CHAPTER 30

Alicia couldn't remember the last time she'd sat on the sofa in the family room, eating high-calorie snacks and watching old sitcoms. It had been one of the best afternoons she'd had in years, and now she knew sleep deprivation wasn't good for anyone. She'd known that all human beings needed a certain amount of sleep to function properly, but she'd learned to live with her situation. She wouldn't settle anymore, though, and she couldn't wait to take another sleeping pill tonight. However, this time she would cut it and only use one-half.

When her phone rang, she picked it up from the rectangular leather ottoman in front of her.

"Hey, Mel," she answered.

"Hey, girl, how are you?"

"I'm great. How about you? You at work?"

"No, I left early today so I could go to my appointment with Dr. Brogan. Just leaving there now, and that's why I'm calling you."

Alicia started thinking of a good lie to tell, just in case Dr. Brogan had told Melanie she'd tried to call her back. "Why, what's up?"

"I told her that I had a friend who was going to be calling her for a reference, and she told me you already had."

"I did, and I left her a message."

"She said she got right back to you, but you didn't answer."

"I took a nap this afternoon, so I didn't realize I'd missed her call until a few minutes ago. I'll call her tomorrow."

"You don't have to. I told her you needed someone who specialized in marriage counseling and grief. So she gave me the name of someone who could help you with both."

"Oh, okay. What is it?"

"Her name is Janice Smith, and she's been counseling for more than twenty years."

Alicia wrote her name in a notebook she had sitting on the table, and Melanie also gave her the counselor's phone number. Alicia went along with this whole scenario just so she could prove to Levi that she'd done what he asked. But she wasn't calling anyone.

"Why were you taking a nap in the middle of the day?"

"I took a sleeping pill last night, and I think it was too much," she said, lying again.

"Are you sure you're feeling okay?"

"I'm fine, and I'm fully rested. I just needed some downtime today."

"That's good, but you're definitely going to call Ms. Smith tomorrow, right?"

"Absolutely. Why wouldn't I?"

"Because I know how you are."

Alicia picked up the remote control and pressed the Guide button. "No worries. I promise I'll contact her."

"Oh and hey, have you talked to your mom since she got back?"

"I called her yesterday."

"I'm glad they made it home safely."

"They did, and they had a great time, too," Alicia said.

"I'm sure."

"Levi and I are driving over to have dinner with them tomorrow."

"Gosh, girl, isn't it amazing how God can turn things around?" Melanie said. "And when you least expect it, too."

"I know. This has been a long year, and I never, ever wanted to stop seeing my parents. But when I married Levi I decided that if a person didn't like my husband, they also didn't like me."

"But you know that's not true. Your

parents never stopped loving you."

"No, but I'm making a point. When two people get married, they become one. So all I'm saying is that if you don't like Levi, you don't like Alicia."

"I hear you on that. I felt the same way about Brad."

"I really wish you would talk to him. I know he messed up. He messed up really bad, but I know you still love him, Mel. You can say whatever you want, but I know you do."

"Doesn't matter. I can't live with the fact that he went out and got someone pregnant behind my back. He had an affair, and he had a baby."

"But both the woman and the baby died in that car accident."

"Yeah, and?"

"It's not like you've ever had to see them. I'm not saying that this diminishes what Brad did or that it makes it any less painful, but I do think it's different than most situations."

"How?"

"When other women go through this kind of thing and they stay in the marriage, they still have to deal with the other woman and be a stepmom. But that's not the case for you."

"No, but it still happened, and I can't pretend that it didn't."

"I'm not saying you should, but if you love him . . ."

"Even if Brad never messed around on me again, I'm not sure I could ever trust him."

"Not everyone who has an affair keeps having them."

"Yeah, well, this is one of those times where you and I have to agree to disagree. I might feel differently down the road, but right now, I say once a cheater, always a cheater."

Alicia flipped through the Guide again, checking to see what she could watch next. "I just don't like seeing you alone. You're a good person with a big heart, and you deserve to be happy."

"I am happy. Being alone doesn't automatically mean a person is miserable."

"No, but I also know how much you loved Brad and how much you loved being married."

"I did, but since my divorce? Not so much."

Alicia heard her phone beep and pulled it away from her ear. Her heart skipped what seemed like several beats.

"Oh my God, Mel, this is Daddy calling."

"Are you serious?"

"Yes. I saw his cell number."

"Well, answer it, girl. Bye."

Alicia took two deep breaths, closed her eyes, and hit the icon on her screen.

"Hello?"

"Hi, baby girl."

"Hi, Daddy."

"Can you talk?"

"Uh-huh."

"I didn't catch you at a bad time, did I?"

"No."

"Well, I'm sure you know I spoke to your mom."

"Yeah, she told me she talked to you last week."

"And she also called me again this morning. We were on the phone a whole hour."

Alicia sat quietly, listening because she wasn't sure what to say or why he was calling.

"I'm so ashamed, I don't even know where to begin. But I guess the first thing I should say is that, sweetheart, I'm sorry. I was wrong about so many different things, and I never should have put my pride and selfish wants before my own daughter. I was being self-righteous, and you didn't deserve that," he said, sighing. "But your mom took me way back in history. She made me remember things about myself that I had tried to forget about. She reminded me of the unspeakable things I did to her when we were married . . . things that you had to witness as a child. Then she asked me the million-dollar question."

Alicia still held the phone steady but didn't say a word.

"Baby girl, are you still there?"

"Yes."

"Well, what your mom asked me was how you were any different from me. She wanted to know why I'd expected you to love and accept Charlotte as your stepmother, but I wasn't willing to love and accept Levi."

"I don't understand," Alicia said.

"Your mom made the point that I got Charlotte pregnant while I was still married to her. I had an affair just like you did, and then I married Charlotte. I married my former mistress, which is no different than what you did, and you forgave me for it."

Alicia heard every word he'd said, but what shocked her was that she'd never looked at things that way before. She hadn't even considered comparing her dad's affair with Charlotte to the one she'd had with Levi.

"So can you ever forgive me?" he asked.

"This has been so hard on me, Daddy.

Harder than you could ever imagine."

"I know, and I never should have put you through something like this. I kept telling myself that you were marrying the man that helped you kill Phillip, and that's where I made my mistake. I know you didn't physically kill him and neither did Levi, but that's how I saw it. Everyone knows I loved Phillip like a son, but I never should have let that cloud my judgment the way it did. I'm your father and a pastor, and I'm supposed to be better than that. I'm supposed to forgive others the same as I expect God to forgive me, and I didn't do that."

"I never wanted to end my relationship with you, Daddy. Not with you or Mom, but I couldn't let you treat Levi like he was the enemy. He and I both made mistakes, but we love each other. We've always loved each other, and that hasn't changed even today."

"I receive that, and I understand it. I would never allow anyone to treat Charlotte badly, either. You and I both know that."

"I have really missed you, though, Daddy. I've missed all of you."

"We've missed you, too, and I've already spoken to Matthew. He was angry because of what happened with Phillip, but he was more hurt over the way you and Levi joined

Dillon's church. He forgave Dillon, because Matthew is a forgiving kind of person, but he doesn't want anything to do with him. And I won't lie, when you left Deliverance to become Dillon's chief operating officer, I resented you even more. It was wrong, but I'm just being honest."

"But Daddy, Dillon isn't the same person. He's changed, and he wants to make things right with you. He just wants to be your son. He wants you to love him."

"I hope that's true, the part about him being changed, because I don't want you to end up hurt."

"With the exception of Levi, no one has been there for me more than Dillon. Not over these last two years. He even stood by Levi and me that whole first year before we got married, and he never judged us."

"Well, I'm not saying that Dillon and I will never have a relationship, but it'll take some time. Trust has to be earned."

"I really hope you'll try, though, Daddy. Dillon did do a lot of horrible things, but so have all of us. And you know that one saying, right?"

"What's that?"

"Don't judge me because I sin differently than you."

"You're right, but this thing with Dillon is

a lot more complicated than that. It's not just that he committed sins. He violated me and Matthew. His own father and brother."

Alicia wanted to remind her dad about the way he'd falsified the DNA test he was supposed to take when Dillon was a baby, but she didn't.

"But enough about Dillon," Curtis continued. "Can *you* forgive *me*?"

"I do forgive you, Daddy, but I want you to call Levi. I want you to welcome him into our family."

"What if I told you I already have?"

"When?" Alicia said, but looked behind her when the doorbell rang. "Daddy, hold on a minute."

"Okay."

Alicia hoped it was only a delivery person because she looked a hot mess. She hadn't even combed her hair. But when she peered through the glass to the side of the door, she took a step backward. She opened the door, and tears streamed down her face. There stood her dad, Charlotte, Matthew, Curtina, little MJ, her mom, and James. But the person who warmed her heart the most was Levi, who stood at a distance, smiling. The only way any of her family could have known that she was home and hadn't gone to work was if Levi had told them, which meant he'd orchestrated this entire reunion. She was so overwhelmed, yet so happy. She couldn't love her husband more. She hugged each and every one of them for more than just a couple of seconds. She was reunited with her family and so at peace. Finally.

CHAPTER 31

Dillon stood by the large window in his office, admiring the property New Faith was built on. The landscaping was immaculate, but it was time to freshly seal the asphalt parking lot. He then scanned the reserved spots for staff and zoned in on the two that said *Pastor Dillon Whitfield Black* and *Lady Raven Jones Whitfield Black.* Dillon thought about how he'd wanted Raven to eliminate her maiden name altogether because to him, using Whitfield Black was enough. Whitfield was his birth surname and Black was the name he'd added legally, but Raven had wanted to keep *Jones* and hadn't relented. She was just that kind of woman, though — the kind who knew what she wanted, when she wanted it, and how she was going to get it. This, of course, was the very reason she was so livid about what had resulted at the board meeting. He just couldn't allow her to have equal position with him, though.

He wouldn't allow anyone to do that, and as much as he loved her, if her not being co-pastor meant the end of their marriage, he would just have to accept that. He wouldn't, however, allow her to leave him or divorce him before the church was bringing in a lot more money. She'd already talked about taking half of everything — she'd threatened him twice now — but it was obvious that she still didn't know him very well; didn't know that he would do whatever it took to keep all that he'd worked for, and that loving her wouldn't change what he was capable of.

He didn't want to do anything cruel to Raven, but when he'd gone into her office an hour ago, the nonchalant, I'm-through-with-you look on her face had told him he'd better be prepared for anything. His hope was that she would settle down, accept that she couldn't be anything more than first lady, and go back to being a happy wife. Because, again, he did love her, but he wouldn't let her take a dime from him.

Dillon looked toward the light-blue sky and thought about Miss Brenda and her cancer diagnosis. The news had hurt him to his heart, but he was trusting and believing that God was going to heal her. He just couldn't lose another mother figure. He needed her in his life, and he had a feeling that with the way things were going with Raven and his father, he would need Miss Brenda more than ever. Of course, Miss Brenda now wanted him to go to his dad, and while he didn't want to ignore her request, he wasn't sure he could do it. He didn't know if it was worth taking yet another chance of being rejected. As it was, when he talked to his father, or on the rare occasion when he ran into him, he felt like a pitiful little boy. He felt scorned, discarded, and like a secondhand toddler whom nobody wanted. He was so confused about what to do. And what Miss Brenda didn't know was that Vincent was carefully arranging things. He was gearing up to carry out their plan so that Dillon could replace his dad as the go-to pastor in Mitchell. New Faith would become the place to be on Sunday mornings instead of Deliverance Outreach. Dillon did have his moments when he wondered if he was going too far, but he also knew his dad deserved what was going to happen and then some. Dillon was doing it for himself, but he was also getting justice for his mom because his dad still hadn't paid for what he'd done to her. As far as Dillon was concerned, he hadn't even apologized the way he should.

Gosh, why hadn't he gone to buy more liquor so he could refill his flask? He had so much troubling him at one time that he needed something to soothe his pain. Something to quiet his racing thoughts and alleviate all the uncertainties that were steadily mounting before him.

But maybe his earlier thought about driving over to Benny's, having a drink, and calling Taylor was his answer. So he reached and picked up the phone from his desk and searched for an entry in his contact list that read *Pastor Thomas Taylor*. In the address section, it stated *Met at the minister's convention in Atlanta*. He liked how he was able to turn Taylor Thomas into Thomas Taylor without having to think up another male name.

He dialed Taylor's number.

"Hello?" she said.

"Hey, how are you?"

"I'm good, what about you?"

"I could be better," he said, moving back closer to his window.

"I was wondering if I'd ever hear from you again."

"I wanted to call before now, but I've had a lot going on."

"Nothing too serious, I hope."

"Well, it's not great, but it'll be fine. So

what have you been up to?"

"Thinking about you and wishing you would call."

"Yeah, right," Dillon said, but in his heart he believed her. He knew it was silly to think you could meet someone by chance and trust them, but it was just a feeling he had. "I'm sure you tell every guy you meet that same thing."

"As a matter of fact, I don't. It's just that I really like you, and I felt a special connection between us. The kind of chemistry I've not experienced with anyone before."

"Yeah, well, all jokes aside, I feel the same way."

"So what next, then?" she asked.

"Where are you now?"

"Still at work."

"What do you do?"

"I'm an investment banker."

"Nice."

"It's a pretty good job, and I enjoy it."

"Maybe you can give me some financial advice sometime. I already have an adviser, but you can never have too much financial knowledge."

"That's true."

"What time do you get off?"

"Normally five, but probably closer to five thirty tonight."

"It's five now."

"So, you coming over?"

"I was thinking about it."

"Then why don't you?"

"I think I will. Is seven okay?"

"Perfect."

"See you then."

Dillon pressed the End button but continued looking out his window. For some reason, he thought about Raven again, wondering what would become of their marriage. Then he thought about Porsha and how it was time to ask her for the lump sum he needed. The marketing meeting had gone well yesterday, but in order to get things going as soon as possible — and at the level he wanted — he needed more than what his CFO had confirmed as the final budget. He would go see Porsha next Monday, though, and say whatever was necessary to get what he needed. He hadn't thought he'd ever end up juggling three women, because two was already a job, but to have everything he wanted, he had no other options. He loved money, power, and women, and he didn't mind working for it.

When someone knocked at his door, he turned and looked in that direction.

"Come in."

"Hey, Pastor," Vincent said.

"What's goin' on?"

Vincent closed the door. "I just wanted to give you an update, and I didn't want to do it over the phone."

"Let's hear it."

"We're finally in countdown mode. I won't tell you the exact day things are gonna go down because I want you to be in the dark as much as possible. But just know that it won't be long. Not more than a week or two."

"Is that right?" Dillon said, hearing Miss Brenda's voice and having second thoughts about this scheme against his dad.

"Yeah, but you don't sound too excited. Not like you have been."

Dillon looked away from Vincent and back out the window. "I just don't know, man. I've wanted this for a long time, but I need to be sure."

"Well, you'd better *get* sure, because once the first half of that money is paid, this is a done deal. There won't be any turning back."

"I know, I know, I know. Can you give me until Friday?"

"That's two days from now, but I gotta tell you, my contact won't be happy. He's already been setting the preliminaries in motion, and he's expecting his down payment. Twenty-five thousand is a lot of money to miss out on."

"I realize that, and if we don't go through with this, we'll still give him five for services rendered."

"It might take ten, but I'll try to talk him into five. It's a good thing you've been depositing money into that special account for months. It was really smart to have me open it in New Faith's name, even though I'm the only person who can withdraw from it. That way there won't be any money trails leading back to you."

"That's why I made deposits little by little. I only took money from my personal accounts that Raven doesn't have access to. I didn't know when we would need the whole amount, but I wanted to be ready."

"If this thing happens, though, that other twenty-five is going to be due. My guy won't want it right away because he'll want things to cool down some, but he'll want it within seven days. And he'll also want it transferred into an account in another state. He's going to give me the information when it's time."

"We'll get it to him, but for now, let me think about this some more."

Vincent put both his hands in his pockets. "If you don't mind, can I ask why?"

"I just need to be sure is all. I had a long

conversation with Miss Brenda this afternoon, and she raised some points I hadn't thought about."

"Like what?"

"Well, for example, what if I just need to give this thing with my dad more time? What if maybe I should go talk to him?"

Vincent chuckled. "Look, man, I hear all that and I get it, but do you really believe your dad is going to change? And if he does, for how long?"

"I don't know, but she made some really good points. She's a wise woman, and she's never steered me wrong."

"You've only known her since you founded the church. So that's for how long? Two years?"

"Still, she's good people. She's a strong Christian woman, and I can't ignore what she told me."

Vincent breathed a sigh of frustration. "I don't get it, man, and I definitely don't see your dad changing anything. But I'll still support whatever you decide."

"I'll let you know soon."

"No later than Friday, right?"

"Yeah."

"All right then, I'm gonna head out," Vincent said.

"Thanks for the update."

"Anytime. See you tomorrow."

When Vincent left, Dillon's mind was made up. He was going to give his dad one final chance. He would do it tomorrow, in person.

CHAPTER 32

Dillon pulled into Taylor's driveway and answered Alicia's call.

"Hey, Sis, how are you?"

"You'll never believe what I have to tell you. Levi told me you asked one of the elders to lead Bible study tonight, though, so did I catch you at a bad time?"

"No, I just had a couple of things to do, but I can talk. What happened? Are you okay?"

"Well, if you want to know the truth, I haven't felt this good in two years. Daddy actually called me today."

Dillon shut off his ignition. "Really? Why?"

"He apologized and asked me to forgive him."

Dillon didn't know whether to be happy for his sister or jealous. "That's good news, but what brought that about?"

"A couple of days ago, my mom told me she was going to talk to him. She spoke with him last week, too."

"I'm still shocked. After all this time, he just up and apologized? And he accepts your marriage to Levi?"

"Yes. I told him why I had to end my relationship with him, and that he needed to apologize to Levi personally and welcome him to our family. But what I didn't know was that Daddy was calling me from his cell phone, and the next thing I knew the doorbell was ringing. I went to the door, and everybody was standing there. They were here for three hours."

"Who? Charlotte and Curtina?"

"No, everybody. Daddy, Charlotte, Curtina, Matt, little MJ, my mom, Dad James, and Levi."

Dillon resented the fact that no one had invited him. Even Levi hadn't bothered to say that Curtis had called him. Although, in all fairness to Levi, it would have been too awkward for him to tell Dillon, "Your dad called and apologized to me and is heading over to my house. But he still doesn't want diddly-squat to do with you."

Dillon was angry and hurt at the same time, but he didn't let on to Alicia. Instead, he reached over on the passenger seat, pulled a beer from the brown paper bag, and popped it open. "This is definitely a serious turn of events. Hard to believe this happened."

"Tell me about it, but Dillon, I have to say I am so relieved. I've struggled with being estranged from my parents for a long time, and it really took a huge toll on me. I've experienced feelings that no one would ever imagine, and I thank God for everything that happened today."

"I know you've had a tough time, and I'm glad for you."

"But you know what?" she said.

Dillon swallowed some beer. "What's that?"

"I think there's a great chance for you and him to get things right, too."

"I wish that were true, but who knows."

"Daddy has a lot of pride, and can I be honest?"

"Go ahead."

"So do you. And when you have two people with lots of pride, no one wins."

"Funny you would say that, because Miss Brenda said something similar. She was on me about going to see Dad."

"I really think you should. I know when you've called him before, things haven't gone well, but I believe the conversation could be different now. You and Daddy both just have to have open minds. You have to meet each other halfway and try to find some way to trust each other."

"I've been willing and ready to do that all along, but I can't do this by myself. You can't fix things with someone if they don't want anything to do with you."

"I agree, but why don't you go see him?"

"Well, actually I was already planning to do that tomorrow."

"Good for you."

"I debated it, but I decided to try one more time. But know this: If he rejects me again, I'm done, Sis. That will finally be the end for us."

"I'm not going to think about that. I'm just going to pray for everything to work out the way we want it to."

"I think I'll go see him at the church, but I'll definitely let you know how it goes."

"I'll be waiting to hear."

"All right, well I need to get going, but you guys have a good night."

"You, too," she said. "Love you, and I'll see you tomorrow."

"Love you back."

Dillon ended the call and set his phone in his lap. He leaned his head against the backrest and turned his beer can all the way up. He'd drunk one before getting on the road and heading over to Taylor's, but he hadn't planned on drinking any more until he got inside her condo. This news about his dad, though, had interrupted his whole evening. He was genuinely glad for his sister because he loved her, but what if his dad still didn't want to renew his relationship with Dillon? It hadn't been that long ago when Dillon had told Alicia that their father still loved her. They might not have been speaking much or seeing each other, but Curtis Black loved his other three children and his grandson. It was Dillon whom he could take or leave or have no problem not seeing again.

Dillon crumpled the beer can and dropped it inside the bag with the rest of the beers he had left. He got out of his car, locked his doors, and walked up the sidewalk. When he rang the doorbell, Taylor opened it right away.

"That was quick," he said, walking in and pecking her on the lips.

"I saw you when you pulled up."

"Oh. I was on the phone with my sister."

"Can I take that for you?" she asked, reaching for his bag of beer.

"If you don't mind."

"Not at all. I'll put it in the fridge. But go ahead and have a seat."

Dillon strolled into the living room and

sat on the charcoal-gray leather sofa.

When Taylor walked back into the room, he gazed at her from head to toe. She was beautiful. He'd known that the night he'd met her. But she had a sweet spirit about her, and the long, flowy sleeveless top she had on with matching lounging pants seemed exactly like the kind of thing she would wear. She was classy, down-to-earth, and compassionate.

She sat down next to him. "So, I don't mean to sound like somebody's mother, but were you drinking and driving?"

"No, but I did drink one while I was talking to my sister."

"Well, I was just wondering because not only was there an empty can, there were only four full ones left."

Dillon laughed. "Now you sound like a private investigator."

She smiled. "I just don't think drinking and driving is a good idea is all, and I almost said something to you last week. You know, the first time you were here. But it wasn't like I could suggest that you spend the night."

"I wasn't drunk. I mean, maybe a little, but I was able to drive home fine. And just for the record, I drank the other beer right after I bought it and then threw the can away in a dumpster."

"But you still shouldn't be drinking in your car, either."

Dillon raised his eyebrows.

"What? I'm not trying to judge you or tell you what to do, so please don't be mad. I just don't want you to get stopped or in an accident."

"Advice noted."

"Have you eaten? Can I get you anything?"

Dillon pulled off his suit blazer. "No, I'm fine. I grabbed a burger when I left the church."

"I had a salad before you got here, but we can order something if you want."

"No, but if you have something to drink, that would work."

"I have soda but only diet. Is that okay?"

"I was thinking of something stronger."

"I have some red wine, but that's pretty much it."

"I'll take that until my beer cools back down. It got kind of warm while I was driving."

Taylor got back up and went into the kitchen.

Dillon picked up the remote and turned on the television. He searched through the channels until he found one playing slow

R&B music.

After a few minutes, Taylor returned with two wineglasses and passed one to Dillon.

"Thanks," he said.

"You're welcome."

Dillon took a few sips and breathed deeply.

Taylor did the same and set her glass on the table. "You must be having a bad day."

"Is it that obvious?"

"Kinda."

He set his glass down. "Come here."

Taylor moved closer so that she was leaning into him, and he wrapped his arm around her.

She rested her hand against his stomach. "Wanna talk about it?"

"Not really. But why don't you tell me a little about you."

"Not a lot to tell, except I was born in South Chicago, near Calumet City; I have one sister; and after high school I went to Northwestern. I graduated, and I've lived here in the northwest suburbs ever since."

"What about your parents? Do they live nearby?"

"No, they both passed away when I was in my twenties. My dad had a massive heart attack, and two years later my mom died of pneumonia."

"I'm really sorry to hear that. It's never easy to lose your parents. No matter what age you are."

"Very true. You learn to live with it, but you never get over it."

"I lost my mom when I was just a newborn, so I never even got a chance to meet her. But I'm sure you already know that from news stories."

"Yeah, I do."

"So are you and your sister pretty close?" he asked, drinking more wine.

"We are. Always have been."

"Does she know I came home with you the other night?"

"No. My sister is one of the sweetest people I know, and she would never be okay with me seeing a married man. She loves me, but she wouldn't be happy about that."

"Did she know who I was?"

"No, and I never told her. When I got up from the table with her to come meet you, she just thought you were some random guy at the bar."

"That's actually good, because no sense taking a chance on anyone else knowing about us."

"I agree. So what is your father like? I've read things online, of course, but how is he really?"

Dillon set his empty glass down. "He's not what you'd probably expect. He's a well-known pastor, but he and I don't talk much. And we never see each other."

"Why is that?"

"Partly because of the way he treated my mom and denied me as his son, but also because of some stupid stuff I did, too. It's not all his fault, but what bothers me is that he doesn't want to forgive me for it."

"Have you tried to talk to him?"

"More than once, but he's still angry."

"I'm sorry. If my parents were alive, I can't even imagine not being around them all the time. So I know that must be hard."

Tears filled Dillon's eyes. "You have no idea how painful it is."

Taylor looked up at him and saw tears falling. She raised up and hugged him.

"I didn't mean for this to happen," he sniffled. "How embarrassing."

"Why? Because you're hurt over your dad? You don't ever need to feel ashamed about something like that."

Dillon held her close and then kissed her. She kissed him back, and Taylor unbuttoned his starched white shirt and slipped it down his shoulders. He pulled her top over her head. They gazed lovingly into each other's eyes, and Dillon couldn't remember feeling so at ease with a woman. He didn't even know her well enough to feel this way, but she gave him comfort. She was good for his soul, and right now that's what he needed. Someone who didn't care about money, brand names, or anything else that didn't matter. Someone who seemed to care about him as a person and for no other reason.

CHAPTER 33

Dillon was exhausted. It was going on midnight, and he'd just left Taylor's about twenty minutes ago. He wasn't sure if he was just tired in general or a bit fatigued from drinking the couple of beers and glasses of wine he'd had. But either way, he was glad he'd at least gotten an hour of sleep before getting dressed to leave. If he could have, he would have stayed at Taylor's until morning, but he'd known it wasn't a good idea. Raven was already fired up, and his not coming home would have only made difficult matters worse. He'd actually thought she would have called him by now, but she hadn't. He wasn't sorry, of course, but the fact that she hadn't tried to contact him did make him wonder what she was up to. Knowing her, she thought the silent treatment she'd been giving him and her demand for him to sleep in one of the guest bedrooms would eventually get him to change his mind about vetoing the board's decision. She was also likely acting as though she didn't care where he was or what he was doing tonight, trying to pretend she no longer wanted him. The Raven he knew wanted him to believe she was preparing to file for divorce, so he would beg her not to. But he wasn't falling for it.

When he'd gone to her office to try to reason with her, he'd been hoping that she would accept what was and they could move on. Because truthfully, he didn't want a divorce, for all the reasons he'd thought about. But now, after tonight, he wasn't sure. He didn't want to cause a church scandal, but if there was some way for him to divorce Raven and be with Taylor, he would. He'd heard a number of married men say that no matter how many women they'd dated in their lifetime, no matter how much they didn't want to be tied down, that one special woman had gotten their attention. They'd willingly (or in some cases unwillingly) met their soul mates, and their lives had been changed forever. Once upon a time, Dillon had thought the same thing about Raven, but when he'd begun seeing Porsha he'd known something was missing. Otherwise, he couldn't and wouldn't have started sleeping with another woman. Even if he'd made a mistake and had a one-night stand, he wouldn't have kept a full-fledged affair going for more than three months, not even for money. Then there was Taylor, who was making things even harder for him. He hadn't gone looking for her, he hadn't seen her coming, and they'd met in the most unlikely place — that is, since most pastors didn't frequent bars. But he was falling for her with record speed, and he couldn't stop himself.

He was sure Taylor wasn't perfect, because no one was, but he liked everything about her. He felt good when he was with her, and almost as if he were cheating on her instead of Raven. He knew it was a strange way to think, but he was contemplating not seeing Taylor anymore until he saw how things were going to play out with his marriage. She deserved better, and if there was a chance he could marry her and be with her for good, he didn't want their relationship to begin like this. He didn't want it to be based on lies and adultery.

Dillon drove down I-90 and turned on his radio. He wasn't all that in the mood for music, so he searched through talk show segments. He stopped when he saw the Christian channel he'd heard his dad on last week. Ironically, the same interview was replaying, which Dillon wasn't shocked about, because lots of shows were repeated late at night. It also didn't have to be the same show that had aired earlier that same day, if the station had a popular segment that had attracted a large audience.

Dillon kept listening and heard his dad say, "I appreciate that, Jacob. I'd be glad to."

Then Jacob asked, "So do you meet pastors like this all the time?"

"Unfortunately, I do, and I'm ashamed to say that I know one of the young men very well. He lives right here in Mitchell. And in his case, he'll do anything to get what he wants, and he has no moral values. He even once had a fiancée who he treated like an animal, and he slept with his own brother's wife. He's also done things to other family members, yet he has a pretty sizable congregation."

Dillon had heard every word the first time he'd listened to the interview, but it still hurt as though he hadn't. After talking to Alicia, he'd been sure he was going to go see his dad in person, but now he wondered if he should even bother.

A commercial break aired, and Dillon realized that last week his dad's words had made him so angry, he'd turned off the radio. But it sounded like the interview wasn't over, so Dillon kept the channel right where it was.

When Jacob returned, the conversation continued.

"So, Pastor Black, while reading your bio, which I must say is very lengthy and most commendable, I noticed that you have children. In particular, a son."

"Yes, my son Matthew is twenty-three."

"The reason I mentioned your son is because I'm just wondering if he's planning to follow in your footsteps."

"Well, I can't say, but first of all, if he were to become a minister I would hope that it would only be because God has called him. That's something I can't stress enough, just like I was saying earlier. However, if God were to call Matthew, I wouldn't be surprised because he's always been the kind of child that most parents pray for. He isn't perfect, and he's made mistakes just like any of us, but he is a great person with a huge heart. He always thinks about others first and tries to do the right thing. So needless to say, his mother and I couldn't be more proud of him. He's always had a kind spirit, and if he'd been an only child he would have been more than enough. But thank God, we also have two other wonderful children, my oldest daughter, Alicia, and our youngest, Curtina. And of course, we also have our precious grandson, MJ."

"That's great," Jacob said. "So you have one son, two daughters, and a grandson."

"Yes."

One son? He meant two sons, and Dillon waited for his dad to correct Jacob. But he didn't. Curtis moved on to a whole other subject, and what Dillon also thought about was how he'd even counted Alicia as one of his children, even though this interview had aired days before their little reunion this evening. If Dillon hadn't heard this broadcast with his own ears, he might not have believed it, but now he knew the truth: His dad wasn't even claiming him publicly anymore. He was acting as though Dillon weren't his son, the same as he had when Dillon was born.

Dillon drove his car onto the shoulder of the road, threw it in park, and pressed the lever that opened his trunk. He got out, walked around to the back, and opened his cooler. There was no ice in it, which was the reason he hadn't bothered putting his beer in there before heading over to Taylor's. But he also hadn't wanted Raven to see it inside his car when he got home tonight. He doubted she'd come out to the garage, but if she left before him in the morning, she might casually glance over into his car or open it all the way to take a look. If she did, he didn't want her to see it.

He pulled out one beer, pushed the auto-close button for the trunk, and walked back around to the driver's side. He got back in and downed the beer almost nonstop. Then he opened his window and threw out the can. As a few cars zoomed by him, he sat thinking. Miss Brenda had been dead wrong about there being a chance to make things right with his dad. It was too late to repair all the damage that had been done. The more he thought about it, had his dad wanted to reconcile with him, he would have called him the same as he'd called Alicia this afternoon. He also would have invited Dillon to join them when they'd all driven over to Alicia's to surprise her. They'd held a planned family gathering without so much as thinking of him, and no one had to knock Dillon in the head to get their point across. He understood very clearly.

So much so that he dialed Vincent's number, shifted his gear back to drive, and drove back onto the highway. When Vincent answered, Dillon never even told him hello.

Instead, all he said was, "Do it, and do it quickly. My mind is made up."

CHAPTER 34

Alicia sat at her desk, smiling. She couldn't have been happier, and she thanked God for all that had transpired two days ago between her and her dad. Even Matthew had shown up with little MJ, and they'd hugged for longer than usual. They'd laughed and talked like old times, and Alicia could tell her baby brother had missed her as much as she'd missed him. Then there was her four-year-old nephew MJ. What a sweet, handsome little thing he was. She'd always loved him, but after missing two years of his life, she was planning to spend as much time with him as possible. Wednesday had proven to be one of the best days ever, and she was in awe of how fast things had changed for the better.

Alicia did wonder, though, why she hadn't slept very well last night. She'd been so relieved when her family had left on Wednesday and so relaxed that she hadn't bothered taking another sleeping pill the way she'd planned. Yet she'd still slept six hours straight, which had seemed more than enough, because when she'd gotten up yesterday morning, she'd felt fully alert and energized. This was the reason she hadn't taken anything again last night, thinking she would rest well a second time. But, oddly, that hadn't been the case. She hadn't worried about anything and had only indulged in happy thoughts; however, she'd still tossed and turned for hours. If she'd gotten two hours of sleep total, that was all, and she didn't understand it. Nonetheless, she was definitely taking something before lying down tonight.

Alicia picked up her office phone and dialed her brother's extension, but he didn't answer. It was unlike him not to already be at the church by now, although maybe he had an outside appointment she didn't know about. She was somewhat concerned about him because yesterday when she'd asked him how his visit had gone with their dad, he'd told her he'd changed his mind. He was leaving things as is, and he wasn't planning to contact Curtis again. Alicia still hoped he would, though, so she pressed the Contacts icon on her cell to call his mobile number. But before she scrolled down to it,

Raven burst into her office and slammed the door behind her.

"You know, I've waited three days to decide how I was going to confront Dillon, but then it dawned on me. You're the one I need to talk to."

"Raven, why are you here?"

"Because my husband founded this church, and I have more right to be in this office than you do. I have more rights than you, period, although I can tell you think otherwise."

"I don't think anything. You're just upset because the board voted against you. And rightfully so."

"They voted against me because they saw right away how you, Dillon, and Levi felt. They knew that whatever they said or wanted wouldn't matter. Ever since you and Dillon reconciled your differences, he's basically kissed your behind and done whatever you tell him."

"That's not true."

"It *is* true!" she yelled. "I've just never said anything, but sweetheart, people talk. I found out a long time ago that you and Levi are the reason I wasn't named CFO. I heard you were both against me handling the finances because of my past. That's why Dillon went along with hiring Lynette. He was worried that Levi might not invest all the money he was planning to give, and that was the end of it."

Alicia stood up. "Raven, I'd really like you to leave."

"I'm not going anywhere. You're Dillon's sister, not his wife. Actually, you're only his half sister, yet the two of you walk around here like you grew up together. He loves the ground you walk on, like you're the light of his life, and that's why I never liked you. Well, no, that's not really true . . . I never even liked you when I worked for your no-good father."

"Raven, I'm not going to ask you again. Please leave."

"No, I'm staying, because you need to know how things are going to work from this point on."

"What are you talking about?"

"You're going to go to the board and have them vote again. They're going to make me co-pastor. Then you're going to get your brother to have legal documents drawn up so I can also be named co-founder."

Alicia wasn't sure if Raven had lost her mind, or if she was telling some sort of deranged joke.

"You must be crazy."

"No, I'm fine. I'm the reason this church

thrived so quickly. I'm the reason a handful of members turned into a thousand. But now you, Dillon, Levi, and the rest of the elders are trying to dismiss me? Well, I'm not having it."

"No one's trying to do anything. That nonsense is all in your head."

"Really? Well, not only are you and Dillon trying to walk all over me here at the church, your brother has a mistress."

Alicia tried not to react, but she knew the look on her face told another story.

"Yeah, that's right, your precious brother who stands in the pulpit every single Sunday is sleeping around with some tramp. I've never said one word to him about it, though. The whole time, I've acted as if I didn't know a thing. As a matter of fact, once I found out, I became a better wife to him than I had been. I gave the man sex, even if I didn't want it, I cooked, I did anything I thought he wanted me to do. And if you wanna know the truth, I was more than happy to let him sleep with whomever he wanted, as long as he shared his role as pastor with me. That's all he had to do, and everybody could've been happy."

"I don't believe there's another woman, but even if there is, that's between you and Dillon. I don't have a thing to do with it."

"Oh, you have *everything* to do with it. You run all this, remember? Your dear brother founded New Faith, but you're Miss COO. *Chief . . . operating . . . officer.* So either you convince Dillon and the board to give me what I want, or this Sunday I'm telling the congregation who their pastor is. I'm telling them about his mistress, and that I'm divorcing him."

"Raven, save your threats for somebody who cares. Now get out of my office."

"You have two days. And if I don't hear from you by first thing Sunday morning, things around here will never be the same. Your dad will also have to deal with another family scandal. I can see the headline now: 'Dillon Whitfield Black: The Apple That Didn't Fall Far from the Tree.'"

Alicia frowned. "You know, Raven, why is it that you want to be co-pastor so badly? Or better yet, why do you need to be co-founder? You didn't *found* anything."

"Because over the last two years, I've watched this church grow like wildfire. Even putting the physical church aside, New Faith Ministries, Inc., will eventually make millions. I realized that a while ago, and I want what's mine. I don't want to have to fight for it years down the road, which means I need to make sure I have just as much control as Dillon."

Alicia sat down and didn't look at her again. "It'll never happen, so deal with it."

"Oh, I think it will. Did I forget to tell you that I have proof that he's messing around? The kind of proof that will stun the members of this church and all of Mitchell? Now, you get me what I want or else."

Alicia watched as she walked away, and she wanted to cry. Not because of Raven's threats and demands, but because for no reason she could think of, the voice in her head was back.

You and Levi are going to lose everything you've worked for here, and so is your brother. This is all punishment because of what you did to Phillip. You can't hurt people and think you're going to be successful. You have to reap what you sow, and there's still only one way for you to do that.

CHAPTER 35

Dillon drove into the church parking lot and pressed the speaker button in his car. "Hello?"

"Dillon?" Alicia said. "Where have you been?"

"Hey, Sis," he said, laughing. "So did you hold down the fort . . . while . . . I . . . was gone?"

"Dillon, what have you been doing?"

"Nothing."

"You sound like you're high or drunk."

"Girl, I'm not . . . drunk. I'm . . . just glad to hear from my . . . sister is all."

"I've been trying to call you all day. Nobody knew where you were, and I've been worried sick. So was Miss Brenda."

Dillon pressed the button in his car to open his home garage, but then he remembered he was at the church.

"Dillon, are you there?"

"I'm here. Are you?" he said, cracking up.

"Where are you?" she shouted.

"Are you mad, Sis? What's wrong?"

"Where are you, Dillon?"

"Well, I thought I was home, but I'm really at the church. Guess I took the wrong turn," he said, still laughing.

"Don't you go anywhere," she said. "Levi and I are on our way."

"Sis, it's really dark out here," he said, rolling down his window.

"I know, and that's why I'm telling you to stay where you are."

"Okay. You coming to get me?"

"We'll be there in a few minutes."

"Okay, bye."

"No, don't hang up. I want you to stay on the phone with me until we get there."

"Awww, you missed me today, didn't you? You love your brother, don't you?"

"Of course I do. We all love you."

"Oooh, Alicia, you're telling a lie."

"What kind of lie?"

"You said you *all* love me, but . . . that's . . . not . . . truuuuuue," he sang. "Dadddd . . . doesn't love me. He . . . never . . . loved me."

"He does, Dillon."

"No, he doesn't. That's why I had to get him back."

"What are you talking about? Get him

back how?"

"You'll seeeee," he crooned. "But when are you coming to get me?"

"We're on our way."

"I'm glad, because . . . it's dark out here."

"I know, but we'll be there soon. You just hang in there."

"You know what else . . . Sis? I finally . . . found the woman of . . . my dreams."

"Really? Who is she?"

"Her name is . . . Taylor, and you would . . . love her."

"Who's Taylor?"

"That's a secret, and if I tell you I'll have to kill you," he said, laughing again.

"We'll be there shortly, okay?"

"If you say so."

Dillon laid his head back and closed his eyes. He thought he heard someone talking to him, maybe Alicia, but he was too sleepy to tell. He blinked his eyes, trying to stay awake, but they became too heavy. So he closed them, and he was out in a second.

Chapter 36

Dillon stared at the light fixtures attached to the ceiling fan, but he still didn't move. It was Saturday morning, he was lying in one of his sister's bedrooms, and he couldn't have been more ashamed. He'd gotten so wasted at Benny's that when he'd gone outside to look for his car, he'd barely been able to find it. He couldn't even remember how many drinks he'd had, and he still didn't know how he'd made it back to Mitchell without being arrested. He hadn't planned on drinking as much as he had, and he was only supposed to stop for one or two cocktails before meeting Taylor at her condo. But he'd never gotten there, and he hadn't called her. She, of course, hadn't called him because she knew he could have been with his wife.

He raised his head up from the pillow but felt dizzy. What in the world was wrong with him? He'd been sure he wouldn't fall all the way back off track, yet last night, he hadn't been able to stop drinking. He'd found himself finishing one drink and then ordering another. He would down the next and then ask for a new one. He was out of control, and he finally knew he couldn't continue like this. He could no longer deny what he'd learned in treatment. Once an alcoholic truly did mean always an alcoholic.

Alicia knocked on the door. "Dillon, are you awake?"

He thought about pretending to be asleep so he wouldn't have to face her, but it was better to just get this over with. "Yeah, I'm up," he said, swinging his legs onto the floor.

"Levi is with me, too," she said, easing the door open.

They walked in, and Dillon stared at them in silence. He was completely hungover, and his head throbbed.

Alicia leaned against the tall wooden dresser. "What happened?"

"It's a long story."

Levi stood just inside the door with his arms folded. "I knew something was wrong when you were at my mom's on the Fourth, and I should have called you on it."

"I wouldn't have admitted anything."

"Maybe not," Levi said, "but at least you would have known I suspected something."

"What made you start drinking all of a sudden anyway?" Alicia asked.

"Everything."

"Does it have anything to do with someone named Taylor?"

Dillon looked at Alicia, wondering what he'd told her last night. He certainly didn't want his sister, or anybody for that matter, to know he was having an affair.

"Why do you ask me that?"

"Because you said you'd found the woman of your dreams, and her name was Taylor."

Dillon could kick himself. "Wow."

"Who is she?" Alicia asked.

"I'd rather not say. It's just best not to talk about that."

"Well, after yesterday I don't think you have a choice, because your wife knows everything. That's why I kept trying to call you."

The pounding in Dillon's head thumped harder. "What does she know?"

"That you're messing around on her. She says she's known all along, but she never said anything to you."

"Man, man, man," Dillon said, but he wondered how Raven knew about Taylor. He'd only been with her three times. The first night he'd met her and again on Wednesday. Then, when he'd discovered

346

that Raven still wasn't speaking to him, he'd gone back to see Taylor on Thursday evening.

"But that's not the worst of it," Alicia continued. "She says if she doesn't get what she wants, she's telling the congregation about your mistress. She also says she has proof."

Levi shook his head. "Dillon, please tell me this is all a lie. Tell me you haven't been sleeping with another woman."

Dillon cast his eyes at him but quickly looked away, feeling more ashamed than he had been.

"After all I did to help you with the ministry?" Levi said. "You've been playing with God all this time? Standing in the pulpit saying one thing, and doing something totally different outside of it?"

"No, that's not what I've been doing at all," Dillon told him, but his response didn't sound convincing even to himself. "I made a mistake. I met Taylor at a bar last week, and things happened. I didn't mean for them to, but they did."

"I can't believe you've been doing this," Levi said. "I did a lot of wrong in the past, but you always knew I was serious about my faith in God. When I turned my life around in prison, I was sincere. When you hear me say I love God, and that I try my best to live by His Word, I mean that. And I thought you were doing the same thing. I thought you'd changed from the person you used to be."

"Levi, I'm not perfect, and there are things you and Alicia don't know about me."

Alicia seemed irritated. "Like what?"

"When I left Mitchell three years ago, I was severely depressed. I'd lost everything, and eventually, I started drinking. Before long, I was a chronic alcoholic, and I couldn't stop. That's the real reason I had to sell my aunt's house. I needed the money to pay bills, and I drank a lot of it away, too. But I thought I had it beat. I swear I did."

"Beat?" Levi yelled. "No addict ever just *beats* anything. You stop using, then you either go into treatment or attend meetings or you do both. But you never get to a point where you're cured. You just do what you need to do to stay sober."

Dillon tried to defend himself. "Well, it's not like I was using drugs, so I thought I was fine."

"Using is using. I don't care whether it's alcohol, drugs, sex, or shopping. It's all the same, and you have to treat it that way. You should've been going to AA meetings all along."

"I didn't think I needed to. I went a few times in Atlanta, but I didn't want to bring that part of my life back to Mitchell."

"Dillon, man, we all have problems. And covering things up is the reason you're in this mess. That's why so many people struggle. That's why marriages break up, and most importantly, it's the reason people die. They pretend like nothing's wrong or they become ashamed of the issues they're dealing with. But when it's all said and done, all they end up doing is hurting themselves and the people who care about them."

Dillon sighed but didn't respond. He wanted to, but he couldn't.

"I don't understand," Alicia said. "Why did you start drinking again? Why now?"

"I know you don't get it, but not having a relationship with our dad has me crazy. Every time I think about him, I'm either hurt or angry, and I needed something to help me with that. Something to mask it, even if only for a short while."

"I get all that," Alicia said, "but you should've come to me or Levi. And even if you couldn't stop yourself from taking a drink, you didn't have to start seeing another woman. Raven isn't my favorite person, but I thought you loved her."

"I do, but I've struggled with so many different issues."

"Well, you'd better pull it together, because this Raven situation has to be dealt with. She said she has proof, and I believe her."

Dillon held the top of his head with his hand. "What does she want?"

"To be co-pastor. But that's not all. She also wants to be named co-founder."

Dillon scrunched his face. "What?"

"I just can't get over all this," Levi said matter-of-factly. "It was your idea to start the church, and we invested all the money, yet she wants to claim half of the proceeds? We're trying to build up a ministry, not shell out money for Raven's material possessions."

"Surely she doesn't believe we're going to allow that," Dillon said. "There's no way."

"She does, and she's not playing," Alicia told him.

"I just need to talk to her. Let her know that I won't see Taylor again," Dillon explained, but deep down, he wondered if it was Porsha that Raven knew about. Especially since he hadn't been seeing Taylor long enough for Raven to find out anything.

"I hope that works, otherwise this is going to cause huge problems," Alicia said.

Levi threw up his hands and turned to walk out of the room. "This is too much. I gotta get out of here."

Dillon couldn't have felt worse. He hadn't wanted to let Alicia down, but he definitely hadn't wanted to disappoint Levi.

Dillon looked at his sister. "I'm sorry. I'm sorry for everything."

"I don't know what to say, but let me ask you something else. What did you mean last night when you said, 'That's why I had to get him back'?"

"I don't remember saying that."

"We were talking about Daddy, and you were saying he didn't love you."

A chill shot through Dillon's veins. He wondered what else he'd said that he shouldn't have. Especially since Vincent had told him on Thursday that he was paying his contact the down payment sometime tomorrow. What if he'd alluded to any of that while he'd been drunk? What if he'd confessed to more than Alicia was asking him about?

"It must've been the alcohol talking," he said.

"Maybe, but it sounded real to me."

"I was out of my head. It was almost like

351

I blacked out."

"Well, like I already said, you'd better pull it together, Dillon."

"I promise you, Sis, I'm going to fix this. I'll make it right."

"I hope you can, because if not, New Faith is about to be in an uproar."

CHAPTER 37

Dillon had been so hoping that the idea of getting drunk last night and having to spend the night at his sister and brother-in-law's had been nothing more than a bad dream, but sadly, this was his reality. Then there was the whole Raven fiasco that Alicia had told him about earlier. Could it really be? Could Raven actually have proof that he'd been having an affair on her? If she did, who was it that she'd found out about? He still doubted that it was Taylor, but there was just no way to be sure until he questioned Raven. Worse than that, though, was her threat of exposing him to his congregation unless she got what she wanted.

Dillon wasn't sure how he'd allowed this thing to happen, but he knew he had to do something. This was part of the reason he'd asked Alicia if he could lie back down for a few more hours, as he'd needed some time to gather his thoughts and plan a way out of the mess he'd created. He'd, of course, told his sister something different, that the reason he wasn't ready to go home was because he needed to sleep off more of his hangover. But as it had turned out, he hadn't come up with anything and had dropped off to sleep after all. Now, however, he was awake and knew he had to think, and think fast.

When he heard a knock at the door, he sat up. He hoped it was Alicia and not Levi, because he just wasn't ready to face him again. His brother-in-law was hurt, disappointed, and furious with him, and Dillon didn't blame him.

"Come in."

Alicia opened the door. "I know I probably should've asked you first, but I didn't want to give you the chance to say no."

"About what?"

"Someone's downstairs to see you."

"Who? Raven? Please tell me you didn't call her over here."

"No, it's not Raven, it's Daddy."

Dillon wasn't sure whether to jump for joy or tell her he wanted nothing to do with the man. "Why is he here?"

"I called him."

"Why?"

"Because enough is enough. The two of

you need to sit down and talk, man to man, once and for all."

"I don't think so."

"Dillon, please. Do this so you can stop hurting. You'd said you were going to go see him anyway."

"Yeah, but then I also told you that I decided not to, and that I was done with him for good."

"I know, but we've all made mistakes. Daddy has, I have, and so have you. None of us are innocent, and until we can fix this, things will never get better for us as a family. So I really need you to do this. Just talk to him."

Dillon didn't see how this meeting of the minds was going to help anything, and he honestly wasn't interested. But it was the pleading look on his sister's face that he had a hard time ignoring.

"Why is it so important to you?" Dillon asked. "You've repaired your relationship with him, and that's all that matters."

"No, that's not all that matters. You're my brother, and you're in trouble. You have a drinking problem, and you said yourself that you drink because of your issues with Daddy."

"I'll get over it, trust me."

"Oh yeah? And what about all the drama

that's building with Raven? How will you deal with that?"

"I told you, I'm going to fix things."

"Look, D, all I'm asking is for you to do this one thing. Even if you don't have anything to say, just come downstairs and listen to Daddy. Let him do all the talking."

"You're not going to let up on this, are you?"

"No, so please."

Dillon sighed loudly. His father was the last person he wanted to see and talk to, but he got up and followed Alicia out of the room. When they arrived down on the main floor, Dillon glanced toward the family room, half looking out for Levi, but thankfully he didn't see him.

Alicia pointed toward the kitchen. "Daddy's outside."

Dillon headed in that direction and walked through the patio doors. Then he went inside the gazebo. "You wanted to see me?"

Curtis was sitting on the padded sofa dressed in a pair of white shorts and a navy-blue-and-white-striped T-shirt. "Son, have a seat."

Dillon sat as far away from his dad as possible in one of the chairs.

"We have to stop this."

Dillon stared at him as though he couldn't

care less.

But Curtis continued. "First I did that awful thing to your mom when she forced me to take a DNA test. Then I pretended for twenty-nine years that you'd never been born. And actually, the only reason I finally owned up to everything was because you conspired with Mariah to have me beaten nearly to death. Not to mention, you went on television and told everyone how I had denied you from the time you were born. Still, I forgave you. But then it wasn't long before you tried to blackmail me and cause a public scandal. On top of that, you slept with your brother's wife. Then, if that wasn't enough, you married the woman who stole a lot of money from my church."

"Why are you talking about things we already know? What good is that going to do for either of us?"

"Just hear me out."

What a pure waste of time. This had been the very reason Dillon hadn't wanted to see or talk to his father.

"The reason I'm reminding you of all of this is because neither of us is blameless. We've both done some heartless things to each other. But ever since Tanya got me to see how wrong I was about Alicia's marriage to Levi, I've done a lot of soul-

357

searching. I realized that I hadn't truly forgiven you. I know I told you I had, but to be honest, I just wanted you to go away. I wanted to pretend all over again that you didn't exist."

Dillon rested his elbows on the arms of the chair. "So is that supposed to make me feel good or something?"

"No, but what I'm trying to say is that I was wrong for that. I teach and talk about forgiveness all the time, but somehow when it came to following my own advice, I wasn't able to. I was just so angry at you for so many different things. And it seemed easier to simply stay away from you. But I'm very sorry about that. Alicia also told me this afternoon how you've always felt left out. Like I treat my other children much better than you. At first, I didn't see that, but as I thought back to three years ago, I couldn't deny it. I didn't purposely try to treat you differently, it's just that I've had a relationship with my two girls since birth. And with Matt since he was seven. Then when I finally met you, it happened on bad terms. But now that I know you're struggling with alcoholism, it's time for me to be a father to you. It's time for me to be a loving dad to all my children, and not just Alicia, Matt, and Curtina. My own father was an alcoholic, and he made life miserable for my mom, my sister, and me. It was like I never even had a father."

Dillon wasn't sure what to say, and he'd had no idea his grandfather had suffered with anything.

"So you see, son," Curtis continued, "we can't go on the way we have been. We need to come together so you can get the help you need. And there's one other thing I need you to understand."

Dillon stared at him in silence, still thinking about his grandfather. Dillon had heard alcoholism was hereditary, but because he'd never seen his father drink, he hadn't thought much about it.

His dad spoke again, though. "Alicia told me that when you first moved back to Mitchell, you always talked about how lucky she was to have grown up in the same house with me. And that had you been able to do the same, you would've turned out a lot differently. But truth is, you suffered because you *didn't* grow up with me, and Alicia suffered because she *did*."

"Why do you say that?" Dillon asked.

"Alicia had affairs on Phillip twice, but it was me who she learned that kind of behavior from. When she was growing up, she saw firsthand how to commit adultery. I slept around on Tanya, Mariah, and Charlotte, and it wasn't a secret. On top of that, Tanya and I got a divorce and Alicia had to struggle through that, too. Then, as far as you, when I falsified that DNA test, you were forced to grow up without a mom or a dad. You've been searching and crying out for a parent's love ever since. I know you had your aunt, and thank God for her, but it still wasn't the same. And for that, son, I'm sorry. I apologized when I first met you, but I really mean it this time. I handled so many things with you in the wrong way, and I want us to start over. Can we do that?"

Dillon wanted to tell him how much he hated him and that he didn't need him, but the words wouldn't leave his mouth. Instead, tears fell from his eyes, and he couldn't stop them. He was thirty-two, yet he felt more like a five-year-old who just wanted his daddy to love him. That's all he'd ever wanted, and now that his father had finally admitted his mistakes, Dillon knew he needed to ditch his pride. It was time he and his dad stopped doing all the tit-for-tatting that Miss Brenda had talked about. Time to call a truce and be a family.

It was time to call off the vicious level of revenge Dillon had planned for his father.

CHAPTER 38

"I just want out," Levi said coldly.

Alicia continued pacing back and forth in her office, something she'd been doing since finally getting in touch with him by phone. "Baby, look. I know you're upset with Dillon, but please don't take that out on me."

"I'm not. But I just can't deal with your brother. I don't even want to be around him."

"I know, and it's like I told you, he's gone. He left a little while ago."

She waited for Levi to respond, but he didn't.

"Baby, I'm sorry that my brother disappointed you. He disappointed me, too, but now that he and Daddy have talked I think he'll be different. Things'll be better for all of us."

"I don't care about any of that," Levi said matter-of-factly. "I worked hard to get my life right, and I surrendered completely to

God. But I also believed that Dillon was sincere. I thought he was serious about his faith, and now I find out he was playing games the whole time."

"I just think he has a lot to learn," Alicia tried to explain. "You said yourself that we all have problems."

"Yeah, but Dillon has been misleading a lot of innocent people. I thought he wanted to grow the church so we could save more souls, but this was all about him. Becoming a minister wasn't a calling like he claimed, it was simply a career decision."

"I don't think we can decide that, because we don't know what's in his heart."

"You're right, we don't. But that's how I feel, and like I said, I just want out."

"Are you on your way home?" she asked, switching the subject.

"Yeah, but I'm not changing my mind. I want out, and that's all there is to it."

"But maybe —"

"Baby, I don't wanna do this, okay?" Levi said, interrupting her. "I'll just see you when I get home."

"Fine," she said, but before she could say anything else, he ended the call.

Alicia dropped down in her chair, stunned like never before. Levi had actually hung up on her, and he sounded as though he was just as mad at her as he was at Dillon. When Levi had said earlier that he'd needed to get out of there, she'd just thought he'd meant he was leaving the room Dillon had slept in. But when she'd come downstairs looking for him, she'd discovered that he'd left the house altogether. He'd gone to his mom's without telling her — when normally he didn't go anywhere without informing her — and it was then that Alicia had known how hurt and upset he was. Although, as she thought back, she'd seen the angry look in his eyes while they'd been questioning Dillon, and it had made her a bit nervous then, too.

Alicia sat for another ten minutes, trying to settle her racing thoughts. But she was so exhausted and tired of trying to fix one problem after another. She'd been so sure that once she reconciled with her family, all would be good for her. And it had been. That is, until last night, when she'd learned her pastor brother had gotten drunk and was out driving around. Then, if that hadn't been enough, she'd learned a few hours ago that he was an alcoholic. She'd also learned that Raven had told the truth about his having an affair, which meant the church's reputation and financial status were at risk. As the daughter of Curtis Black, Alicia had witnessed and experienced more than a few church scandals in her thirty years, and no good ever came from them. Some members of the church would leave and never come back, and rumors would circulate for months. It would take a very long time for New Faith to recover from something like this, and Alicia wasn't sure it was possible. More than that, she didn't know if she had the strength to battle any more pain and humiliation.

She just didn't understand why bad things kept happening to her. Why they'd been happening ever since she was a child. When she was a small girl, her parents had argued daily and finally ended up divorced. Then when she was fourteen, she'd left school and had gone to meet a boy she'd met online, only to discover that this *boy* had been a grown man — who had raped her.

Alicia leaned farther back in her chair, and tears filled her eyes. She'd worked hard to block that part of her life from her mind, so why was she remembering it now? Why was her childhood tragedy taking root as though it had occurred yesterday?

You know why. Your family is cursed, and it's the reason you've never really been happy. Not your whole life. Then you made Phillip unhappy. You hurt him, and he's dead. And if you don't do something to end this, you're going to hurt someone else. You're going to cause harm to someone you really love. And didn't you hear Levi? He said he wants out of the marriage.

Alicia pressed the front of her wet face with both hands. "Oh God, please make it stop. Please, God, I'm begging You. Levi just means he wants out of New Faith. Not out of our marriage. Dear God, please, no."

Her heart rate sped up, and the voice got louder in her head.

No, he meant that he wants to leave you! He wants to get out before he ends up like Phillip!

"No!" she yelled. "Stop it! I'm not crazy. I'm not. I'm not. I'm not. Father, please help me."

There's no one who can help you except you. So go ahead and open the drawer so you can be at peace. It'll fix everything.

Alicia slowly removed her hands from her face, glanced down at her lower right drawer, and pulled it open. She lifted stacks of unopened office supplies from the back, moved them toward the front, and then she picked up three boxes of thank-you cards. When she set those on her desk, she pulled out four small reference books on writing and then the black leather box at the bottom. It was a case that one of her writing awards had been delivered in years ago.

She closed her eyes, trying her best not to open it, but she didn't see any alternative. Not when she was as tired as she was, and she actually *was* responsible for Phillip's death. But worse than that, now Levi was going to leave her.

You've made a lot of mistakes, but you're finally doing the right thing. For the first time in your life.

Alicia opened the box and pulled out the loaded gun. She held it in front of her, pointed it toward the floor, and closed her eyes.

You know you're doing the right thing. You've tried your best to handle things in other ways, but this has always been your only solution. That's why you feel so much calmer now.

"I do," she whispered, and cried more silent tears. "I know this really is the only answer."

She thought about Levi, her parents, her siblings, her nephew, and Melanie and closed her eyes again. Then she raised the gun up and turned it toward her chest.

But that's when Levi rushed in.

"Oh my God, baby!" he shouted. "What are you doing?"

Alicia gazed at him strangely, not wanting

to let go of the gun.

Not for herself, not for Levi . . . not for anyone.

CHAPTER 39

Dillon drove in front of his house but not into the driveway. As soon as he'd finished talking with his dad and had left Alicia's, he'd gotten in his car and tried to call Vincent. Now Vincent was ringing him back.

"Hey, man," Dillon said.

"Hey, what's up? Sorry I missed your call."

"There's been a change of plans."

"With what?"

"That whole thing with my dad. I'm calling it off."

"Why?"

"I had a talk with him, and he apologized for everything. Wants us to start over."

"And you believe that?"

"I have to. It's the only way I can have some peace. Plus, right now, we have another family issue to deal with, and I just want to forget about this. If you want to know the truth, I can't believe I got myself angry enough to want to do something this evil."

"But it was all for good reason. Your dad did you dirty more than once, and he deserves what he gets. We agreed on that, remember?"

"Yeah, but it's over. Call it off."

"I don't know if that's gonna be possible. You can't just hire someone to burn down a church and then walk away from it."

"Well, it's not like any money has been paid."

"I paid the first twenty-five thousand yesterday."

"I thought you said you were doing that tomorrow?"

"They wanted it sooner."

"Well, you still need to call it off. Tell your guy they can keep the down payment, but this is over."

"It doesn't work like that. Remember, I told you. Once the first payment is made, there's no turning back from this."

"Look, man, I need this to go away. I don't want my father's church being destroyed."

"But what about New Faith? The whole reason we were doing this was so your dad's members wouldn't have a place to worship. That way, we could immediately start doing all kinds of advertising and inviting them over to our church. You'd even mentioned spreading a rumor to make people think that your dad would be speaking at our services. Your idea was brilliant."

"It was also wrong. I must have been out of my mind to even think about burning down a church. Let alone my dad's. So I'm telling you, Vince, make this go away."

"If I could, I would."

"What's so hard about it?" Dillon asked. "Why can't you at least try?"

"Because I already promised them the other half. When you're dealing with criminals, you can't be all wishy-washy. When you hire them, they expect to be paid."

"Well, I need you to call them. Do whatever you have to. Even if it means paying them the whole fifty thousand dollars."

"As long as they're getting the full amount, that might work. But are you sure about this?"

"I know you don't understand it, but I'm very sure. I finally have a chance to turn over a new leaf and do the right thing, and I'm taking it."

"Okay, well, I still say this could've been good for us. Because even though your dad is building a larger sanctuary, it won't be done for a few months, and a lot of his members would have started coming to New Faith. I guarantee it."

"Maybe, but like I said, this is over."

"Okay, I'll let my contact know."

"I appreciate that, man, but let me get going. I just pulled up at home. I'll have to tell you about my Raven situation later, too."

"Uh-oh. Sounds like trouble."

"I'll fill you in tomorrow, but it's got to be handled."

"Like I always tell you, whatever you need. Just let me know."

When Dillon went inside the house, he'd half expected to see Raven rushing toward him. But instead, she sat at the kitchen island like normal. Dillon was almost afraid to approach her, because she seemed too calm for a woman who supposedly knew her husband was cheating on her.

"Where were you?" she asked.

"At my sister's."

"Why?"

"It's a long story, but you can call her, Levi, or my dad. Any of them can confirm it."

"Your dad?"

Dillon set his key fob on the counter and leaned against it. "That's *another* long story."

"Well, I'm sure your sister told you about

our little conversation yesterday."

"As a matter of fact, she did."

"And?"

"And what?"

"What are you going to do about it?"

"I don't know."

"She did tell you what I want, though, right?"

"I guess."

"Either she did or she didn't, Dillon."

"She said something about you wanting to be co-pastor and be named co-founder."

"That would be correct."

"And is there a reason why you think you should be co-founder? Because I founded the church before I married you."

"I understand that, but that's all you did. I'm the one who showed you what to do after the fact."

"Well, I can't offer you a partnership."

"I'm really sorry to hear that."

"Given the situation, though, I am willing to make you co-pastor."

Raven laughed at him. "Now, that's funny."

"What's so funny about it?"

"That's all I wanted at first, but you didn't. So now I want both. I need to know that my future is secure, and this is the only way to make that happen."

"Do you really think I'm going to just turn over one half of everything involving the church?"

"If you don't, I'll be announcing your little secret."

This was the subject Dillon had been waiting for her to bring up. He also wondered which woman she knew about and how.

He still pretended he didn't have a clue, though. "I don't know what you're talking about."

"Of course you do. You've been laying up with Porsha Harrington every Monday afternoon for the last three months. Sometimes on other days of the week, too."

"That's not true," he said, wondering how she knew the length of time he'd been seeing Porsha.

"Well, I've got video footage that says otherwise."

Dillon felt like he might have a panic attack. Had she actually said *video footage*?

"You don't have *anything*," he said matter-of-factly, trying to call her bluff.

Raven picked up a large white envelope that he hadn't noticed until now. "Don't I?" she said.

"What is that?" he asked.

She slid the package across the island to him. "Open it and see."

Dillon pulled out a DVD, but he couldn't tell what was on it. "For all I know this could be a Disney movie."

Raven took the DVD from his hand and slid it into her laptop. It only took seconds to load, and once it did, Dillon knew he had a problem. One of his and Porsha's sexcapades was in plain view, including sound bites of every moan and groan and word they'd said to each other.

"Where did you get this?"

She smiled. "I figured you might want to know that," she said, and turned around, looking toward the hallway. "Porsha, can you come in here?"

When Porsha walked into the kitchen, Dillon thought he would die.

Porsha tossed him a look of disgust. "Hi, Dillon. Surprised to see me?"

Dillon wasn't sure what to say or who to punch first. "So let me get this straight. The two of you were in on this all along? You planned this whole thing to try to take over my church?"

Raven smiled. "No, see, that's the beauty of the whole thing. I told your sister that I've known about your affair the whole time, but that was just to get her attention. To be honest, though, I didn't talk to Porsha for the first time until yesterday morning."

"Porsha, why would you do this?" Dillon wanted to know. "What can you possibly gain by it?"

"I told you not to try to use me, because if you did it wouldn't be good. I told you that the same night you stood me up. I knew you were lying about being home with Raven, so I hired someone to follow you, starting the very next day. So imagine my surprise when I found out you were seeing someone else. You saw her twice this week, and I'm sure that's where you were last Thursday, too. So, needless to say, I called Raven right away yesterday. Wanted to let her know who you really are."

Dillon didn't see a reason to keep playing around with these witches. He wanted to know exactly what he was up against. "What is it that you want, Raven?"

"Unless you want this played for the entire congregation and released to every media outlet, I want papers drawn up. I want to be named co-founder *and* co-pastor. I also want fifty-one percent control. That's the most important part of all."

Dillon glared at her. "You must think I'm some child."

"I don't think anything. I'm just telling you what I want and what the consequences will be if I don't get it."

Dillon looked at Porsha. "And I suppose you've got your list of demands waiting, too?"

"No, just standing here watching all the smoke blow up in your face is more than enough for me. My father left me millions, so I don't need a thing from you. I just want Raven to take what's hers. I was wrong for sleeping with a married man anyway, and I'm making up for it now."

Dillon gazed back and forth between the two of them. No matter what they said — no matter how many threats they made — he would never let Raven take over everything he'd built. But he also knew that if he didn't give her what she wanted, she would in fact play that DVD for the congregation and send it out to the media. It would go viral, and he would instantly lose all credibility as well as each of his parishioners. There was no winning with this for him, but again, he couldn't let Raven have New Faith. He wouldn't let anyone steal what was his.

It was the reason he left both women standing there, went outside to his car, and called Vincent again.

When his friend answered, Dillon got straight to the point. "Man, there's been another change of plans."

"Really?" Vincent said. "I was hoping you'd come to your senses."

Epilogue

Three Months Later

Dillon had tried to stop drinking on his own, but after losing everything he'd worked so hard for, he'd become depressed and hopeless. It had been one thing to realize his marriage was over, but burning down his own church had been another. The irony of it all still stunned him. Who would have guessed that planning to burn down his father's church would ultimately cause the ruin of his own? But there had simply been no way Dillon was going to allow Raven to have controlling interest in New Faith Christian Center. He hadn't known why she'd gotten that foolish idea in her head, but in the end, he'd had to remember she was a criminal. She was a very intelligent one who didn't mind manipulating, deceiving, or doing whatever became necessary to get what she wanted. Dillon had certainly coveted top-level status himself, but ultimately, Raven had yearned for the same thing. She'd become drunk with the idea of becoming rich, powerful, and famous, and two people with that same tenacious thinking couldn't stay married. Or if they did, there would be constant bickering and downright dirty battles to contend with.

When he'd first married her, he had in fact loved her and thought that they'd be together forever. However, slowly but surely, he'd realized that it had been her ambition and business knowledge that he'd been most attracted to. He'd seen where she could help him get to where he wanted to be, but he hadn't counted on her wanting to take over New Faith Ministries, Inc. He hadn't even expected her to want to be co-pastor, but she'd suddenly become obsessed with the idea. She hadn't just wanted to partner with him equally, either. She'd wanted 51 percent. So Dillon had decided he didn't have any other option except to destroy the church altogether. He'd known there was still a chance that Raven would send out that trashy video to the media — especially since he'd stopped her from taking his church from him. But he'd promised her that if she did, he would tell the world how she'd stolen a hundred thousand dollars from a church and had served time in prison. In the past, she'd talked about it locally and to their congregation, but Dillon would make sure everyone knew nationally, guaranteeing that she wouldn't find employment or be able to start her own church anywhere.

There was some good news, however, because after having Vincent pay someone to commit arson, the fire investigators hadn't been able to determine a definite cause. They did believe that someone had set the church on fire, but they didn't have any real evidence or promising suspects. This had been Dillon's hope all along, and as wrong as it was, he'd still gone ahead and filed an insurance claim. He wasn't sure when or how much he would be paid, but his goal now was to do the right thing. He didn't know what that was exactly, but he wanted to be a better person. He no longer wanted to play with God or pretend that he'd been called to lead His people. What he wanted was to walk the straight and narrow the way his father kept telling him. This, in itself, was the real reason he had fully acknowledged his alcohol addiction and had checked himself into a twenty-eight-day treatment facility. He hadn't wanted to, but he'd known that if he didn't, alcohol might control him for all eternity. He would never get back to being an upstanding citizen, and he wouldn't have an ounce of a chance with Taylor. The two of them had made the decision not to see each other until his divorce was final, but they talked all the time and were planning to be together. Dillon was also relieved to know that Miss Brenda's surgery had gone well and so had her chemotherapy. She'd been hurt about the destruction of the church, and until the day he died, he would never tell her — or another living soul besides Vincent — that he had masterminded it, but she still loved and supported him like a son. His dad had also kept his word in terms of being a better father, and that gave Dillon more hope than anything else. Levi and Matthew still didn't have much to do with him, but his prayer was that they'd eventually change their minds. This had also made him realize that he needed to nix his grudge against his former fiancée, Melissa. It was hard, but if he was truly going to try to live his life right, he knew he had to.

Then there was his dear, beloved sister Alicia, who'd finally gotten the help she needed. To this day, though, he still wondered what he could have said or done to help her before she'd nearly killed herself. Months had passed, yet Dillon couldn't shake the guilt he felt. Especially since he'd always known Alicia struggled with her past. But thank God Levi had shown up when he had. Alicia was doing well, and Dillon couldn't be happier for her.

So now, all he had to do was figure out how he was going to live the rest of *his* life. Right now, his father paid the rent and utilities at the apartment he'd been forced to move into, but he knew he had to become self-sufficient. Whether he found a job or started some lucrative business, he had to be responsible. He had to map out a plan to take care of himself and become a great provider for Taylor, the woman he loved and was going to marry. She and his family were the reason he had a future to look forward to, and for that, he was grateful. For whatever reason, God had seen fit to bless him in spite of his awful sins, and a person couldn't ask for any more than that. He wouldn't expect anything more, either, he would just be thankful. He would try to be satisfied and content from now on.

Alicia and Levi lay in bed holding each other close.

Levi sniffled, and Alicia wondered why.

"Baby, what's wrong?"

"Three months have passed, and I still

wonder: What if I hadn't come straight home that night? I just can't imagine what my life would be like now."

"But you did come home, and I'm right here. And we're always going to be together."

"I know that, but I still can't help thinking about it sometimes. I've always told you that you're the love of my life, but that night at the hospital changed everything. My love for you rose to a level I didn't even know existed. I finally get how it must feel to not want to go on without someone. And I don't ever want to find out."

Now tears fell from Alicia's eyes. "I love you exactly the same. I always have."

Alicia and Levi had been through so much, but strangely enough, they were more in love than before. Alicia knew it sounded odd and that most people would never understand her reasoning, but while her near–suicide attempt had been the worst thing that had ever happened to her, it had also been the best thing. The reason: Like so many others who had successfully taken their own lives, she'd been in denial, was too ashamed to talk about her symptoms, and thought she'd soon get better. Alicia knew all of the above was possible because she'd walked around with a serious form of psychosis for two whole years — and hidden it from everyone who cared about her. Both Levi and Dillon had seen signs of trouble, but they'd never imagined she was having audible hallucinations. When Phillip had died, she'd become depressed, yet she'd learned to live with it. She'd become functional and very good at smiling and pretending to be happy when she was supposed to. Her marriage had still suffered, but she'd somehow found a way to make it through the day-to-day motions. Then, by having her worst psychotic episode ever, this was how Levi had learned the truth. He'd been closer to home than she'd realized, and he'd stopped her from pulling the trigger. To this day, Alicia knew for sure that she never would have found the courage to tell him or get the help she needed. So having the truth come out had freed her from carrying a burden that had become heavier and deadlier than she'd imagined. The hard part, though, had been seeing the broken, severely distraught looks on her parents' faces when they'd arrived at the hospital. They'd been in total shock, and they'd blamed themselves, thinking that if they'd accepted Levi none of this would have happened. Alicia wasn't sure if that was true or not, but as far as she was concerned, no one was at fault, and the blessing was that God had seen fit to save her life. He'd allowed her to reach her darkest and lowest point, and she'd lived to tell about it. She was now able to give testimonies to others and speak openly about the seriousness of mental illness. She was no longer ashamed of anything that had happened to her, not even her long-term hospital stay on the floor reserved for patients like her.

And she was grateful for Dr. Brogan, too, who had still ended up referring her to a psychiatrist by the name of Dr. Kasey Meyers. Alicia now saw Dr. Meyers as a gift from God, and it hadn't taken her long at all to diagnose Alicia with psychotic depression. Through Alicia's online research, she had believed she might have that very illness, but because she'd experienced certain symptoms early on and some more recently, she hadn't been sure. But after talking to and being thoroughly evaluated by Dr. Meyers, she'd learned much more than what she'd read on the Internet, some of which had deeply concerned Alicia. In short, Dr. Meyers had told her that having even one isolated occurrence of psychotic depression increased a person's chance of becoming bipolar. It also left more opportunity for recurring episodes of PD, mania, and, like with Alicia, even suicide.

So by covering up her symptoms and acting as though she were well, she'd set herself up for more harm than good. She also couldn't agree with Levi more as far as the damage people did when they were miserable or depressed, and from now on, she would be an open book — not just about her illness but about everything. She wouldn't care what people said or thought about her, she would merely be honest about who she was and how she was feeling. She would stand in her truth and not waver from it for anyone.

This was also what she hoped for her brother Dillon. He'd spent time at a treatment facility, and he went to AA meetings regularly. He seemed to be doing well, but Alicia and Levi were still saddened by the church fire. They'd tried to figure out why anyone would want to burn down the Lord's house, even more so because they hadn't received any threats, and to this day, there was no motive and no arrests. It didn't make sense to anyone, but they, the same as Dillon, had found a way to accept what had happened. It had been a huge loss to all the members of New Faith, but as God would have it, their dad had stepped in and helped in every way he could. He'd even taken on the task of holding a third service at his church to accommodate all the members of New Faith. Deliverance Outreach's new building would be finished in another three months, though, and once that happened everyone would be able to worship together. It was interesting how things had turned out, too, because not only had their dad and Dillon become closer, Dillon had become a member of their dad's church. He never talked about being a pastor anymore, but he attended service weekly. Alicia knew that when Dillon had led New Faith, he'd wanted to become the largest church in the city, but because of the arson attack, Deliverance still held that position.

So life was good. Alicia was taking her medication on schedule, preparing to write again, and Levi worked at Deliverance for her father. This was yet another blessing and great miracle from God, and it just went to show what could happen when forgiveness became the center of a person's life. Mistakes had been made, resentment had taken root, and there had seemed to be no possibility of reconciliation. This hadn't just been the case for Alicia's dad and her husband, either. It had become a way of life for all of them. Now everyone tried to get along and love each other the way they should. Matthew and Levi still had work to do when it came to having a relationship with Dillon, but Alicia believed with all her heart that it would happen. Because of her faith and trust in God's promises, she had to. Many times she'd heard her father say that God was true to His Word, and thus far, she hadn't seen otherwise. Maybe things didn't happen when she wanted them to, but at some point they finally did — if it was in God's will, of course.

So it was all of that — her love, trust, and faith in God — that she would continue to count on. She would hold those sentiments for dear life — always.

ACKNOWLEDGMENTS

As always, I thank God for absolutely everything. I also thank all my family members who continue to support me in a huge way: my dear husband, Will, of 25 years; my brothers, Willie, Jr. (and April) and Michael (and Marilyn) Stapleton; my stepson and daughter-in-law, Trenod and Tasha Vines-Roby, our grandchildren, Alex (Lamont) and Trenod, Jr. and the rest of my family (Tennins, Ballards, Lawsons, Stapletons, Youngs, Beasleys, Haleys, Romes, Greens, Robys, Garys, Shannons, and Normans). I love each and every one of you with all my heart.

To my first cousin and fellow author, Patricia Haley-Glass (and Jeffrey), my best friends, Kelli Tunson Bullard and Lori Whitaker Thurman, and my cousin, Janell Francine Green. You four ladies are my sisters for life, and I love you dearly. Also, Kelli, thank you for giving this book such a fitting title! To my loving spiritual mom, Dr. Betty Price and my spiritual sisters (the Price daughters), Angela Evans, Cheryl Price, and Stephanie Buchanan — I love you all.

To the 19 family members and friends who so graciously traveled all the way to Jamaica to attend Will's and my 25th anniversary vow renewal ceremony: Trenod & Latasha Vines-Roby, Jeffrey and Patricia Haley-Glass, Bianca Roby, Pastor Brian and Kelli Bullard, Lori Thurman, Venita Sockwell Owens, Ben Walker, Gwyn Gulley, Charles Brown, Clint and Venae Jackson, Kasondra McConnell, Kaprisha Ballard, Kiara Bullard, Connie Dettman, and Linda Duggins. Will and I are forever grateful, and we will never forget your kind generosity. You all helped make our anniversary trip our best ever, and we love you so very much.

To my attorney, Ken Norwick, my amazing publisher, Hachette/Grand Central Publishing — Beth de Guzman, Linda Duggins, Jamie Raab, Elizabeth Connor, Caroline Acebo, Maddie Caldwell, Stephanie Serabian, the entire sales and marketing teams, along with everyone else at GCP; and to my talented freelance team: Connie Dettman, Luke LeFevre, Pamela Walker-Williams, and Ella Curry — thank you for everything and then some!

To all the bookstores and retailers, every media organization, website, and blog who sells and/or promotes my work, and to all the fabulous book clubs that select my novels for their monthly discussions — thank you a thousand times over!

To all my fabulous readers — you are the people who make writing worthwhile, and I am forever indebted to all of you.

Much love and God bless you always,
Kimberla Lawson Roby
E-mail: kim@kimroby.com
Facebook:
Facebook.com/kimberlalawsonroby
Twitter: @KimberlaLRoby
Instagram:
Instagram.com/kimberlalawsonroby
Periscope: @kimberlalawsonroby

READING GROUP GUIDE

1. Dillon Whitfield Black decides to become a pastor and start his own church despite not being called by God. How does this affect his ability to really become a changed, better person? Do you think that his drinking and cheating are the reason he's fallen off the path? Or are they just a symptom of a false calling?

2. Alicia doesn't like Raven from the beginning. Do you agree with Alicia? Why or why not? Do you believe Raven's childhood is the reason she treats people the way she does?

3. Even though she knows there is something wrong, Alicia is too ashamed to tell anyone about the voice in her head. Do you think this is the case for many people

who struggle with mental illness? Should Alicia's family have done more to help her?

4. Despite saying that he truly loves Raven, Dillon repeatedly cheats on her. Do you think it's really love? Have you been in a situation where you hurt someone you thought you loved? If so, please share why you handled things this way.

5. Alicia has an especially hard time being separated from her family, but she feels strongly that she shouldn't have anything to do with them until they accept Levi fully. Do you agree with her? Why or why not? Have you ever had to stand up to friends or family to support someone you love? If so, what was the outcome?

6. Alicia's mother eventually sees the error of her judgment of Levi. Why do you think it takes so much longer for Curtis Black to change his mind? Do you think you could have forgiven Levi despite the mistakes he and Alicia made?

7. Dillon's drinking and cheating escalate after interactions with his father. How do you think his relationship with his father affects his relationship with God? What

advice would you give to someone in this situation?

8. Were you surprised at Raven's reaction to Dillon's cheating? Do you think this justifies the way she treats him as her husband? Why do you think that Raven doesn't learn from her mistakes and change?

9. Even today, many people don't believe women should be pastors. So what are your feelings on the subject?

10. More than once, Levi stresses the importance of getting help after a traumatic situation even if you feel fine, but Alicia doesn't listen. Do you think there is a stigma related to mental illness and PTSD? And is there enough awareness about how to talk to a loved one or know when it's time to see a professional? What advice would you give someone who you knew or suspected was suffering from mental illness?

11. Given Alicia and Levi's history, are you happy that they are finally married? Why or why not? Do you think their marriage will survive for years to come?

12. Were you surprised that Curtis was finally able to forgive Alicia, Levi, and Dillon and bring them back into the family fold? Why do you think this happened? Are you happy that they repaired their relationships? Do you think it will last?

The employees of Thorndike Press hope you have enjoyed this Large Print book. All our Thorndike, Wheeler, and Kennebec Large Print titles are designed for easy reading, and all our books are made to last. Other Thorndike Press Large Print books are available at your library, through selected bookstores, or directly from us.

For information about titles, please call:
  (800) 223-1244

or visit our Web site at:
  http://gale.cengage.com/thorndike

To share your comments, please write:
  Publisher
  Thorndike Press
  10 Water St., Suite 310
  Waterville, ME 04901